Spirits of St. Louis: Missouri Ghost Stories

An Anthology

Cover design by Shannon Yarbrough, St. Louis, Missouri
Copyright © 2013 by Rocking Horse Publishing
All rights reserved.

The characters and events in this book are fictitious.
Rocking Horse Publishing
All on the Same Page Bookstore
11052 Olive Blvd.
Creve Coeur, MO 63141

Visit our website at www.RockingHorsePublishing.com

ISBN 10: 0989568598
ISBN 13: 978-0-9895685-9-3

Table of Contents

THE HOUSE ON WOLF CREEK

A Story of Slavery and Terror

Pablo Baum

The world had spun off its axis. Humanity, despite its brilliance, beauty and creativity, had turned on itself with callous claws. Seclusion, for the defenseless, seemed the only shield from the evil.

Beautiful brown-eyed Rebecca lived on a small farm in western Missouri in the mid-1800s with her brother and father, her mother long dead. This once barefoot and scrawny child had blossomed into a buxom, auburn-haired woman, at the pinnacle of her femininity in her twentieth year. The back-woods farm provided them with a modicum of prosperity but the world around them seethed with barbarity.

At the end of what seemed a routine day, her father, swarthy and graying in his mid-fifties, and her muscular brother Robert, ten years her senior, entered the cabin with their hands dripping from their scrubbing at the pump. Their usual chatter did not occur. Rebecca noticed.

In the two-room, one-window log cabin were three straw-mattress beds, a wobbly table with four straight-back chairs and a century-old cook-stove that cowered darkly in the corner. Forks clanked noticeably against chipped plates. Something was on their minds.

"Rebecca, dear," said her father, breaking the burdensome silence, avoiding eye contact, steam from his boiled potato rising toward his lowered face. "Robert and I are leaving tomorrow . . . early." Her fork fell noisily onto to her plate.

1

"To Marshall, for supplies, Father?" she asked, but expecting an explanation not nearly so mundane.

"Rebecca, dear, you know those Kansans have been releasing slaves to live anywhere and now some folks've seen 'em in blue uniforms carryin' guns and they picked a fight, a big one, with our Bushwhackers at Island Mound, that place where Robert and me been huntin' deer."

"This is just too close," added Robert, elbows on either side of his plate, his hands clasped before his mouth. "This ain't the Lord's way, Rebecca, it's just wrong so me and Father'll be helping those wiser Missourians that know the truth and we'll fix this quick in a week."

Rebecca, her face flushing red, was speechless.

Their pre-dawn bustling about the cabin by the light of a single candle was tense. Beige water-gourds and cloth bags of biscuits swung from their belts, flintlock rifles rested on their shoulders while unspoken doubt as to the wisdom of leaving Rebecca hung in the air like smoke from charred bread, doubt that gnawed at them though they intended to perform only a quick and vital chore. Ready, straw hats perched on their heads, they looked toward Rebecca who sat at the table, her face in her hands.

"Robert and me'll be back so quick you'll never even notice we was gone, sweet Rebecca." He leaned down and kissed the top of her head, while Robert managed to place a fraternal arm across the shoulders of the little sister he had always defended. He pressed one cheek against the top of her head and heard her muffled weeping. She could not look up at them. The door squeaked open and the strains of awakening birds filled the cabin with the new day, but nothing could console her. The door closed and their boots clomped across the porch. The horses' hooves over the rocky soil told her they had actually done it.

Rebecca's first night alone was like the next and the next and the next. The sound of every pesky raccoon was that of a stealthy intruder lurking in the thick woods surrounding the cabin; the whisper of the most innocent breeze was the voice of phantoms. Her heart would pound wildly in her chest, then rest, then leap into frenzy again at the thump of a falling walnut outside her window. Holding her breath only allowed her to mistake the slightest rustle as a villainous attack in this, her state of utter vulnerability. Her loyalty to that higher power – to which she whispered faith and oaths in exchange for being allowed to see just one more dawn – seemed impotent in the face of certain death leaping at her from the nocturnal secrets of the tomb that was that cabin.

That week, that one week, so vehemently promised, became a month, then another, then another. Sleep was rare, terror constant, hope fading.

It did occur to her to risk a trip into nearby Marshall to inquire if anyone knew of Robert and Father but that would announce her solitude on the secluded farm. The cabin, even in winter with all foliage gone, was beyond the view of passers-by on the main road to town but there was a circuitous path that wound through the woods, stopping at the porch, a porch that she allowed to become increasingly veiled by vines. Isolation. Concealment. It was her only defense. Thus, her survival depended on the farm itself, fish in the creek and she could slaughter a goat when necessary – never losing from mind that her goal was to wait out the long nightmare. There could be no trips to Marshall.

By the anniversary of their disappearance, additional torments commenced: militias. One evening she crouched in the wooded roadside and observed the passing of two cavalry units within minutes of each other, all heading to perform some dreadful deed, gear rattling from their saddles, and the second unit consisted of blue uniformed black soldiers.

All soldiers were here enemies. Won't remaining on this farm be suicidal? She pondered. What won't those soldiers do upon finding me? And find me they will.

Marriage occurred to her. Not marriage for passion, compassion or love, it would be marriage for survival, plain and simple. But are not all the young men swallowed up by armies and are thus doomed to endure whatever has claimed Father and Robert?

Rebecca was stooped in her garden behind the cabin, her hands and arms soiled to the elbows, when she heard, "Hello! Anybody about?" She startled, gripped the metal-bladed trowel, wondering if she should flee or hide or confront what might be a friend, for a friend she indeed needed, but the voice was masculine and not young. Perhaps a gentlemanly grandfather, she pondered, with a grandson my age and disinclined to soldiery.

Pushing her hair from her face, she remained unsure if a quick dash into the woods might be wiser. Terror overtook her. A mounted man attired in black atop an ashen nag rounded the corner of the cabin, reined to a stop and removed his straw hat.

"Afternoon ma'am. I just followed that little path wonderin' where it led. Everything alright?" His grayish long hair remained smashed against his head and his salt and pepper beard reached halfway to his shoulders.

"All's fine here, sir. My father and brother'll be back from the fields shortly," she lied. His eyes fixed on the alluring woman, her beauty not diminished by her tattered beige dress and soiled sweaty face.

"I'm Theobold van Vorhees. Got a plantation 'bout an hour's ride from here. Got slaves too," he added with emphasis.

"And your family, sir?"

The man said nothing. Dismounting, he dropped the reins as Rebecca gripped her trowel. He walked along the edge of the sunny garden, limping slightly, and she thought out-running him might be easy. . .but then what? Her seclusion was gone. The cabin would be a trap. He approached the backdoor and peered in. Two unused beds and empty rifle racks on the walls belied the claim that her men-folk would soon return from the fields.

If only I'd said they'd gone hunting, she lamented.

"Got a name young lady?" he asked turning back toward her.

"Rebecca."

"Well, Rebecca, your men are on their way, eh?" He replaced his hat.

Rebecca remained silent. He stepped toward her. She stepped away, but subtly, hoping not to appear fearful lest he accelerate any intentions to seize her. Closer, his muscular body towered over her and she smelled his unwashed clothes. The age in his eyes – and something unexplained – exuded an unsettling eeriness.

He smiled then turned toward his horse. "You're not safe here, Rebecca. I'll avoid that little path so's not to leave any more tracks. Maybe those soldiers won't find you. Just maybe. Good day ma'am."

Rebecca dropped her trowel and fell to her knees, attempting to regain her composure. Returning to her tasks, tending to her potatoes and squash, her brain raced: "You're not safe here," echoed among her thoughts. He knows I lied about the men-folk. Is my seclusion now broken? Will he return? Do I want him to? He is odd. . .but is he evil?

That night she felt scrutinized, no longer secluded. Finally, sleep took her to places unimagined; there were flames and skeletons and moans in thick smoke, there was dark smiling beauty and things to long cherish, an ax and a cameo all wafting about in a blue-gray miasma of things without shame.

By dawn, she was drained. Seated on the edge of her straw-bed, faint light entering the little window, she ran her fingers through her hair, pulling it back

4

from her face, shaking her head to fling away her nocturnal tormentors. Typical imaginings of silly dreams.

She fed her three emaciated goats, caught a perch in the creek and returned to her garden. The images persisted.

In a week, perhaps more, she heard the grinding of metal-rimmed wheels over the rocky ground near the cabin. It was Theobold again, in his one-horse buggy.

"How's about a ride somewheres, Rebecca? We can take back roads. Nobody'll see ya."

Stepping onto the porch, vines hanging untidily from its edges, trowel in hand, she looked vacantly at her guest. His offer to take her about the bucolic Missouri countryside was tempting, for the farm had been her prison, but above all, survival was her obsession and her peculiar visitor might be a tool to exploit, but was he honorable? Uncertain, she slipped the trowel into her dress-pocket, stepped down from the porch and a raspy hand pulled her onto the front board of the wagon. As they bumped along, conversation with her rigid suitor was hollow.

"Nice day, eh Rebecca? Not as hot as yesterday."

His voice was severe and ghoulish like the rumble of distant thunder and she struggled to respond, then settled on, "Yes, very nice." Nothing lively or amusing would leave her lips as she endured his unwashed odor. His sweat-soaked straw hat, pulled down over his ears, gave him an impish look. The breeze fanned her hair then lifted her dress slightly. He noticed.

When they reached his lush plantation south of Marshall, he pointed proudly to his two field slaves and to his two-story red brick house. She noticed the family burial plot near the barn and its leaning flat stones – no crosses, only stones. Rebecca could not help the daringly premature notion that in that house she would at least be safe.

"Like a tour of the house, Rebecca? I keep it real nice."

"Perhaps another day, Mr. van Vorhees."

"Theobold, please, Rebecca."

His invitation to enter, just the two of them, was not difficult to decline.

The return trip was bumpier, by a different route, and all attempts to converse ceased. Nearing home, jostling through the trees, avoiding her meandering path, the oaks towered overhead and she felt relief upon seeing her cabin ahead. Bidding him farewell was liberating, but as the rattle of his wagon faded, the silence descended upon her once again, reminding her that

5

the first military brute to happen by, with his soldierly command at his heels, would end it all for her. Will the militias find me tonight? Oh Lord, where are Father and Robert?

She sat at the table, preparing the day's harvest of potatoes and carrots and reflected. Theobold won't tell others about me, he'll keep me as his prize. But if I reject him, and if he himself doesn't turn on me, he may seek revenge by revealing my location to the worst of reprobates. Is he salvation or damnation?

The months dragged on through cold and heat and a pitiless drought descended. Two goats died, rotten before she found them the following morning and there would be no more milk. She butchered the remaining one, but food reserves dwindled while her former garden hardened and cracked.

Theobold would bring her minor, and inadequate, amounts of food, accompanied by rambling chats while seated on the edge of the porch. On cool days, he would enter and sit on Father's chair at the table where he, with faint whiskey-breath, would ramble on about the glories of his farm, luxurious house, and something about him was uncanny, though he never menaced or even neared her. As he spoke, his grayish eyes under abundant eyebrows would wander randomly within their sockets. He ranted about "life beyond life," which she gathered to be some netherworld or abyss or lost world that he had visited or inhabited or perhaps imagined; all of which left Rebecca in a quandary. What was this man?

Despite it all, he seemed so harmless. Will he defend me . . . until war's end or . . . until . . . Father and Robert return?

Reality: her options were gone.

The day of the wedding, Theobold, having shaved off that decades-old beard, smelled of strongly scented soap. Rebecca graced his parlor attired in a floor-length gown, on loan by her fiancé, a gown once white now yellowed – about which she cared not the least. Her straight-combed hair hung nearly to her waist and her lashes were as the strokes of angels' wings in a viper's lair. Theobold's acquaintances in attendance – gray-bearded merchants wishing to please a customer – stood in awe of the woman . . . and the man . . . and the union that was about to occur, a union in a house that was more orderly than welcoming, more heartless than caring and, and above all, they knew of Theobold's ancestors, recent and legendary, of their lusts that tainted lives, the slaves they had tortured, the brownish daughters they had battered, impregnated and discarded, their crematory rituals that were heard and smelled for miles around. All had hoped that the repugnant van Vorhees blight would end with Theobold's bachelorhood, but now ...

Justice of the Peace in place, his back to the stone fireplace, book open, somber couple before him, he pronounced the familiar words.

Last word said, Theobold pushed her flowing hair aside and clasped a generations-old cameo around her neck, the tarnished chain pulling its pendant against her throat.

It will do, he thought, forgetting the traditional kiss.

The guests' departure was rapid, claiming urgent tasks elsewhere. Too suddenly, Rebecca and Theobold, husband and wife stood in the drab room and all was in such contrast with the radiant Rebecca.

I will be safe, she told herself, looking up into the eyes that bewildered her.

Then came her conjugal duty, upstairs, to the right and onto the nuptial bed. It was a price she had to pay.

The next day, their first 'business' meeting took place in the kitchen; there were pots that hung neatly overhead, dishes that hid behind cabinet doors and a wood-burning stove that promised varied uses. She was no stranger to domesticity but the commanding authority towering over her, stubble faced with pungent breath, almost made her long for her cabin, now abandoned. Rebecca's husband was clear about her obligations in his home.

Thus, her day would begin at dawn, the kitchen her raison d'etre. Theobold's routine, high-noon appearance at the kitchen table was without the slightest greeting, for ill temper was his reward for twelve hours of whiskey the previous day. Rebecca learned the value of silence as she placed his desired food and drink before him. Strong coffee would momentarily return him to a semblance of civility but the first mug of whiskey would launch him, once again, into his cabalistic world.

The months dragged by, but safely, revulsion replacing fear, though the air in the house seemed heavy, its dark corridors darker than the gloom of a moonless night, and on occasion, colder than death in a silent tomb. Faded paintings of the forgotten ones glowered across moldy rooms and the dwelling seemed to exist as an entity apart.

Daily, Theobold would progress from his hangover at noon, to his slurred speech at sunset, to his mumbling at midnight. Rebecca's only solace were the twice-per-week visits from the brothers Donny and Adam, the field slaves who brought firewood for her stove, along with some lively chatter.

The two graying men, lean and shiny in the sweat of their toil, were humorous, pleasant and Rebecca relished their company. Donny could pluck hilarity from the barest of utterances.

Donny and Adam enjoyed a luxury that Rebecca could not: fields – fields of toil that were their insulation from the abrasive authority. Since childhood, from the shadows, they had watched Theobold and his now deceased family. He was the last of those who had shattered cherished lives as if toys to cast upon flames, flames before which Theobold had once stood with arms raised in homage to some greater power.

The clouds hung low one afternoon as Rebecca heard the creaking wagon's approach, bearing monthly supplies. Pushing the whitish curtain aside, she noticed things arranged differently in the cargo area. Stepping onto the front porch, drying her hands on her apron, hair collected into a bun at the back of her head, she noticed not one but two kegs of sorrow.

Donny and Adam, grasping an old blanket that covered the purchases, removed it and startled. Rising to her knees, with eyes that flitted nervously, was one enchantingly lovely slave girl. The two women, nearly the same age, locked eyes on each other . . . and wondered.

Within a few days, Donny and Adam had constructed for Missy, as she was called, a second cabin, down the hill toward Wolf Creek and next to their own. Rebecca noticed, to her disappointment over several days, that Missy did not approach The Master's house and it was a mystery just what her duties were. It was a mystery, that is, until Theobold's nightly romantic appetite declined slightly, as his nocturnal tasks around the property correspondingly increased, "to avoid the heat of day," he explained to Rebecca. Missy's responsibility to The Master became clear.

With that doubled dose of whiskey, his customary slurred speech late in his day became deep, demonic moans. The noxious drink seemed to be releasing something frightening, not merely distasteful, from deep within him as stumbling replaced groping by midnight.

On what appeared to be just another morning, she arose and left her snoring, odiferous spouse where he would remain for hours. Entering her chamber of toil, she startled when she saw Missy, standing near the stove. "Massa Theobold, he tell me to help you work, Miss Rebecca. I help what I can."

Missy's snow-white eyes contrasted with the ebony of her skin and the perfect form or her African face accented her womanly dignity. Rebecca's initial astonishment was replaced with delight as the two women bustled about that day, and every day thereafter. Missy's slight figure permitted her an unusual grace as they performed tasks, chatting and giggling as time flew by. Their souls bonded as there was the shared obedience to The Master. Obedience was the law of the land: white wife, black slave, it did not matter, for neither could legally deny The Master, be he owner or husband!

It was midnight when the first blow was struck. Rebecca had appeared for her nuptial duty standing near the foot of the bed. Theobold lurched toward her, steadying himself by placing a hand on her shoulder. Repulsed by months of sickening submission, she stepped backward. He seethed at such defiance. His eyes bulged, inflamed, but his next step resulted in the same response. In his fury, he emitted a cavernous moan and raising a fist high overhead, it plunged impacting her mouth, smashing her lips against her teeth, spattering blood and saliva as he managed to throw her onto the bed. He could not follow as he crumpled to the floor moaning, snarling, drooling, losing consciousness.

Seated on the edge of the bed, she reluctantly raised one hand to examine the remains of her lips but, barely touching one front tooth, it dislodged, falling onto her hand and she clutched it, blood dripping onto the white nightgown that barely reached her knees. Throwing her head back, looking upward toward the dark ceiling she screamed, "Oh Lord, what's next, what's next?"

She dared to leave the bed, that hellish workbench of a fiend. Down the creaky stairway she stepped, irrationally fearing seizure from behind by the brute who was at that moment an incapacitated sot.

Stepping out into the cool night air, she hurried barefoot over the rocky ground down the hill to where she had never ventured, to those two slave cabins and she pounded on the door crying, "Missy, Missy, Missy!"

The door opened and her sleepy-eyed friend whispered, "What happened Rebecca?"

The two women, accompanied now by Donny and Adam who had heard the clamor, sat at Missy's table and, in the orange lantern light, saw Rebecca's once beautiful mouth. Missy gasped. It was Donny who said, in his fatherly voice, "Open your hand, Rebecca." She extended it toward the lantern. More gasps as the bloody tooth fell out onto the table. Donny spoke for all four when he uttered Rebecca's words of moments before, "What's next, what's next?" The two young women did not yet know of Theobold's family history and the gravity of the gathering peril: The last of the ethereal van Vorhees was being the only thing he could be.

So it was, the little family of brothers and sisters, an alliance of peaceful people, dedicated the remainder of that night to constructing a plan, a plan that was not peaceful, and was not righteous, and was not loving; it was a plan for survival, plain and simple. The Plan would determine every breath and every step, The Plan could not fail, for life was precious and lives were hanging by a thread.

The dawn brought a new day, its golden warmth rescuing them from a sleepless night of unimaginable things which included Donny's recounting of the horrors of the van Vorhees. Their daily labors were the farthest things from their minds as their tormentor slept, so the foursome strolled down the hill toward Wolf Creek. There they sat at the water's edge, peacefully dropping pebbles into its flow, chatting, searching for humor, attempting to avoid, however momentarily, the burden of The Plan. As they sat with their arms around their knees, Rebecca saw Donny and Adam in a new light, not just as congenial fellows, but as gallant warriors, reluctantly willing to stand and confront a powerful foe. The gray at their temples, the wrinkles about their eyes and the depth of their voices spoke of men who had survived savagery and the societal brutality that enslaved them, forcing them to endure the unimaginable. She affectionately leaned her head on Missy's shoulder, thus avoiding the slightest risk of catching a glance of her reflection. Wolf Creek wouldn't lie.

As the sun neared its zenith, Donny and Adam stood, shattering the reverie of their hours together, then, clad in their loose white cotton, they turned toward their fields as Missy and Rebecca ascended the hill, hand in hand, toward whatever awaited them in that house. The only thing they couldn't know was how soon they would have to unleash the beast that was . . . The Plan.

That night, upstairs in the nuptial bedroom, normalcy was teetering on a cliff. Theobold, having achieved his maximum inebriation for the day, approached his beautiful Rebecca. Her planned, even practiced, steps backward once again ignited his ire.

"Come, Theobold," she said, vexingly. His hideous moan, this one of rage, meant nothing to her now. "You can have me any time. Come, Theobold!" Feeling the corner of the room pressing on her shoulders, that corner from which there was but one escape, she repeated her taunts as her victim neared. Reaching back into the corner she felt that ax handle. Raising it high she brought its blade down with all her force upon his skull. There was a cracking sound, his body stiffened and fell to the floor in a dull thud. Directing her face to the dark ceiling, she unleashed a scream that split the night. Then, stepping over the motionless mass, she descended the stairway not at all concerned that the creaking boards might awaken her surly oppressor.

Into the night air, stumbling down the hill, shouting the names of the only family she knew would never abandon her, she saw them running toward her. "I did it. I can't believe I did it!" Feeling weight in her right hand, she saw that dripping ax and released it with revulsion.

The family of four brothers and sisters ascended to that room, a grim duty to perform. Each grasping a wrist or an ankle, they began their descent, coordinating each step. "Next step now," Donny would say as that dead head thudded, disgorging its cranial contents.

Down the hill they struggled, only Donny and Adam doing the work now dragging their burden by its ankles while Missy and Rebecca noticed its head and arms jogging in and out of every wagon rut. Down they went, down, down, down past the two slave cabins, down, down, down onto old Wolf Creek.

There, at the water's edge, the four of them hefted their macabre load onto a carefully crafted brush pile. Adam knew flint and steel. One spark, then another and a minute flame came to life, then two, then ten. Grasping each other's hands, the family stepped away, seating themselves on the dry leaves, transfixed by the flickering and dancing of the nascent flames, flames that explored its clothing, inexorably making their way through it, then finding that beard, causing it to explode into a crackling and malodorous conflagration hurling sparks and smoke toward the stars.

For the remainder of that night they watched as the spectacle branded its way onto their souls, and they – especially with the brothers' memory of crematory rituals – relished the ghoul's erasure from all existence. The Curse of the van Vorhees was ending. The enormous brush pile, with its once burdensome load, slowly collapsed. In the last moments before dawn, the foursome stood, approached the edge of the coal-bed and looked down at what they had done. There they saw one bright, red glowing skeleton – and it moved! Perhaps it was a mere re-positioning of the embers under the skull, surely this and nothing more, but it turned its hideous head toward them, flames reaching upward through the eye sockets as if seeing them, berating them, daring them; the jaw then dropped, emitting the evilest . . . moan.

With this, they grasped their satchels of meager belongings, turned toward the West and undertook their trek, but Rebecca stopped. Curling her delicate fingers around that cameo, she pulled until its clasp relented and flung it toward the noxious heap. Having ascended the hill, feeling the dawn's early light, they paused, glancing back to see for the final time that valley of the shadow of death, and they feared no evil . . . but they heard it. Echoing through that valley below was an unmistakable, deep, resonant, satanic moan.

They turned their backs, never again to look upon such a place. With their early morning shadows stretching out before them, pointing their way toward the West they strode unstoppably now, to see for themselves if it was really true that there was a freer land, a slaveless and fertile land . . . called . . . Kansas.

Thank You, Mary Ann
Larry G. Brown

The alarm went off, jarring Mary Ann to consciousness. She gathered her senses and shuffled to the kitchen to start the coffee and retrieve the newspaper.

"Here I go again," she said, "scouring the want ads for job possibilities. How could I have gone from a career, to four jobs in three weeks?" First it had been the downsizing (yeah, right) and being too old. Then it was part-time fast food delivery, until she was scheduled out the door by the incoming college students who would deliver all night. Then it was receptionist for a day, until two men in suits came in and carried out boxes and furniture and left her standing in an empty room. And lastly, the nursing home, "I'm sorry," she said, "I just can't do THAT to those people."

But, here she was, mid-50s, divorced, four grown kids and their families scattered across the map, and now she was looking at want ads. Just then, her eyes were drawn to a little box, which simply read, "Part-time driver needed, must like children, call 505-6729 for an interview."

"Must be a preschool or daycare center," she thought. "I like kids, have my chauffeur's license from the delivery job… what the heck." Mary Ann picked up the phone and called. "Greenview School, Miss Schusler speaking, how may I help you?"

"Uh, yes, I was inquiring about the driver needed," said Mary Ann.

The pleasant voice of Miss Schusler expressed delight, "Come right over if you can. Mr. Hanson will interview you."

After she had gotten directions, Mary Ann hung up and couldn't quite believe the enthusiasm from Miss Schusler, "Were they that desperate? What's the catch?"

Mary Ann dressed and drove out to an older suburb that was a part of the city not familiar to her. She turned onto Greenview Street, not remembering ever having heard anything about this school. She wondered if it was a public or a private school. She hadn't asked if it was a preschool or what. But, as she approached the address, there it was, Greenview Elementary School, looking like every other off-white brick institutional school building she had ever seen. Mary Ann thought to herself as she walked to the main entrance, "It does remind me a lot of my elementary school. I wouldn't be surprised to see Mrs. Woods, who was our school secretary forever."

Mary Ann walked down the hallway to the right, noticing the shiny marble floors, glazed tile walls, and bulletin boards filled with children's artwork. She heard the muffled sounds of classroom activities echoing down the hallway. "It hasn't changed much since I was a kid," she thought.

As she entered the school office, a smiling Miss Schusler greeted her, "We've been looking for you. Come on in and meet Mr. Hanson." Mary Ann stepped into the principal's office and a short, balding man in a blue suit came around the desk to shake her hand. "A little too friendly," she thought, "and right out of the fifties."

"I'm Theo Hanson, Miss Sparks. Sit down and let me tell you about the job." Mr. Hanson went on to explain that the school needed an occasional bus driver at least twice a week for special trips and excursions to places like the zoo, the park, the museum, and sports events; usually one class or small group at a time. It would be minimum wage, but consistent work. And she would begin the very next day.

Mary Ann was surprised at the minimal number of questions asked her, the scant paperwork, and very, very low pay; but it was part-time. "No wonder nobody else had taken the job," she thought.

"You're just the one we're looking for," Mr. Hanson beamed. Mary Ann stuttered, but said, "OK," and signed the paperwork. "Come, come," Mr. Hanson said, "let me escort you down to the garage and introduce the staff. They turned left and hurried down a series of hallways, past the gym and cafeteria, and into a large garage with a couple of buses and various pieces of automotive equipment scattered around. Three more buses were parked just outside the big open garage doors.

"Ira, meet Mary Ann," Mr. Hanson called. To Mary Ann, he said, "Ira is our head driver, he will be your immediate supervisor. Pete is our number one mechanic, and Gary is the assistant to everybody." One-by-one they shook hands. Ira took her over to a big yellow bus. "This is it, the bus we usually use for special runs. You have time for a trip? I'll show you how it handles."

Mary Ann mumbled, "OK" and looked over the bus as they boarded. It looked old, but yet was as shiny and clean as if it had just been purchased. "School buses do live forever," she thought to herself.

Within minutes, Ira was driving out of the school lot with Mary Ann, seated in the front seat across and back from the driver's seat, listening to Ira explain things and watching his moves. "We usually take the same basic trips," Ira explained, "and I'll accompany you on the first few trips until you're comfortable."

She watched the neighborhood streets go by and as they turned off Greenview Street onto Jasper Street, Mary Ann reflected that the neighborhoods looked much the same as her childhood community, and that was a comfortable feeling. Oddly, at that moment she remembered glancing at a calendar in the garage; a calendar with a picture of President Richard Nixon on it. "It must have been one of those calendars featuring past presidents," she thought. "Was Nixon born in September?" She couldn't remember and it really didn't matter.

"Be careful at the Santa Fe railroad crossing here at Jasper Street," Ira turned to tell her. "The signal will warn you of oncoming trains, but the law requires that we stop whether a train is coming or not. Stop, open the door, look up and down the tracks, and proceed with caution."

In a few minutes, Ira drove the bus into a park and pulled over. He encouraged Mary Ann to drive the bus back to school while he coached. "No problem," Mary Ann thought. "Tomorrow, September 14, 2000, will be a new start for me."

The alarm jarred Mary Ann awake. "This it is, my first day at work." She showered, had coffee, and retrieved the newspaper, but did not look at the want ads. She took her time getting dressed and drove leisurely over to the school, arriving well before 10:00 a.m. Mary Ann walked into the school building, waved at Miss Schusler, and proceeded down the corridors to the garage.

Ira warmly welcomed her. "Ready to begin your bus driving career?" he said.

"You bet," Mary Ann answered.

"Mrs. Rumbaugh will be bringing out the third grade class at 10:30; we will pick them up at the east door." Ira went on to explain, "They will have their lunches to eat at the park before the nature tour. Then we'll be back at 2:00. If I know Mrs. Rumbaugh, she'll have the kids singing all the way."

The third graders marched out of the door precisely at 10:30 and onto the bus. Once seated, Mrs. Rumbaugh had the class greet their new driver with a loud unison "Hello Miss Mary Ann!" Ira took his seat behind Mary Ann, and they were off.

They pulled onto Greenview Street, proceeded north to Jasper, and in a few minutes came to the Santa Fe Railroad crossing. The signals were silent as Mary Ann stopped the bus, opened the door, looked left and right, and proceeded into the crossing. But no sooner than it was on the tracks, the bus chugged, sputtered, and came to a stop. Mary Ann tried the ignition, but got no response from the bus. Ira stood and asked if there was a problem. "It just died, and now it won't start!" Mary Ann snapped back.

"That's strange, everything checked out yesterday," Ira commented.

Mary Ann and Ira could hardly hear each other speaking for indeed, as Ira had predicted, the class was singing loudly. Ira said he would look under the hood, and Mary Ann reached to open the door for him. She heard the sound of a whistle. Turning to her left, she looked in horror straight at a train engine bearing down on the bus, whistle blowing, lights flashing, and the scream of steel wheels against steel rails as it tried to stop. Mary Ann yelled for the kids to get off the bus, but they were singing and totally oblivious to the impending doom.

Ira turned at the bottom of the steps just as the train struck the bus broadside. To Mary Ann, it all seemed to happen in slow motion, the bus surged sideways, she heard the screams of the children, the shattering of glass, the tearing of metal, felt her own body slam against glass, metal, and the head of the train engine, and blood splattering amid the twisting wreckage…

Mary Ann sat upright in bed, eyes open wide, heart pounding, gasping for breath. "Oh, oh, oh, oh my God! It's a dream, just a horrible nightmare." For a few moments, she lay back on the bed and shut off the alarm before it rang. Then, when her heart and lungs began to relax, she sat on the edge of the bed. "Just a nightmare," she said. "I had no idea I was so anxious about my first day."

16

She showered, had coffee, and retrieved the newspaper, but did not look at the want ads. She took her time getting dressed and drove leisurely over to the school, arriving well before 10:00 a.m. Mary Ann walked into the school building, waved at Miss Schusler, and proceeded down the corridors to the garage.

Ira warmly welcomed her. "Ready to begin your bus driving career?" he said.

"You bet," Mary Ann answered.

"Mrs. Rumbaugh will be bringing out the third grade class at 10:30; we will pick them at the east door." Ira went on to explain, "They will have their lunches to eat at the park before the nature tour. Then we'll be back at 2:00. If I know Mrs. Rumbaugh, she'll have the kids singing all the way."

Mary Ann looked intently at Ira and hesitantly asked, "Would it be all right if we took a little different route to the park, maybe on Broadmore?" Mary Ann thought she remembered there was an overpass over the railroad rather than a grade crossing at that intersection.

"No problem," said Ira, "traffic should be OK this time of day, and after all, you're the driver." Mary Ann gave no hint of her dream, but she was relieved to have permission to take the alternate route on Broadmore.

The Third Graders marched out of the door precisely at 10:30 and onto the bus. Once seated, Mrs. Rumbaugh had the class greet their new driver with a loud unison "Hello Miss Mary Ann!" Ira took his seat behind Mary Ann, and they were off.

They pulled out onto Greenview Street and went on south to Broadmore. But in a few blocks, to Mary Ann's surprise and horror, there were roadblocks ahead and a detour took them back to Jasper Street and the Santa Fe Railroad crossing. The signals were silent as Mary Ann stopped the bus, opened the door, nervously looked left and right, and proceeded into the crossing. But no sooner than it was on the tracks, the bus chugged, sputtered, and came to a stop. Mary Ann tried the ignition … no response. "This can't be happening," Mary Ann thought. Ira stood and asked if there was a problem. "It just died, and now it won't start!" Mary Ann snapped back. "That's strange, everything checked out yesterday," Ira commented.

Mary Ann and Ira could hardly hear each other speaking for indeed, as Ira had predicted, the class was singing loudly. Ira said he would look under the hood and Mary Ann reached to open the door for him. At the moment she anticipated, she heard the sound of a whistle and turning to her left, she looked in horror straight at the train engine bearing down on the bus, whistle blowing, lights flashing, and the scream of steel wheels against steel rails as it tried to stop. "NO, NO, THIS CAN'T BE HAPPENING!" her mind screamed.

Mary Ann yelled for the kids to get off the bus, but they were singing and totally oblivious to the impending doom. Ira turned at the bottom of the steps just as the train struck the bus broadside. To Mary Ann, it all seemed to happen in slow motion, the bus surged sideways, she heard the screams of the children, the shattering of glass, the tearing of metal, felt her own body slam against glass, metal, and the head of the train engine, and blood splattering amid the twisting wreckage . . .

Mary Ann sat upright in bed, eyes open wide, heart pounding, gasping for breath. "Oh, oh, oh, oh my God! It's a dream, just a horrible nightmare!" For a few moments, she lay back on the bed and reached to shut off the alarm. Then, when heart and lungs began to relax, she sat on the edge of the bed.

"OK, OK, I have been warned – this isn't going to happen." Mary Ann quickly showered, dressed, had her coffee, and drove to school. She hurried past Miss Schusler's friendly wave and on down the corridors to the garage where Ira warmly welcomed her, "Ready to begin your new driving career?"

"Ira, listen to me, we can't go!" she said as seriously and calmly as possible. "What do you mean we can't go, the trip is scheduled. We have to go," he answered.

"No, no, you don't understand. We can't take this trip. Postpone it, change it, we can't go!" she pleaded. "I'm sorry, Mary Ann, we can't change anything. We thought you were the one," Ira said a bit hesitantly.

Mary Ann continued to plead with Ira and she noticed that Pete and Gary had gathered close by and over near the door, Miss Schusler and Mr. Hanson stood quietly, looking intently at her.

"I don't know what is going on here, but I am not driving this bus! Something horrible is about to happen and I am not going to be a part of it!" Mary Ann said emphatically. She turned and in sobbing tears ran past Miss Schusler, out to her car, and drove away.

It was nearly 10:00 as Mary Ann arrived back at home still sobbing. It dawned on her as she walked into her apartment, "stop the train! Stop the train!" She fumbled with the telephone directory, found the Santa Fe number and called. "You have to stop the train, the one coming through the city this morning about 11:00!"

There was a pause, and then a voice said, "I'm sorry ma'am, but we have no trains coming through the city."

Mary Ann didn't give up. "Yes, there will be, about 11:00, you have to stop it from crossing Jasper Street!"

Again a pause . . . "Ma'am, I don't know what you are up to, but it is not funny! The Santa Fe tracks were taken out of that location nearly 25 years ago." Click, the phone went back to dial tone.

Mary Ann was stunned. "What is going on?" she thought. But with only a few moments hesitation, she dashed out of the house and drove out past the school and turned on Jasper. She slowed and then parked her car on the side of the street. Mary Ann left her car and walked up to the crossing. It was a bike and hiking trail; she couldn't believe her eyes. She looked up and down the trail before slowly walking toward her car.

It was after a while walking, that she spotted off to the right of the trail, a granite monument with a bronze plate. She stared at what was written there. *"In loving memory of the children of the Third Grade Class of Greenview Elementary School who, along with three adults, died at this crossing on September 14, 1970. This memorial is placed here by school mates, family, and friends."*

"1970? Thirty years ago, today? What on earth is going on?" Confused and faint, Mary Ann turned back toward her car, and as she pulled back onto the street, she saw the yellow school bus coming up from behind. She knew immediately what she would do.

Mary Ann whipped her car onto the trail crossing and turned it sideways, blocking both lanes of traffic. Mary Ann looked out to Jasper Street and saw the bus slow and stop. The driving was waving, he honked the horn and flashed the lights, and then he stepped out of the bus and ran toward her. It was Ira.

At that moment, Mary Ann turned to look up the track, facing the oncoming train. To Mary Ann it seemed to happen in slow motion, the car jerked backwards as she was thrown into the windshield. She heard the shattering of glass and tearing of metal, she felt her body slam into glass and into the face of the train engine, and blood splattering amid the twisting wreckage.

Thursday morning, September 14, 2001, an old pick-up truck pulled off to the side of Jasper Street. An elderly Ira Bloom walked over to the granite monument placed near the crossing of the Santa Fe Bike and Hiking Trail. He fingered the bronze plate that read, *"In loving memory of Mary Ann Sparks, who was killed at this crossing September 14, 1970. This memorial is placed here by the Third Grade Class of Greenview Elementary School, their families, and friends."*

Ira wiped his face with a handkerchief and walked back to his pick-up. "Thank you, Mary Ann," he whispered, "we knew you were the one."

PASSING TIME
Kenneth W. Cain

In the mornings, before Jonathan woke, Paula would stare out their front window at the Arch. Such incredible architecture, but it reminded her of some discarded halo to this city, left half-buried in the earth. Especially when the sun rose and was caught within the structure. Then the sun would shift behind the Arch and the sky would ignite with red and orange hues that illuminated the Arch. This was her cue to wake her husband.

She always woke him before the alarm sounded. She liked to hum into his ear until he stirred. But waking him in this way so early never made anything better between them. The emptiness would still be there.

Their time together was often uneventful, no longer any need for words to pass between them. That did not mean she didn't love him. Most of these problems came of her doing, because she had somehow lost the knack of expressing her love for him. Some people claimed that was what happened when you had a child together, but she was not so sure. And because of her uncertainty, their relationship had evolved into something rather devoid of life these last few months since Heidi was born.

He rose, stretched his lanky body, palms opened to the ceiling. He glanced to a photo of them together, back when they were happier, that rested on the dresser. Then he made his way to the bathroom and she followed, laughing to herself when he scratched his ass and yawned all at once. He ignored her merriment, still not fully awake. And he would not be awake at all until he walked out the front door. That also saddened her.

The bathroom light flicked on and he stood in front of the mirror forcing his eyes wide. There had been more life in those blue eyes several months ago. They had lost the glimmer they had back when they took the time to speak of their dreams, possible futures. Now, he was but a shadow of the man he had been then. The scruff on his chin cemented this visual, and he did not bother to shave it away as often as he once had. Who would have known things like having a child could bring such sadness to her man?

She missed his body next to hers, his sweet embrace each night when he kissed her goodnight. They were distant now, slept on opposite sides of the bed. Her side was always so cold, and she rarely made it through the night without waking. And she also longed for the days to return when he kissed her every morning before he left for work, and then again when he arrived home. They never kissed anymore, not since Heidi was born. But she supposed there could be no point to dwelling on the past.

Their cat, Chester, curled his tail around her calve and mewed. It made her smile and she snuck a peek at Jonathan, wondered if he would be caught smiling. His expression remained solemn as ever, but at least he had bothered to glance her way. She felt uncomfortable standing there at the bathroom doorway under his gaze. She shifted and Chester sped to her other leg, looked up to her and cried. The poor thing must be hungry.

She ignored the cat for now, stayed focused on her husband. She enjoyed observing on the days when he shaved, wished he would do so more often. The process of shaving mesmerized her and a clean-shaven man could be so handsome. He was so meticulous with each stroke, slicing off the stubble without nicking himself. She loved the way he smelled afterward, the cologne he splashed on his neck and cheeks to keep from getting a rash.

Today, his eyes were too dreamy and he did cut his chin. A red pearl of blood trickled along his jaw, dripped into the white porcelain sink. He stared at the droplet, watched as the running water rushed it down the drain. He remained in this position, gazing into the steaming sink while another droplet formed and then fell, was swept away in the swirl of water.

A loud meow drew his attention back to them, his gaze on Chester and then to her. He opened his mouth, as if to say something. But then he stopped. The discomfort returned and she had the odd sensation he had not been looking at her. Still, she waited, hopeful. He forced a half-hearted smile and went back to shaving. This, too, would suffice.

If nothing else, he had continued being a snappy dresser. He still wore dress shirts, although they had grown more wrinkled as of late. Even the pleats of his slacks were uneven. The jacket could use a good dry-cleaning, but he kept his ties knotted neat as ever. She expected no less and it made her proud that she was his wife. Now and then, he even took the time to polish his shoes a brilliant black while they watched prime-time television together. Regardless of how flawed their relationship had become, she thought still thought him appealing after all these years. Even on days when he was not so clean-shaven or sharp-dressed man. Maybe this was why she had stayed.

She sat at the breakfast bar, watched as he prepared his breakfast. After all these years, he still made the best omelets. Even Chester mewed with approval. And together, the cat and she watched Jonathan eat. He ignored them for the morning paper, engrossed in the day's affairs. Before he finished his eggs, he rose and placed the plate in the sink. Chester whined a complaint, but Jonathan had already left the kitchen and would not return.

Together, Jonathan and she stood in the doorway of their daughter's bedroom. They took a moment to observe the baby breathe. She was so young, so new, so beautiful. She could not think of a single thing she had done in her life that could even be compared to what they had created together.

He stepped into the nursery, stood over Heidi and wavered. Then he had her in hand, propped her up against his shoulder and smiled. This had been the first smile she had seen this morning. A sigh of sleep escaped their precious little one, and Paula followed when he passed her in the hallway. She lifted herself on tippy toes behind them, to catch glimpses of her daughter's face.

He eased Heidi into his arms, rocked her for a bit and then placed her in the car seat while he gathered supplies into her diaper bag. She took note of what he grabbed to make certain he forgot nothing. He was such a good dad and had not missed a single item. Then he slung the bag over his left shoulder and grabbed up the car seat in his right hand.

She trailed him to the door and he opened it, stood in the doorway and gazed back at her. And she beheld him. Then his eyes fell to their baby, and he smiled again.

"Maybe after work we can stop by and say hi to mommy," he said.

This made her both happy and anxious.

The door closed and she hurried to the front bay window. There she saw the Arch in the distance and again thought how magnificent it appeared. Jonathan set Heidi in the backseat, locked her into place. Then he climbed into the driver's side and sat behind the wheel where he stared up at their house. She could see a frown form on his face. And tears leaked from the corners of his eyes.

He backed the car out of the driveway, and she watched it all the way down the street, until it disappeared around the corner and was out of sight. She stayed by the window for a long time, reflected upon their marriage. She could not help but have a sense of pride for her husband, but she also worried because he was so sad. She decided to wait in this spot for them to return. If she had to, she would spend an eternity trying to make things right again. And then it occurred to her that he had not bothered to kiss her goodbye. But that was how most days went, always together but so very far apart.

PATIENCE, I PRESUME
Malcolm R. Campbell

Lo, are my songs like birds
Within a wicker hung, and thou,
Beloved, hast loosed the latch
And let them free!
  - Patience Worth

The power went out when Prudence Lowe began reading chapter two of *Hope Trueblood.* The darkness startled her and the book fell to the floor with a thud. Her bedroom window rattled in the wind bringing St. Louis its first snowfall of the year. She knocked her hairbrush and several makeup bottles off the vanity while searching with gloved hands for the power outage candle. Frugal to a fault, her father kept the house colder than a morgue throughout the winter.

When she lit the candle, the tri-fold mirror displayed three Prudence Lowes looking back at her. Chances were none of them were less prudent than she, for here she was on a snowy night with nothing but a candle for writing a procrastinated book report.

"Read and report on an old book," her college English teacher announced three weeks ago, demonstrating that she was faultlessly cruel.

Hope Trueblood, rescued earlier that evening from the downstairs crypt her father called a library, lay face down on the floor. Her second floor bedroom with its canted bay window was not only cold but drafty, and those drafts made the candle flicker enough to bring the book's golden egg-shaped illustration, "*Hope Trueblood*" and "By Patience Worth" in and out of the dark. The book seemed to breathe or have a heartbeat.

Prudence felt an unpleasant jolt when she picked up *Hope Trueblood*. Static electricity or something else, the current that flowed through her black leather gloves was colder than snow. She was colder than snow, too, and was certain one of the Prudences in the vanity mirror was frowning at her.

The last words she read before she dropped *Hope Trueblood* were '*When I waked the rain roared upon the roof and the chill of night filled up the room. I sat up in my cot and rubbed my eyes open, yawned and looked to her cot. The light was still pale.*"

Her mother and grandmother loved virtue names, names like Prudence, Patience, Temperance, and Chastity. Like the kid in the book, Mother's name was *Hope*. Grandmother's name was *Grace*. Her older brother was *Destiny*.

"Live up to your name, Sweetie," Mother said.

"We're a Puritan family with positive virtues," Grandmother said.

"Listen to your mother and grandmother," Father said. His name was Randy. Proper to a fault, Mother and Grandmother called Father "Randolph" because they thought it was impossible to be both randy and virtuous.

Prudence heard a voice when she resumed reading chapter two. Since the raspy whisper startled her, *Hope Trueblood* hit the floor with another thud or, perhaps, a cry of pain. Her bedroom window was empty of everything but snow. The voice was in the room.

Prudence crept across the cold, hardwood floor, turned the knob slowly, and yanked open the bedroom door, thinking Destiny lurked on the landing. Nobody there. The house was quiet as a tomb and twice as dark. She took a deep breath. It didn't help. Her skin from head to toe and back again itched inside and out. In spite of the voice, her bedroom was less forbidding than the landing. The candle welcomed her back to her vanity and so did the three red-haired Prudences within the brass frames of her mirror.

She sat face to face with her selves and listened. The snow fluttered against the window like caged birds. Cold air from an unknown source whispered through the heating vent. A siren wailed down DeBaliviere Avenue toward Forest Park. The snare-drum beat of her gloved fingers on her vanity were the loudest sound in the room.

"Patience, Prudence," Mother would say.

"She has flaming red hair, Hope, and will never be patient." Grandmother would say.

Destiny would laugh at that.

At dinner, when the house was warm and filled with light, Destiny said, "I can't believe you're writing a report about a dead lady's book." He made a ghostly sound and wriggled his fingers in the air.

"That's the assignment," said Prudence. "The book has to be old."

"Patience Worth was dead when she wrote *Hope Trueblood*," said Destiny. "Right Dad?"

Mr. Lowe, who believed — to a fault, of course — that dinners were meant for eating rather than talking, came alive when Destiny uttered what must have been a magical incantation. He put down his fork for Patience Worth.

"Patience was a pure spirit from the land of Everspace," he said. "She became quite a celebrity when she spoke via Pearl Curran's Ouija board almost a hundred years ago. For twenty-five years, Patience dictated poems and novels that were well received."

"Through a Ouija board — are you kidding?" asked Prudence.

"Only at first," Father said. "Soon, Pearl began speaking for Patience with archaic words and phrasings outside her knowledge."

"How did I never hear of that?" asked Prudence.

"The Currans lived in a first-floor flat right around the corner when it all started," said her mother. "The traffic to and from their living room was endless. By the time you were born, Pearl and Patience were forgotten."

"A dead lady writing books right here in our own Skinky-D," said Destiny. "I love it."

"Which house is it?" asked Prudence.

"The brick one," said Destiny.

"They're all brick," said Prudence.

She punched Destiny's arm. He punched her arm and moved his chair out of reach.

"One wouldn't know you two are college students," Father said. He scribbled scarcely legible words on a napkin as though he were writing a prescription at his clinic. "Here's the address. It's a nice old house with real people who probably won't appreciate your snooping."

"I'll drive by in Jitterbug. They won't know I know."

"I hope they don't," Mother said. Mother was ever hopeful.

"So, you're the work of a ghost," Prudence said as she returned to *Hope Trueblood*. "Grandma once told me that opening a ghost story book is like opening a portal into Everspace or the spirit world or the astral plane.

Figuratively speaking you are a ghost's story, are you not, Miss Trueblood?"
The brat, as some called her, didn't answer.

The book was tedious and perhaps infinite. Nonetheless, she crawled through the next line: *"I shivered and arose to hasten to her side. She lay huddled, shivering."*

The words further chilled the room. Prudence could see her breath and breaths of the Prudences in the mirrors. Were her reflections as cold as she? Left Prudence looked dead already, indicating that hyperthermia attacks images faster than people. Prudence leaned in close and kissed Left Prudence's cold blue lips.

"There now, we'll have our heat back soon."

The Prudences looked unconvinced. Behind the three Prudences, the vibrant moon and stars quilt lay warm and inviting on her bed. They could share, she thought, as the temperature dropped low enough to freeze perfume, hairspray and blood.

A fourth, Almost-Prudence sat on the bed, watching them. *Hope Trueblood* fell on the floor again, provoking a sharp cry from the book and the mirage above the moon and stars. Prudence spun around in her chair and saw no one there. That sharp cry had been brittle cold as though the quilt were a deep space portal.

"I would speak with thee."

The voice was behind her. Almost-Prudence was still in the mirror. She was young, but wore an old lady's cape made of dark, homespun fabric that matched the color of night in the quilt. Her hair was dark red, more mahogany than fire and her eyes were brown and staring and desperate as her blood red lips repeated the words *speak with thee* with a gale force wind that tore the flame off the candle.

Prudence needed to breathe.

She was colder inside than outside and felt watched from both the mirror and the moon and stars. Spirits can see in the dark because they are the dark. She had read that in a dark book in the downstairs crypt.

"Speak with thee."

The words were far away and weakly said.

"Okay," said Prudence.

"Nay here."

"Where?"

"Thou knowest."

"I do?" asked Prudence as the power came on.

Almost-Prudence disappeared. Light flooded the room followed by a wraith of lukewarm air from the heating vent. Prudence released her death grip on the edge of her vanity. She could breathe now. She scanned the room for the ghost and saw that the left, right and middle Prudences did the same. They were alone and lonely as though a part of them had vanished.

Prudence stuffed *Hope Trueblood* into her book bag and bolted out of the room. She had a book review to finish. As Grandmother said, "time doesn't put on its brakes for anyone." She ran downstairs making more noise than was prudent, insuring that Mrs. Lowe would be standing like a security officer at the front door.

"Patience, Prudence," she shouted with more volume than the moment required.

"You're absolutely right, Mother. I must find Patience's house."

Mother was stunned, though Prudence wasn't patient enough to ask whether it was due to the mission at hand or the lack of an "Oh, Mother!" response.

"What about your book report?"

"This is research," said Prudence, slipping around her and out the front door.

"In my day, we just read the book and wrote down what we thought about it," Mrs. Lowe was saying, or potentially saying, as the front door clicked shut.

The blustery weather had moved east. The first snow on the ground was minimal. Jitterbug started without protest. A good omen, thought Prudence. She put the napkin on the passenger seat even though she didn't plan to forget the address.

Kids out past their bedtimes were playing in the streets and yards. The neighborhood was more people friendly than car friendly. Streets curved around to adjacent streets where intersections once provided options. Trees stood close to curbs lined with parked cars. Snowball fights added another driving hazard.

Prudence had never paid attention to Patience Worth's two-story brick house snugged in between other two-story brick houses with side yards so small neighbors could shake hands and borrow cups of sugar by leaning out their windows. A light was on in the front room of the flat where Pearl channeled Patience. While the rest of the house was dark inside, the outside was overexposed from a nearby streetlight. Two kids were having a snowball fight on several adjoining bright white lawns. Prudence could hardly sit there without attracting attention. Her ancient, lime green Volkswagen always attracted attention. She drove past the children, an old man walking a small dog, and a young couple guiding a laughing toddler down the sidewalk.

Prudence thought about going home, borrowing her folks' boring grey Buick and coming back. But, she didn't have a key to the Buick. She circled around several large blocks, figuratively speaking, and by the time she returned, nobody was there. The downstairs light was off. Prudence turned off the engine, rolled down the window, and watched for signs.

The neighborhood was quiet. Quiet and bright. If there were a sign, a voice or a wispy cloud that turned into Probable-Patience, they could hardly talk here. The house was dark, but who knew how many eyes the darkness held? Probable-Patience's house was either a Queen Anne with Craftsman influences or a Craftsman house with Queen Anne influences. Her mother would know. Her mother knew everything about the Skinker-DeBaliviere-Catlin Tract- Parkview Historic District including how many minutes Prudence had been sitting there in front of the house.

"Patience?" she whispered.

"Nay here — women watch," said a cloaked figure crouching between two parked cars.

"Where?"

"Mayhap Kennedy Forest is dark enough to hide a shade."

Probable-Patience vanished. Prudence's only option at hand was driving over to DeBaliviere and following it south into the park. Jitterbug's heater was working, and that was a small comfort. Prudence liked DeBaliviere — it was spacious, especially at night. When she said the name, she felt French, French and fiery.

Once she emerged from the Jeep-trail tracks centered in the neighborhood's white streets, driving was easy. Earlier traffic on the main streets had worn away the snow. The night was too warm for black ice and the clearing sky gave Prudence the stars.

"I threw my small arms about her and let my lips press her cold cheek, saying: 'Sally Trueblood, I love you.'"

Jitterbug swerved and almost hit one of the trees in the median. *Hope Trueblood* was reading itself to her from inside the tattered book bag.

"Bad Jitterbug," snapped Prudence with a touch of guilt for her complicity in the near accident.

"She did not wake and I crept to her side beneath the covers that she might warm upon my body."

Prudence checked the rearview mirror for police cars. None were present. She didn't want to get pulled over with a talking book bag because that meant somebody would end up going to jail and it probably wouldn't be Hope Trueblood.

Like an old radio tuned to a station on the far side of the country, *Hope Trueblood* was talking in scattered nouns and verbs when Prudence passed the history museum. *"I heard the dog arise and shake."* Her cell phone rang. It was beneath the book. She pulled over and fished it out while the book kept talking.

"Yes, Mother."

"Are you okay?"

"I'm fine, mother."

"It's late. I thought you'd be home by now," Mother said.

"I've expanded the scope of my research," said Prudence.

"Sally Trueblood, it is morning!" the book said, loud enough to wake the dead.

"Who are you with?"

If there was one thing Prudence disliked to a fault, it was being smothered by a mother hen of a mother. After all, she was in college. Parents were not one of the perks of living at home. *It's Patience, Mother*, she wanted to say.

"It's the radio," said Prudence. "I pulled over to answer the phone. I can't sit here and talk."

"Be careful."

"My mother suddenly arose and clung to the coverings, wrapping herself within them and coughing. She seemed like a slender reed in the wind, the cough swayed her so."

"I will," said Prudence, pressing the *End* button before her mother could ask what station had such programming.

Prudence wrapped a sweatshirt around Sally and Hope and shoved the book to the bottom of her book bag to muffle the coughing. Mother vexed her so, but Prudence worried about her. Her hair was greyer than the paint on the Buick, she had a persistent winter cough, and like Sally, she was like a slender reed in the wind.

Kennedy Forest was deserted, dark outside the range of the streetlights, and the branches of the trees were shrouded in white. In the summer and fall, Prudence loved the sanctuary of oak, hickory and walnut, but now even the delicate, feathery silhouettes of the pin oaks were stark and forbidding in the weak light. While the tangle of winter creeper and honeysuckle appeared as insubstantial as frost patterns on a window, they were faultless in their ability to snag a hiker's foot. If she had to walk, she wanted a trail. She parked Jitterbug beneath a streetlight across from a flight of wood steps leading up a gentle hill.

When Prudence stepped outside, her shoes plunged deep into slush. Why hadn't she taken the time to put on boots? Mother was right: it was late and she should be home by now writing her book report.

"Is anyone here?" she asked, tentatively.

"When I awoke the sun was not come. Silence hung about, like unto a shroud, pierced but by some waking bird that called to its mate," said *Hope Trueblood* from the depths of the book bag.

"Hush, you dusty old book or I won't hear your author."

There she was, then, that cloaked Almost-Prudence fresh out of her vanity mirror, descending the wood steps out of the woods the way a grand lady makes an entrance in a ball gown. She was remarkably present within the here and now for a ghost who hadn't haunted St. Louis for seventy-six years.

When their eyes met, as mirror images of each other, Prudence said, "Patience, I presume."

"Aye, thou seeth me," she replied as they met in the middle of the street. She raised her eyebrows, adding, "Impatience, I presume, dressed to naught in pantaloons without a pettiskirt."

"I am Prudence. You've been haunting me long enough to know I wear jeans."

"Sitteth with me?" asked Patience, returning to the bottom step.

Prudence watched her brush off the snow with a branch. Brushing snow off a step was so overtly normal that it scared her.

"I'll sit if you'll tell me in modern English what you want."

Patience pushed the back her hood and smiled.

"I can stick out a modern tongue," she said. "Please, sit."

When Prudence sat, the left side of her body merged with the right side of Patience Worth, and the partial intermingling of their selves was sweetly painful and cold.

"You are spirit to a fault," said Prudence.

"Speak no more of fault for it's a poor shield even though you wear it bravely," said Patience. "It is late, as your vexing mother told you and *Hope Trueblood* grows tired of talking to herself inside your cloth sack. I also say it is late and ask when you planned to write about a book you have not read while the dawn is growing near."

"I meant to do it sooner, but the assignment was long and tedious," said Patience.

"The chore does not grow shorter through delay."

"You're right," snapped Prudence. The conversation was going badly. Patience spoke the way her mother spoke when she wanted something. "The report was going to be wonderful."

"You bask in the imagined fame of having written rather than in the joy of writing."

"Are you handing me parental injunctions or proverbs?" asked Prudence, shifting away from the cold zone where her left arm was the same as Patience's right arm.

"They are apothegms," said Patience.

"What?"

"Helpful sayings."

"Fine," said Prudence. She stood up and stared down at the tiny woman. "You led me to your book, to your house and to this forest. Why?"

"Each of us needs something."

"Do we?"

"You need a book report or else you will fail your English class and I need a voice. I called you because I saw a mutually beneficial opportunity."

The words were gentle, but there was guile in between them. If she failed English, she wouldn't have enough credits for graduation. That was faultless logic.

"You have a voice," said Prudence. "I've been listening to it."

Patience vanished and where she had been sitting, the step was no longer free of snow.

"Patience?"

"I am here."

But she wasn't *here*. She was within or above the small trees alongside the steps.

"You are floating over me as a cloud."

Even though no spindrift rose up along the stair, a cold wind tossed Prudence back into the street. She skidded on the slick pavement but didn't fall.

"I am naught but cloud, wind and mirage," said Patience, reappearing on the step. "When Pearl Lenore Curran died in December of 1937, she took my voice with her to the grave. Though you are but an impatient girl, you have ears to hear the *me of* me in the old neighborhood and here amongst powerful oaks where I have awaited such as you. Otherwise, I am mute."

"You want me to speak for you?" The notion was both flattering and troubling. When Patience nodded, Prudence added, "To what end?"

"To your end," said Patience. "Until then, I have more books to write while you bask in the fame Pearl Lenore Curran enjoyed. Dignitaries sought her out. Critics praised her writing. Spiritual experts debated her existence and the manner in which the relatively unschooled Pearl knew what she knew and said what she said."

Prudence remembered thinking when read the Seth books channeled years ago by Jane Roberts that "it must be nice."

"It can be nice," said Patience, prying into her thoughts. "Think of it, the fame and money of having written without the long and tedious chore of having to write."

"There is that," admitted Prudence. There had to be a downside, though. Genies, gods and ghosts always took something when they gave away blessings requiring no human effort.

"The downside as you call it," said Patience, "is that you will never be shed of me. The *me of me* is pervasive and persistent."

Patience's dark brown eyes missed nothing, piercing the night and Prudence's impatient soul like hot coals on a block of ice. Those eyes held blessings and curses, and she had to wonder if Pearl Lenore Curran knew that to a fault. But Prudence did not know how to turn away.

"If we started, how would we start?" she asked.

"Open your book bag and give *Hope Trueblood* back to me. Then, sit beside me, my beloved, and with pen and paper we will embark upon our first collaboration, a learned and stunning book report that will give you sufficient credit for your graduation. Do you consent?"

"I do," said Prudence before she took a breath.

ONE MILE SHY OF DEATH'S DOOR
Janet L. Cannon

Ragged breaths hissed in then out one cool, fall night on Des Peres River Road. Neon orange flashed just beyond the beam of a dim streetlamp. The quiet rhythm of feet pelting pavement resounded against the evergreens on one side and the swelled ditch of a river on the other. In and out the strained breathing continued. The scents of lemon sports drink and sweat mingled with the odor of pine and car exhaust. A whisper of fabric against fabric harmonized with the rustling of autumn leaves. Chirping crickets accompanied the ghostly concerto.

The deep inhales and quick exhales sped up as did the cadence of the pounding. Drops of sweat appeared then vanished on the cracks of the black asphalt. Faster! Another streetlamp, another flash of orange. *Faster*!

Shelby Monohan arrived at the southern corner of the boulevard that indicated the two-mile mark from home. She reduced her pace back to tempo speed and exhaled a relieved sigh. Leaves and twigs and bits of candy wrappers swirled in all directions. Glancing at her watch, she smiled. Shelby was on track for setting a personal time record for a ten-mile run. All she had to do was keep her current pace, enjoy the cool evening breeze and the adrenaline high she often got from running long, and arrive at her front door. Easy. She'd done it a hundred times before.

As Shelby passed the boulevard and the four lanes merged again, she sensed a change in the atmosphere. She glanced around, searching for what was wrong. A moped passed her in the far northbound lane. On instinct, she flipped the switch on her pepper spray. There weren't many places for people to hide and it was decently lit, but she was always hyper-aware of her surroundings when running alone. Vance knew her route and when to expect her back home. He'd come for her in the car if she didn't show in the next 15 minutes, but a lot could happen in 15 minutes.

She was so focused on locating the danger around her she forgot to watch traffic. As she looked forward again, she realized the oncoming car wasn't swerving away. They had a whole other lane! Couldn't they see her reflective orange jacket? Shelby screamed and dove for the grassy edge.

In the movies, the heroine had the dexterity to curl and roll through the fall, perhaps even land back on her feet. In real life, however, Shelby wasn't that coordinated. She fell spread-eagle and skidded and bounced across the grass, feeling every pinecone, exposed root, and tossed beer bottle. When she opened her eyes, she was level with the newly mown lawn.

Perfect. She had probably just blown out a knee and road-rashed her arms and legs. Didn't experts say most accidents happened within five miles of home? How was she going to make it two more miles? Shelby rolled to sit up and assess the damage.

It was too dark to see, but she was betting her outfit was covered with green streaks. Annoying but washable. Nothing felt bruised or was bleeding on her face. She patted her arms, her chest, and examined her legs. Nothing. No injuries. She didn't even feel bad. Shock, perhaps. That must be it. The ground was soft enough to dull the blows, but the bruises and aches would kick in tomorrow.

"Ma'am, can I help you?" a man's voice asked.

Shelby yelped, surprised that someone had sneaked up on her. The wind shrieked through the trees around them. She turned to find a middle-aged man kneeling in the street. He was dressed in the most ridiculous running outfit she'd ever seen: a white sweatband over his salt and pepper hair, white sneakers, a white cotton t-shirt that barely covered his beer-belly, and blue shorts with white piping. The man even had his white socks pulled up nearly to his knees! His pale skin seemed almost translucent under the harsh glow of the streetlamp.

"Ma'am, you okay?" he asked again. "You took quite a spill there."

"You're not from around here. Your accent is strange." Shelby rolled to her feet.

"You're right, ma'am. I'm originally from parts south o' here. Would you like some help?"

She stepped away so he was out of arm's reach. "No. Thank you. I just need to walk it off." Shelby took a few steps and found her legs didn't hurt.

For now, at least. She was certain that if this guy turned out to be a psycho, she could outrun him. With her thumb, she checked the pepper spray tube. It was still unlocked and ready. "I'm okay. You can go back to whatever you were doing."

"I don't think I can, ma'am. Ya see, my wife would yell at me if I left you helpless on the side of the road. I have to make sure you get home safe."

On the grass, Shelby jogged a few steps beside the curb. Still, nothing hurt. "My husband is expecting me home soon. When I don't show up in time he'll drive out and pick me up. I'll be fine."

The man smiled, his teeth too white and perfectly shaped under the lights. Falsies at his age? "I don't mean to make you nervous." On the street, he jogged parallel to her position. "I'll just keep my distance, okay?"

Seeing she had little choice in the matter, Shelby nodded and continued north, staying on the grass. "So what brought you to Saint Louis, Mr...?"

"Heath. Rob Heath." He kept pace with her but in the street. "I'm a detective. Transfer from Georgia."

"Georgia? Why would you want to move here?"

He laughed. "Ghosts."

"Ghosts? There are no such things as ghosts."

Rob threw her a sidelong glance. "You live in Saint Louis and don't believe ghost stories?"

"No reasonable person believes ghost stories."

He chuckled again. "When I do murder investigations, I like to imagine I'm discovering what the ghosts are trying to tell me. Some people say I'm psychic. Everyone has a story. Especially people who die before their time."

"Ghosts tell stories to the living? Right." Shelby tightened her grip on the pepper spray. She glanced over and studied Rob, trying to figure out his game. Besides his odd dress and his accent, he didn't <u>look</u> like a sexual predator. But what did a sexual predator look like? It was then she noticed that his footsteps didn't make a sound on the pavement. She sped up and so did he. "And that's what you do for a living? Murder investigations?"

"Well, I do whatever the chief tells me to do, but I specialize in murder." He laughed. "Investigating murder. You know. Figuring out what kind of weapons leave no mark, how to hide a body so no one will find it, how to break into people's houses without a trace, what's the best way to sneak up on people, gain their trust, things like that."

Shelby sped up. So did Rob.

Another car headed their way and refused to yield. Rob cursed and leapt up onto the curb with Shelby, forcing Shelby to surge forward out of his way.

They stopped and stared at the back of the truck as it zoomed south.

Rob waggled his finger at the truck. "I'm gonna report that driver. He had plenty of room to move over. Could've killed me. Crazy people. Probably some pimply kid out to prove his manhood to his friends." He pointed ahead. "Let's stay on the grass. Probably safer anyway."

A few seconds after they'd started running again, Shelby turned her head. "Did you hear that?"

"What? A ghost?" Rob grinned.

"No, I told you, there are no ghosts. Listen!" Shelby held her breath and tried to filter out the hissing of the leaves, the choir of crickets, and the howl of the wind through the trees. Footsteps. Breathing. She looked behind and saw nothing but empty black pavement but she swore she could hear someone following them. And a buzzing noise, like a small motor. "Let's run a little faster."

"Okay." Rob looked around but apparently didn't see anything either. Together they ran in the grass at a quick pace toward the Landsdowne Bridge.

The sound of footsteps and heavy breathing behind her was getting louder. She glanced back again. Nothing.

"Do you see anyone?" Rob asked.

"No, but I swear I hear somebody!"

"Let's keep going."

She pushed the pace faster. Although he appeared out of shape and much older, he kept up. He might not know how to dress for a run, but he was definitely fit.

A mile from home, yards from the Landsdowne Bridge, Shelby heard soft laughter behind her. Stopping, she turned and saw a flash of a knife. Shelby screamed. She sprinted across the street dodging past another northbound moped with his lights off. Or was that that the same one? She could almost feel the breath of her assailant on her neck, his hands on her shoulders, his cackle of delight as he caught her and pulled her down, his weight pressing her body on the ground, the knife sinking into her chest....

But when she reached the rocky river's edge and turned, no one was there. Shelby turned, confused.

Rob, in the meantime, had started running across the street after her. She watched in horror as a ghostly car swerved off the Landsdowne Bridge and directly for him.

He heard the screech of tires and looked up just in time to see a pair of halogen headlights outlining a sports car's bumper.

Rob cringed, unable to avoid the impact. Shelby cringed, too, anticipating the crackle of bones pulverizing into shards and the rending of muscles and ligaments into shreds. Instead, the car passed <u>through</u> him and skidded to a halt, skewed 90 degrees, halfway in the grass. Then it faded away.

They stared at each other for several silent seconds.

The moped made a U-turn on the bridge and pulled up between the two on the grass.

A young man pulled off his helmet and glanced at each of them. "Shelby Monohan and Rob Heath, I believe?" They both nodded. "You've both witnessed the replay of each other's deaths and experienced evidence of your own unlife. You can now move on."

Shelby frowned. "I'm not dead, I--"

"Shelby Monohan, you were reported missing by your husband three years ago. Your killer confessed to your murder but wouldn't reveal where he stashed your body. I imagine it's under or around the bridge."

"I'm not dead!"

He pointed to his moped. "I've been tracking both of you all night and I can tell you, your behavior is not that of the living. First, you took a fall that would have put most runners in the ER. That's why we think your killer was able to catch you. Second, according to reports, you've been repeating this run every fall since your death, terrifying every psychically sensitive person in the area. Which happens to be quite a few. You are a danger to the living. I'm sorry. You're dead, and it's time for you to stop."

She stared down at her clothes. In the bright lights of the intersection, Shelby realized they weren't stained. Furthermore, she had no injuries. None. The fall should have incapacitated her. No way could she have run that far that fast after a fall that bad.

"And you've been creating havoc at this intersection for even longer, Rob Heath. You died 40 years ago, killed by a drunk driver. I think your death revelation was pretty obvious. Especially when the cars wouldn't yield for you."

"Like a skunk in the kitchen, son." Rob frowned. "But who are you? What's your part in this?"

"I'm a peace maker. I track ghosts like you two who are in denial of your deaths. I watch you play out your deaths then help you come to terms with your fate." He laughed. "It's a gift I inherited." The young man's wan smile encompassed them both. "Go. Be at peace. Run with the wind, or whatever souls do on the other side."

The ghosts faded.

Quenton Heath smiled. "Good rest, grandfather. Glad I didn't inherit your taste in clothing."

WELCOME
Shenoa Carroll-Bradd

I was born in 1868, and throughout my long life, I have gained and lost a family, played host to millionaires, businessmen, down-on-their-luck boarders, and many a soul in between. And while I have known great joy and triumph, I have also borne witness to lingering tragedy.

In 1876, my family spent a great amount of time and money to make me over, turning me from a stately (if drab) wonder, to a gorgeous Victorian showplace with thirty-three rooms. My heart and arms were big enough to embrace the whole family, and times were good. Beneath my feet lay caves of wonders, boasting an auditorium, a theater, bowling alley and swimming pool. For a short time, my family was happy.

The world began to dim for them in 1901, when young Frederick's heart gave out, and he collapsed like rotting beams. He had always been a sickly man, and though I did my best to keep him safe and warm, there is only so much one can do to stall nature.

His father, William Sr., withdrew into my company after that, no longer venturing outside unless forced. The whole family seemed to carry a pall over them, and William Sr.'s mental and physical self shriveled, until he shot himself in the head in February of 1904.

I have overheard reports of my guests hearing someone running up the stairs and kicking at the door of that room, just as William Jr. had at the sound of the shot. William Sr. had locked the door, of course, but grief made his son violent, and he tried to kick it down.

William Jr. headed the family after that, what was left of it. He, his pretty little wife, Lillian, and their son William III, were my constant companions.

They brought even more beauty into the family with clothing and carriages and great works of art

Soon came the gatherings beneath my feet, the laughter, the excitement that I was not invited to join in, but could hear. I could feel the vibrations of their voices as they swam and talked and bowled, and I had to wait for them to come back to me, always worried that this time, this time maybe they wouldn't.

They did come back though, and one night William Jr. brought an addition to the family, a little secret boy whom I loved very much. I lifted him up and held him above the rest of the family, with the servants. He was a little strange, not like the others, but I loved him best, and he stayed with me his whole life. He never tried to leave me like the others. I heard some call him the monkey-faced boy, but I thought of him as my little angel.

The family broke apart in 1909, and both lovely Lillian and William Jr. III left me behind.

William made me over once more in 1911, a little insulting perhaps, but anything I could do to make him happy, to keep him with me, was worth the trouble and expense. Despite the work, William spent an increasing amount of time down by the Meramec instead of with me, and married another woman, Ellie, in 1915. Neither of us could keep him happy though. William Jr. became gloomy and depressed, preferring my company over society's, and slipping into ill health. While I cherished the increased time with him, I could feel something was not right. But what could I possibly do?

On December 29, 1922, William shot himself in the heart, in the very same place his father had died eighteen years before.

I feared I might be alone after that, but the family always returns to me.

William's brother, Charles, came to me, and lived with two servants and my little angel, the monkey-faced boy. Charles was an odd man, and did not revive the kind of joy the family had known in the old days. He wore gloves at all hours and washed his hands constantly.

My little angel died around that time, somewhere in his thirties. They took him from me, and buried him out of my reach, without his name on the marker.

To this day, visitors claim to see his sweet face peering out of the windows, and that if you leave toys out for him, they will be strewn about the room on your return. I love that my little angel finally has a chance to make friends, now that he's dead.

In 1949, not long after my angel's death, Charles went to the basement and shot his beloved Doberman Pinscher, then went to his room and shot himself. While the second shot did its work neatly, the first was imprecise, and the unhappy dog climbed halfway up the stairs before expiring.

After Charles' death, the family abandoned me to strangers, who came and went, but never forged a connection with me, or the history I held. My new visitors were poor, and complained often of ghostly knocks and phantom footsteps. As they spread their stories, the volume of my guests trickled away, until I was nearly forsaken.

In 1970, the last of the family (who never seemed to like me much) died of old age, and ordered that all of my paintings, documents and keepsakes should be taken from me and burned. You cannot imagine the loss I felt, watching my family's history and treasures consumed by the fire.

I thought for sure that I would be next to feel its heat, but I didn't, and in 1975, I got a new family. Dick Pointer and his family gave me my last makeover, returning me to my former glory. Many of their workers fled before the job was completed though, citing tools that vanished and appeared, strange sounds, and a feeling of being watched.

Many of my guests claim to have seen my first family, though I have not. Stories abound of apparitions that appear and then vanish, of unexplained voices and sounds, and even of glasses that will rise up and fly through the air of their own accord. Doors lock and unlock themselves at will, lights flash on and off by themselves, and the piano is even said to play when no one else is near. When the wind blows just right, I can hear the sounds of horses to the north, though the only beasts in that area these days are made of metal and do not neigh.

And so I stand at 3322 DeMenil Place, changed but not forgotten as the years roll on, a sanctuary for those who wish to visit, and for those who never want to leave.

I am the Lemp Mansion.

Welcome.

THINGS THAT GO BUMP IN THE GYM
Kathryn Cureton

I saw my first ghost shortly after 9:00 on a hot August night, in a high school gym in Cuba, Missouri. I was two years out of college, headstrong and invincible, and a skeptic of supernatural phenomena.

My first varsity coaching job was the only thing on my mind that night. I started volleyball practice for my team at the earliest allowable date, two weeks before school opened. The gym was not air-conditioned. Our workouts were from 7:00 to 9:00 p.m. At the end of practice on Friday of the first week, I lined the girls up to run sprints from sideline to sideline. When they finished, I grabbed the volleyball rack and net bag to put away in the storage closet. The girls trickled out of the gym and into the locker room, and from there into the parking lot through the back door. The rest of the school was locked up with door chains.

I maneuvered the ball rack around the cart holding a deflated high jump mat, and hung the net bag on a hook. The gym was empty when I came out. I crossed the floor to the bleacher side to click off the lights at that end of the gym. Then I continued down the sideline on the bleacher side to get to the other electrical box. I opened the brown metal panel. Just as I reached for the switches, I heard a "click."

Movement to the right caught my attention. The double metal doors on the wall across the gym, beside the boys' locker room door, slowly swung open. Simultaneously. Halfway. They were brown metal. The one on the left had no doorknob, but latched at the top into the doorframe, and at the bottom into a floor plate. The door on the right had the doorknob. Once you unlocked it, you had to unlatch the left door. Yet they both swung open. I looked inside, in the dim light that filtered in from the half-lit gym. There was something white, about three feet tall. I assumed it was one of the players pulling a prank. A girl in a white T-shirt, crouched down to surprise me. I waited for her to say something, still standing by the electrical box. No kid was going to prank me! I was too cool for that.

"Okay. You scared me. Come on out."

Nothing.

"Ha, ha! Very funny. Come on."

Nothing.

By now, I felt foolish. Maybe it wasn't a girl crouching in a white T-shirt to scare me. Oh! It was the deflated, rolled-up, white canvas high jump mat on its rolling cart. That line of reasoning lasted about 15 seconds. I had just walked around that mat in the *other* storage room when I put away the volleyballs. Now things were getting creepy. And I needed to turn out those lights on that end of the gym.

I'd already done it four times that week without incident. I knew I would be in total darkness, save one thin strip of light under the girls' locker room door at the opposite end. Between me and that safe lighted haven was a volleyball net and several guide wires. Running to the light was out of the question. Then there was the little matter of that white thing in the self-opening closet.

I took a deep breath. Clicked off the light switches. Honed in on that quarter-inch strip of light under the girls' locker room door. As with the other nights, I headed across the gym to the concrete-block wall. Not straight across to those gaping doors with the white thing, but not at an angle that would run my head into the net or guide wires. The blind crossing seemed to take forever. I slammed into the wall with hands outstretched. I ran sideways along the wall until I was safe inside that first locker room door, where I had more light from the propped-open inner door, and then into the fully-lit locker room itself. I gathered my things from my office, and went out that back door to the parking lot, making sure to turn off those wonderful lights and lock the back door. The back locker room doors were the only way in and out on nights and weekends, with the rest of the entrances chained and padlocked.

I drove to my newly rented home four blocks away. I was really scared now. Doors don't open by themselves. And what was that white thing? When I had checked out that room at the beginning of the week, all I saw was a big water heater. It was more like a utility room than a storage room.

My plan was to drive to Springfield the next morning, where I had been taking graduate classes that summer, to pack up stuff from my sublet apartment. But I couldn't get that white thing out of my head. What *was* that? What if it followed me? The best thing to do was drive to Springfield *now*. Not sleep in my house four blocks away from the gym with that white thing. Just as I was putting the last of my things in the car, another thought hit me. I didn't turn off the exhaust fans in the gym! They were two big fans high up in the wall *at the end where that white thing was in the storage room!*

I did not want to go back into that building. But if I didn't, and those fans overheated and burned the school down over the weekend, I would be in big trouble. I went back into the house and got a flashlight. My mind kept telling me, "No, no, no! Don't go back in there!" But I had to. I was a responsible adult.

By now, it was around 10:15 p.m. I drove back to the school. I told myself, "If that was a girl hiding in the storage room to scare me, she would have to leave through the back locker room door. And that door will be unlocked now, because you can get out in emergencies, but you need a key to lock it from the outside." I almost had myself convinced that my first instinct had been correct. Until I grabbed the locker room doorknob, and it was locked, just as I had left it.

I went inside and turned on the locker room lights. I had one doorstop. It could prop open the inner door, and let a thin strip shine out under the door into the gym. Or I could prop open the gym door, and get what little light might show under the inner door crack. Darn this school and its doorstop rationing. I opted for propping the inner door as before, leaving a quarter-inch beacon marking my way back from the terror that awaited.

There are not many things scarier than a pitch-dark gym, other than a pitch-dark gym with a thin flashlight beam shining across it. I veered right, ducked under the volleyball net, and took a diagonal path to the light box. I reached to turn off the fan switches. Were those doors still open? Was that white thing still there? I wanted to look, but I didn't want to look. I turned the flashlight that way. The doors were still open. The white thing was gone. Eeeeeeee! The hair on the back of my neck stood up.

I turned off the exhaust fans. The gym was dead silent. I could hear my ragged breathing, and I swear I could hear my heart thumping. I pointed my flashlight back toward the locker room, and took off running. This was the 1980s, the days of the slick parachute-pants style windsuits. SWISH SWISH SWISH through the silent gym. My feet flapped on the composite floor. I wanted to scream. I felt like something was in that gym with me. I got out of that building as fast as I could. Locked the back locker room door. Proceeded straight to Springfield.

I arrived around 1:00 a.m., and nearly gave my summer roommate a heart attack. "You scared me to death!"

"You think *you're* scared, listen to *this*!"

During the next week of practice, I made a new rule. The player who finished last in the sprints had to stay and help me close up the gym. I held the locker room door open so a wedge of light splayed across the court. The daily slowpoke turned off the light switches. Nothing else happened. But I was leery of being in that gym alone after dark.

At the end-of-the-season pizza party, I told the team the whole story. "You made *us* do it because *you* were scared?"

"I sure did. But I stayed to help." They forgave me. But the next year, they ran those sprints a lot faster.

My experience was not the only strange happening in the Cuba High School gym. Coach Steve was in charge of the girls' basketball team. I was his assistant. We returned from a tournament late one night in the midst of a little snowstorm. The bus driver pulled up to the gym lobby. "These doors are chained," said Coach Steve. "Go ahead and park here. I'll run around to the back of the locker room, and come through the gym to open the lobby so the girls can use the phone."

The players and I gave him a few minutes, then went to wait by the glass doors for Coach Steve to unlock the chains. I saw him come through the gym door into the lobby. He looked a bit flustered. Wide-eyed. I could have sworn his hair was standing on end. Must have been the wind as he walked around the building. The girls and I entered. Coach Steve wasn't his usual easy-going self.

"What's the matter?"

"I'll tell you later. Let these girls get a ride." Coach Steve paced around the lobby while the girls used the pay phone. They left one by one, as their rides arrived. When only a couple of girls remained, down the hall at the pay phone, Coach Steve said, "Come here." He pulled me off to the side, out of sight of the remaining players. "Who did you let follow me through the locker room?"

"No one."

"Come on. I'm not mad. Was it Shelley?"

"No. No one followed you. They all stayed on the bus until we got off to wait by the door. Those girls wouldn't walk through the snow in their dress-up shoes. We all stood there waiting until you let us in. What's going on?"

"Are you sure? I walked out into that gym, and when I got about halfway across, I heard someone following me. I thought it was one of the girls trying to scare me. I stopped. They stopped. I went on, and I heard it again. I felt a hand on my shoulder. I threw my arm out and said, 'Get out of here!' and swatted behind me. There was no one there! Then I started running until I got to the bleachers, and I walked out here like nothing was going on. I didn't want to scare the girls."

"I don't want to go through there."

"*I* don't want to go back through by myself. We've got to lock this chain again after they leave."

"I'll stay and go with you. But we're going through together. And I'm holding on to you!"

All the girls got picked up. Coach Steve locked the chain. We linked elbows and entered the dark gym. We both kept talking, and walked as fast as we could with our arms linked. We made it to the locker room, where it was not so creepy.

The next day, we told Coach Mike, the baseball coach, about the incident. "Hey, I've got one, too. I come in here every morning to run laps for an hour. I get here around 6:00, turn on the lights for my half of the gym, and run half-court laps. The other morning, I saw Garland up in the bleachers. He was going from one end to the other, sweeping them off. I finished my workout around 7:00. Garland had been gone for about a half hour. I walked around a minute to cool down, and I saw him go by out in the hall. I walked over to the door and yelled, 'Hey, Gar, what are you doing here so early?' And he said, 'Huh? I just got here.'"

I don't know what was going on in the Cuba High School gym in the early 1980s. I spent three years working in there. After my initial incident, I made sure I was never there alone at night. Around Halloween, or whenever ghost talk came up, students spoke of people who had strange experiences in that gym. I never knew what to believe, whether there was truth behind their stories, or if I was hearing about a local urban legend. The most common tale from the kids was that the gym was haunted by the ghost of a freshman athlete who had been run over by a car walking home from practice one day. I never heard any factual information on this topic. Just hearsay.

It was a bit disconcerting to hear that the alleged accident scene was midway between the gym, and the neighborhood of my rental house and Coach Steve's house.

THE FLEUR-DE-LIS
J.K. Dark

The first time I saw the building, I was convinced we had lost our minds. The old brick building on the corner of Olive and Boyle Streets in St. Louis had seen better days. The windows were all covered with cheap plywood. Weeds growing from every crack in the city street had begun to climb the exterior. The wrought iron gate to the entryway, now rusted and leaning to one side, framed the name of the building that had been etched in the concrete.

Clearly, the "Fleur-de-Lis" had been a jewel in its day. The three-story brick building housed two retail locations on the ground floor, split by a magnificent foyer. The top two stories were dedicated to apartment space. Even in its dilapidated condition, there was a stately appearance and feel to the building. My friend Jack and I had just bought it at auction. He looked on starry eyed and said, "Mark my words, Kevin, this building has good bones." All I could think was that the bones were badly broken and in need of a good orthopedic surgeon. But hey, I was just a friend and investor who came along for the ride, and would help where I could, as he was determined to tackle a renovation of this monster with, or without, my help. Jack had made quite a living flipping real estate; I trusted his judgments, for the most part.

The building was in an area known as Gaslight Square, a remarkable place of St. Louis entertainment history. In its prime during the 1950s and '60s, it housed beatniks and blues clubs, cafés like Jorge's, Smokey Joe's, the Old Palace Theatre, the Grecian Terrace, and also big name acts and performers like Barbara Streisand, Miles Davis, and Woody Allen. Now a victim of urban blight and decay, the area was in the middle of a renaissance of sorts, and based on this speculation Jack bought the building sight unseen at the city auction. I hoped this investment would pay off, but I had my doubts. We took a crowbar and the keys from his truck, and went to the plywood covering the entranceway. It was time for a first look at the interior of the Fleur-de-Lis.

The symbol fleur-de-lis means flower or a lily; it was a widely used symbol common in St. Louis to honor the city's French heritage. I remembered it was also the name of a debutante's ball for the city's affluent young ladies.

As the plywood was peeled back, a beautiful set of mahogany doors framed the glass that let the first light in years filter through to the magnificent marble floor of the grand entry foyer. The foyer was three stories high, there were magnificent wall sconces and a chandelier that hung from the ceiling, and looked to weigh thousands of pounds. I could see Jack smile in the dim light. Looking straight back, an elevator with a gold door came into view. As we walked into the foyer, walls of glass on both sides revealed two distinctly separate retail spaces, accessible by twin sets of French doors that opened to the foyer. We turned on our high-beam flashlights to see more clearly. On the left side of the foyer, a bar was visible through the glass, tables and chairs sat as though it could open for business any minute. It had the eerie feeling of being frozen in time. The bar itself was a work of art with its ornately carved moldings and matching wood frame on the mirror behind it, that ran the length of the bar. Back to the front of the building sat a wall of windows that once the plywood was removed, would make the entire bar visible from the street. Near the wall of windows and the back wall sat a slightly elevated stage. I could picture a jazz, or a blues band playing even now. I shined my flashlight slightly to the right to reveal an old Steinway baby grand piano. I didn't need light to know Jack was smiling broadly behind me.

We marveled at our luck for a minute or two before continuing our tour. In the foyer and bar alone, Jack estimated salvage prices that exceeded the price we had just paid for the building. Though we both knew that moment, the Fleur-de-Lis would live on. We pointed our flashlights forward and continued the dark tour. The other side of the foyer's retail space seemed to have been a coffee shop. Tables and chairs sat in the same positions as the bar, and what looked to be an old newspaper/magazine stand that had sold tobacco products as well. Empty cigar boxes and a cigar-store Indian stood beside the stand. I observed the Indian could be wheeled outside during business hours to lure street traffic. We estimated the bar and the café at three thousand square feet each of retail space. If it could be rented, Jack knew we had a financial winner. His smile grew wider by the moment.

We made our way past the elevator and its shiny brass door, in search of the staircase. We climbed the three floors and headed to the top of the building, or the penthouse. It was a magnificent old apartment. There were high nine-foot ceilings, stained glass windows, hardwood floors, and beautiful woodwork. There were fireplaces in the living room, dining room, and master bedroom. The two bathrooms were done in an ornate tile. The old kitchen, badly in need of renovation, was the only visible flaw. We checked the ceilings in each room and could find only one small area that had water damage.

Jack and I continued downstairs to the other three apartments. All were similar to the penthouse in grandeur, only smaller versions. All of them seemed in very good condition. The kitchens would of course need to be renovated, and all needed a fresh coat of paint. But otherwise, it was as though the old building had held up well to the years. I was impressed with both the trash and laundry shoots in each apartment. Features long ago discontinued in construction.

We ended our first visit with a tour of the old basement. Again, we found it to be in great shape. The old foundation showed no visible cracks, no standing water. It was almost too good to be true, I thought. There was an old central boiler that heated the entire building. It took up six hundred square feet, and would have to be replaced. There was more than enough room for storage and laundry facilities for each apartment, as well as for the retail spaces to store goods and supplies.

We completed our tour and replaced the plywood over the door to the entrance. Jack, perhaps elated or delirious from our good fortune, offered to buy dinner.

We drove the two blocks to the Eat-Rite diner. Jack wasn't frivolous after all. We sat down and ordered coffee and dinner. The owner, a man in his seventies, worked furiously at the greasy looking grill. He delivered our orders and introduced himself as Lee. We knew we would likely be eating many meals here until a kitchen could be renovated. Jack and I introduced ourselves, and we chatted with Lee as business had hit a lull for the moment.

"You bought Lilly's old building? Well I will be damned, welcome to the neighborhood," Lee said, and he hustled back to the grill as another customer entered.

Jack and I went back to our conversation regarding the next steps for the building. A legion of experts and contractors were lined up to inspect and outline repairs and the costs involved. We decided to set up an office in the bar, of course. A great place to meet and coordinate work schedules and negotiate prices.

The next day, the renovations commenced. Jack had three to five contractors lined up to bid on the various projects. I admired his business acumen, and would come to admire his negotiating tactics. He had bought donuts and coffee for the morning shift, and a bottle each of Scotch, Jack Daniel's and vodka; he displayed them on top of the bar.

The electrician and the city building inspector were the first to arrive. And so began the race between renovation and bankruptcy. Most of the building would need to be rewired to meet current code. A hundred-dollar bill slipped to the inspector bought us a two-week window that would allow the electricity to be turned on until the electricians complied with code. The first electrician set the mark we needed to beat with a bid of twenty-six thousand dollars. The commercial space, a potential windfall, also required expensive upgrades to accommodate new restaurant equipment and technology.

The day progressed with similar results as the plumbing inspection and the plumbers convened on us. Upgrades to meet commercial code were the chief culprit; the high bid was thirteen thousand dollars. The water was turned on after additional cash dispersal to a public servant; the unspoken and unwritten cost of code compliance in the city at the time.

Meanwhile, I oversaw the commercial cleaning crew we had lined up to make the building presentable. They removed twenty or thirty years of dust and grime. The plywood came off the windows and doors, the windows were cleaned, the old building was showing signs of life and its original grandeur. This effort alone was a huge effort. A roll-off dumpster was filled with the plywood from over forty windows and doors. I was beginning to understand the magnitude of the job as I watched a crew of fifteen go through the building inside and out.

One of the crew brought me a box filled with framed photos, mostly old black-and-whites, many autographed in the frame. I recognized several old musicians and actors. These would be great when cleaned and hung in the bar, I thought. I set them aside to go through, when time allowed.

The day ended with a mixed bag of emotions. While the building looked great cleaned and lit up, the mood in the bar was a solemn one as Jack went over the latest folly. The roof, which we thought was sound, had to be replaced. Had it not been caught now, the roofer assured us, it would likely cave in with the first heavy snowfall. The old flat roof, with tarpaper and sealed with tar, had not been maintained and had simply outlived its lifespan, a thirty-one-thousand-dollar nightmare.

Jack sat at a table, we opened the bottle of Jack Daniel's and did shots as we totaled up and sorted through the various estimates. We awaited the final contractor of the day, R&H Heating and Cooling. We were fearful of the price tag on replacing the building's largest and major components.

The spreadsheet showed a total of $118,000 before touching the HVAC. We did several more shots; our available credit line for renovation was $175,000. Jack did another shot, under his breath I heard him mumble. It was either a prayer or a curse, perhaps both.

That is when we met Rufus Jones. He wandered in the building and found us in the bar. "Looks the same," he said, startling both Jack and me. He walked in and introduced himself.

"I put the boiler in this building some forty odd years ago, brings back good memories," he said, looking around. "Are you two going to reopen the Voodoo Lounge? This place was happening back in the day, I saw some of the greats right there." He pointed to the stage. "I remember watching Robert Johnson, Muddy Waters, B.B. King, Lena Horne, Billie Holliday... All the great ones loved the Voodoo," he said as he walked around. "But mostly, I remember Miss Lilly." He paused. "So, you boys going to resurrect the Fleur-de-Lis are you?" He chuckled then said, "Miss Lilly would like that. She loved this old building, it was her life."

"Well..." he said, looking at us sitting at the table, "let's have a look." He motioned for us to follow him to the basement. We followed him without question. Rufus had that way about him; you just did as he asked, seemingly without question.

"Well, looky there." Rufus giggled. "She lives," he said, pointing to the old boiler. He commenced to walk around the monstrosity, checking the cast iron, I suspected for cracks. Then he pulled open the door on the front and stuck his head inside to inspect it. After ten minutes of grunting *oohs* and *ahs*, Rufus spoke, "Gentlemen, I need to run out to my truck, I have cold beers there, I noticed you had some Jack Daniel's on the bar. I suggest we sit down at the bar and *neeeeg*otiate." We liked Rufus immediately.

We sat at the table nearest the bar as Rufus laid out our options, but not before insisting we have boilermakers first. "We are discussing a boiler, gentlemen." He cackled and laughed at his own joke. We joined in, Rufus had a way of making you laugh, even as he was about to deliver expensive news.

"See here," he pointed to a brochure. "Most folk want the latest, most efficient unit on the market. I can do that for you, or I can get the old boiler running and carry you through till you can replace it. Meantime, we can work on the air conditioner system. You got to run vent work all through the building. Winter is a good time for me, and I can give you a big discount, provided you keep that bar stocked." He giggled again.

"So you're saying the old boiler still works?" Jack asked. "That would save us a great deal until we could get some tenants in the building."

"Not only am I saying so, I'm guaranteeing it." Rufus cackled and downed his drink.

I wondered if the Jack Daniel's may add up to more than a new HVAC system. Nonetheless, given our current budget, we took the gamble.

Over the next several months, the Fleur-de-Lis underwent a facelift. Jack and I scraped, plaster patched, caulked and painted ourselves. The contractors did their thing, and the building was coming together nicely. Rufus was in and out fine-tuning radiators, bleeding lines, and providing heat from the ancient boiler as he promised. He also provided many evenings of comic relief and storytelling at the bar. He had a remarkable constitution for drink, and a penchant for storytelling. Both suited him.

He told us all about the city of old, our building, and the now legendary Miss Lilly. She was as Rufus told it, a beautiful woman with the voice of an angel. A Creole from Louisiana, of mixed race and neutral color, that allowed her to move among both races in a society that at the time was less than welcoming to blacks in this city. A trained pianist, she was recruited to play in the symphony. She played Powell Hall, and as a sideline every juke joint in St. Louis. She could switch from classical to blues piano in a split second. She did so in order to build this building, according to Rufus.

"Of course, she also attracted money men," Rufus said. "Somebody was always courting Miss Lilly, from the mayor to the porter at old Union Station, everybody loved her. She was smart; she built this building as her own home, with a club and restaurant that made her a fine living, as you boys can see now," he said, waving his arms around. "That is, until things turned bad, but that is a story for another night." Rufus downed his drink and headed home.

By this time, Jack and I had each taken one of the second-floor apartments as expenses mounted on the building. We paid our corporation a fair rent and used the money to keep going each month. We had promises of a restaurant tenant once we had the place in order, and had several prospective tenants for the penthouse apartment. Leasing those two parts of the building would put us in the black with a positive cash flow. Then we planned to keep the bar and operate it ourselves, or sell the entire property once we maximized the revenues.

That day was still months away, so we continued our work with an eye to the future, and a prayer Rufus could keep the old boiler going a few more months. Rufus continued his pesky drilling of walls and cutting through floors to run vents that would carry both heat and air conditioning soon.

It was about this time I sensed Jack was more nervous than he let on. Late at night I could hear him in the bar, pounding on the old piano keys, and hear the sounds of his glass on the bar. I assumed once Rufus closed in the system, the vents would carry air and not noise.

Fall turned into winter, the kitchens were renovated, and the second floor and the penthouse were painted. The old radiators did indeed provide warmth, and provided a wonderful place to lay out your next day's clothing, or keep your coffee warm as you dressed for the day. The unfinished ventilation system carried noises, Jack continued his late night piano playing, and admittedly he was quite good. I was a bit perturbed to hear him arguing with the women he had over on occasion, their heated voices carried through the vents. But I supposed he heard mine as well. We were business partners, not relationship coaches.

Rufus kept us entertained in the winter months with tales of the Voodoo Lounge and Miss Lilly. We went through and hung the old framed photos the cleaning crew had found. The bar was taking shape.

We had our first tenant for the penthouse scheduled to move in within a month. We were about ready to sign a lease with old Lee from the Eat-Rite diner to operate a grill/coffee house in the retail space across from the bar. I had even nearly completed the restoration and painting of the old cigar-store Indian. Things were good. And Jack had taken to playing more jazzy tunes in the evening. I assumed we were both sleeping better.

Rufus was nearing the end of the second-floor vent work and had begun running vent work to the penthouse. We had some more late night history lessons. He told us how Miss Lilly had hooked up with the no-good, womanizing, guitar player Otis Mayberry. Apparently, it was a volatile relationship and one that started the rumors of Miss Lilly being a voodoo queen. It seemed that Miss Lilly found out Otis was strumming more than her strings on the nights his band wasn't booked at the Voodoo Lounge. Legend had it Miss Lilly put a curse on him. He began to lose weight, and his career ended with people calling him "Slim." His luster with the ladies ended and he up and disappeared one day, never to be heard from again. Rufus laughed and downed a shot. He was animated when he told his stories, his arms flailing in the air as a demonstrative gesture to Otis disappearing.

"Don't you boys ever wonder why this building wasn't looted for cooper or the fixtures? It's because the folks around here don't mess with voodoo. They think this building is cursed! See, you some lucky young men." Rufus cackled for good measure. "Miss Lilly always said this building was a testament to her life, not evil," Rufus said seriously.

We all drank a toast to life, and to the fact we were nearing completion of a long renovation. Late that night I could hear Jack playing a nice jazz tune on the piano.

It was in mid-February when the boiler died. We awoke to frost on the windows; I could see my breath in the apartment. Rufus confirmed it and pronounced the boiler dead. The air valve and hot water expansion tank had burst. The basement floor was two inches deep with water. Rufus set up sump pumps and made arrangements to get the new unit delivered to the building. We hired a contracting company to dismantle and haul the old boiler out through the old coal slide in pieces. Rufus was too old for heavy construction. He oversaw the project.

Jack and I sat at the bar near a fireplace, trying to stay warm. We opened the bottle early that day. We were now effectively broke as a corporation. This would cost each of us an additional ten grand each out of our pocket. We swigged Jack Daniel's and cursed our misfortune.

"Well Jack, on the positive side, I guess when the furnace goes in I won't have to hear you playing the piano all damn night." I laughed loudly.

"What the hell, I don't play the piano. I thought that was you," he said. His face was showing confusion.

Just then, Rufus came into the bar. "Come with me, you got to see this," he said. He motioned for us to follow him to the basement. We did as Rufus directed, as we always did.

The contractors had pulled up a long box from the hole recently dug for the new gas line. It looked like an old rifle box. Rufus pointed and said to Jack, "Go ahead, open it up."

Jack did as instructed. He recoiled and said, "What the hell kind of joke is this, Rufus?"

"Ain't no joke, boys."

Inside was a skinny skeleton dressed in a suit holding an old Gibson guitar. We all assumed — correctly, according to the coroner later — we had just discovered what became of old Otis "Slim" Mayberry.

Jack stepped away and called the police with his cell phone. Rufus laughed and handed me a small box. Inside was a legal document. I opened it and read it aloud.

"L.I.F.E. The Lilly Iris Flowers Estate. A trust exempt from probate. Administered by the Boatman's Bank and Trust of St. Louis Mo."

It read, "I, Lilly Iris Flowers, being of sound mind, hereby bequeath my entire estate to the legal owner of the Fleur de-Lis building located at 5190 Olive Street Road. Whoever holds title to said building at the time of this discovery, is the sole beneficiary of my estate held by Boatman's Bank and Trust company. Signed: Lilly Iris Flowers. This 10th day of April, 1957."

Enclosed with the legal document was a bank statement showing a balance of $987,000 as of March 31, 1957.

We contacted our corporate attorney via cell phone. Dealt with the police report, the forensics squad, and watched stunned as Rufus and the crew continued to install the new furnace.

The old Gibson guitar was handed to us by the paramedics. It too apparently belonged to us as there would be no evidentiary value sixty-five years later. We sat it on the stage.

Jack and I sat at the bar, sipping Jack Daniel's as the heat from the new furnace came on—right before nightfall and the temperature drop. We were joined by Rufus. We drank in silence. Our attorney called with the news, the account was held in trust, Boatman's bank and its assets had been sold four times since the legal document was signed. Now Bank of America, the account value was just under 3.2 million dollars.

We sat silently doing shots. Rufus broke the ice by saying, "You know I ain't financing that furnace, don't you boys?"

Later that night, the piano was accompanied by the crisp sound of a Gibson guitar. I swear I heard Billie Holliday sing.

THE UNDELIVERABLE MESSAGE
Gerald Dlubala

Summer in St. Louis was in full effect. The heat could be felt rising in waves from the asphalt. I got out of my car, just wanting to get inside and get a cold shower at the end of another workday. I closed the car door, walked around the back of the truck and headed up the walkway towards our back door.

And then, there it was. "Finally," I said, in a voice only I could hear. "You've finally decided to show yourself."

"Why now, on this day, at this time?" I wondered.

It was a full body apparition, looking directly at me, patiently waiting for me, and in fact, by the looks of it, actually anticipating seeing me. It was positioned in between the houses, meaning our house and the neighbor's. I would honestly have to say that I wasn't totally surprised, because I had been having these feelings all week, you know, feelings that I was being watched. I saw shadows, and fleeting flashes of movement. I now felt strangely comfortable with the somewhat familiar pattern on the apparition's foggy, out-of-focus plaid shirt.

The eyes, though, were a different story. The eyes were very clear, and *very* familiar.

With little hesitation, and really, a minimal amount of fear, I might add, I moved towards it, planning on just going on, getting by, and heading into the house. But as luck would have it, as I approached, the eyes grew more focused and more intense towards me. I put my head down and kept walking, mumbling under my breath, "Please, just leave me alone."

As I approached the form, it spoke to me. It tried, I should say. I could see the jaw line moving. Those shark-like eyes followed me, daring me to look back. The jaws kept moving, kept ranting towards me, but I still couldn't hear what I was supposed to hear.

I kept walking, telling myself that it was my imagination. After all, it had been a very difficult week, and sleep was not on the to-do list any of the past few days. Through the gate to the back yard, a good twelve steps to the deck, and then up the stairs, across the cedar deck boards, to my back door.

My gut feeling was strong, that if I simply turned around, the apparition would be there, still talking, still persistently attempting to communicate with me. My dogs confirmed those suspicions. They were growling and barking in my direction, but not looking directly at me. They were looking behind me, or perhaps through me. "Quiet," I demanded. They stopped momentarily, but just as quickly started up again, growling, whining, and barking while stepping towards me, then back again.

I didn't hesitate. Looking forward, I put my key into the lock, and opened the back door into my home. The dogs ran right through me, and outside in a flash, and as they did I went in, turned and closed the door.

The dogs took a couple of steps out on the deck, then immediately turned back and started barking and snarling in my direction once again. They scratched on the door wanting desperately to get in. Without even getting a chance to set my things down, I jerked around and looked over my shoulder in time to see . . .

Nothing!

Yes, nothing. "What the hell is happening?" I asked myself. I looked outside, and the dogs were normal. They were just happy to be out, running, playing, and jumping around.

Relieved, I sat at the kitchen table to collect my thoughts.

It was then that I felt the temperature change. Just on the back of my neck. It was warm, and very humid. It was definitely someone or something's breath. The stench brought about thoughts of mildew, or standing water. In a flurry of activity, I slid out of the chair, staying hunched over. I turned to see the figure standing over me, but now with a more menacing look on its face. The eyes were furious and determined, the veins protruding in the temples of the forehead, and most strikingly, the bottom jaw was sculpted and unhinged, protruding forward, and moving up and down in a way that meant that whatever it was trying to say was very important.

Extremely important.

Most important.

And yet, I heard nothing.

I looked into those familiar eyes, and they were focused, so focused. The apparition was struggling, trying so hard, using so much energy to tell me something important, but because of my limitations, I could not understand. I was no longer afraid. I wanted to know, wanted to understand what it was trying to tell me.

The figure became increasingly frustrated at my inability to understand. It was angry, and conveyed that perfectly, with no verbal communication needed. I felt so inadequate at the time, but that didn't match my feeling of remorse, for not being able to understand or even begin to try to guess what the whole point of this was. Frustration set in on both of us, and in an instant I yelled out, "Just leave me the hell alone!"

We stared at each other, motionless, and those familiar eyes looked directly at me, deep into me, touching my very soul. That sculpted and strong jaw line receded, and the figure backed up, all while staying seemingly upright.

The eyes went from being direct and demanding to translucent, sorrowful and empty. Those eyes, those black, lifeless eyes, now appeared sad and lost. I swallowed hard, realizing what was happening. The form, once strong and intimidating, now was fading away, with a look of sadness replacing the confidence and arrogance that it initially demonstrated.

I felt immediate panic. Something felt very wrong. "I just can't hear you," I yelled with a voice that begged forgiveness. "What are you trying to tell me?"

It tried once more, with no success. And then with the quickness of someone realizing they've wasted their time, it was gone.

The spirit had tried with all available resources to communicate with me, with zero success. I felt at fault. I was the one with the shortcomings.

This memory has stayed with me, and has impacted my daily thoughts. Those penetrating eyes, the determined actions, and the stench of the stagnant breath on the back of my neck are all still fresh memories, as fresh as the day they happened. And yet I can do nothing but wait. Wait for that moment or event that has yet to happen, that moment or event that my visitor was attempting to inform me about. I don't know when that will be, but I'm sure I'll recognize it when it occurs. And it will be important.

Very Important.

Extremely important.

Most important.

NIGHT LESSONS
Patrick Dorsey

In a quick but sloppy move, I slapped my opponent's blade away from me and lunged at him with my own weapon. With practiced ease, he parried my attack, striking back and hitting me full in the chest. I felt the point as it stabbed at me, blade bowing out. An exasperated sigh rushed past my lips.

"That's five," Diana said, yanking off her protective steel-mesh mask.

I pulled off my own, pushing my fingers through sweat-soaked hair. The one thing about fencing is that it's a hot sport, especially in August. Between the physical activity, the mask, and the heavy, padded jacket, it sometimes seems it was a sport designed for people who enjoy perspiration.

With my free hand, I shook Diana's hand. She'd beaten me, as usual.

"That was all right," Diana began, "you got three. But only the second was a clean one. "

She was right. My other two touches had been lucky, and I shouldn't have gotten them. Even with the lucky hits, I still lost. We walked off the gym floor, heading for the side benches.

"Your footwork's really improving," Diana continued. "And that second touch was beautiful — that's the kind of hit I'm happy to lose to. You had me all the way. You're getting more subtle, controlling the blade less with your whole arm and more with just your fingers." A smile flashed over small, bright teeth. "But there's still a way's to go."

I smiled tiredly and flopped down on the bench as Diana turned off and went outside to the water fountain. I leaned back against the wall, still panting and trying to catch my breath. Everyone had beaten me that night — even

Len, who had started in fencing class with me three months before and was no more experienced than me. Maybe I'd been having an off night. I was tired, though, and I was frustrated. I really enjoyed the sport and I really wanted to do well at it.

But I couldn't. At least that's how it seemed.

Things were beginning to break up. People were packing their equipment, changing clothes, getting ready to go out for the traditional Thursday-night-after-fencing pizza and beer.

I'd been making myself mad thinking about my losing record and needed to work off some steam. With both anger and perfectionist determination, I began doing practice lunges in the corner, my target a small, dark smear on the wall.

"You comin' up tonight?" Tom rumbled from across the gym.

"Our illustrious club president has given to you a personal invitation!" said Diana as she danced through the door past Tom's huge frame. Tom turned and said a few things I'd never repeat to anyone as capable with a blade as Diana.

"Maybe I'll be along later, "I called back.

"Suit yourself. See ya."

Diana's head popped out from behind Tom. "Bye-bye."

The squeaks of tennis shoes echoed softer and softer as they talked and joked down the hall before heading up the stairs to the parking lot. I was exhausting myself quickly with all the lunges I was doing. And the more tired I got, the madder I got. It seemed I couldn't even get the lunges right.

It was nearly ten o'clock, and soon, the janitor would come through and kick me out. He'd already turned off half the lights in the gym — a sort of hint, I suppose — casting odd shadows and a dim gloom over the place.

Stopping for a rest, I turned and noticed someone coming into the gymnasium. He was obviously a fencer — he had on the whole outfit, complete with foil — but I couldn't recognize him. He was too tall to be Len, too slim to be Tom, and far too angular to be Diana.

"So," I called, "you decided you wanted to get one more match in before calling it a night?" My mind was racing as I tried to recall who my new opponent could be.

He approached me slowly, his walk a glide across the floor. Several feet away, he touched his foil to the front of his mask — a salute in fencing — and went to the half-crouched *en garde* position. Scooping my mask up off the floor, I did the same.

Before even our blades met, he stood straight up again, shaking his head. I was about to stand up, too, when his blade tapped my foot.

"Point the toe," I thought aloud.

Another tap, on my thigh. "Straighten the knee," I said.

I felt the blade then press down on my left should "Keep the shoulders level."

His blade then rapped into my middle as if to say, *Good*, then he returned to his initial position and began the match.

His guard was incredible. It was like fencing a propeller, he moved so fast. After a while, I noticed he wasn't just fencing me, but making me practice my footwork, drawing me out, forcing me to retreat, swiping at my leg when I stay out in a lunge too long, just plain making me do it until it was right.

My opponent stopped suddenly, giving me a quick salute with his weapon.

"I'd like to go home sometime, ya know," came a voice from behind me.

Slipping off my mask, I turned and saw the janitor filling the far door, a blaze of pink stomach showing from beneath green shirt.

"We're just finishing up," I called back, turning to my opponent. "Matter of fact – "

He was gone.

The door nearest me, the one Diana and Tom exited through, was still open. I guessed my opponent hadn't felt like dealing with the janitor. And the way he was going on at me right then, I couldn't blame him for slipping off.

Driving home, I tried to piece together just who my opponent had been. It wasn't anyone I knew, that much I was sure of. And his foil — that was something else. Usually, the bell-guard, the rounded part that protects the hand, is made of stainless steel and is plain and smooth except for the nicks and scratches it gets from use. But his was brassy in color. Most odd was that it was intricately designed, almost antique looking. If I'd seen that weapon before, I'd have remembered it.

I wondered why my opponent hadn't spoken to me at all; he never said a word the whole time, and I almost smacked myself in the forehead for missing it. Max. It had to be Max, the only club member I'd yet to meet. I remembered Tom talking about him. One of the best fencers in the state, Tom said. And on top of that, he was from Austria and had a heavy accent — probably, he didn't like to speak in English. It all fit. The next week, I scored two clean hits on Diana, and one on Tom — no small feat considering Tom had been fencing for nearly twenty-five years. I was sitting in the corner cooling off as the last few fencers were leaving for the night.

"Comin' this week?" asked Tom.

I shook my head. "No money. Besides, I've got to be up early for work tomorrow.

"Don't we all?"

I laughed. "I'll see you next week.

"All right, so long."

I waited, and at just about ten, Max showed up. It was odd that he always kept his mask on — protective as they are, they're still not the easiest things to breathe under. What was even odder was that I couldn't see his face behind the mask. Normally, you can see something — eyes, a flash of teeth — but 1 couldn't see anything. The week before, I'd written it off as the gloom of the gym. But all the lights were on this time.

Max saluted me and went *en garde*. I was intrigued by his foil. It was unlike any I'd seen. I noticed a name — *Giscarde* — engraved on it in a rather fancy script. I guessed that it was the manufacturer's name, like Negrini or Prieur. Probably some small, obscure European company, I reasoned.

I saluted him and went *en garde*. Standing up, he came and looked me over. I felt the blade rap into my middle, as if to say, "Very good." He returned to his position in front of me and we began.

His speed and silent skill still amazed me. And Max had one move that was utterly devastating: a way of striking an extra shot without breaking the rhythm of the combat. It was the most bizarre thing, like inserting an extra beat or note into a song without interrupting or appreciably changing it. But it was noticeably, obviously there.

His point tapped my bell-guard and he nodded to me, signing for me to try it. We began fencing, and I tried. His weapon slapped the point of mine, saying, *No. Wrong.* I began again. It was so tiring. First, blade conversation had to be established. That took time. Then I would try when I felt the moment was right. Again and again, I missed. He must have sensed I was tired, stopping suddenly and gesturing for me to sit down. I did, putting my head back and closing my eyes, just for a second or two. When I looked up, he'd left.

My "night lessons" continued this way for several weeks. We did drill after drill, sometimes tiring me so much it all I could look for his foil, Max becoming just an unfocussed blur behind it. But I was learning! I was actually getting better at it! So much that Tom even commented on it one night.

"Oh, "I began," Max showed me some things."

"Before he left town?" Tom asked.

Left town? I thought. "What?"

"He's been in Austria for the last month and a half, visiting family."

Austria? Then who had I been fencing for the last six weeks?

After everyone had left my "friend" showed up. He gave me a quick salute, but I wasn't about to return it.

"Would you mind telling me who you are?" I almost shouted. "And why you let me call you 'Max' for the last six weeks?"

He pointed his foil at me, and then at the place he wanted me to stand. It was one of those commanding teacher-to-student gestures you never argue with. I was still mad, but I acquiesced — for some reason, I still trusted him.

The lesson began. He drilled me over and over on this extra-beat move he'd been showing me, except this time his point would rap into my bell-guard, saying, *correct.* He always parried my blows, never allowing me to get a *touché* or touch against him, unlike Diana or Tom or anyone else who'd ever given me a lesson. But I had the maneuver, the rhythm, right! I was so excited, I forgot my anger.

When we were through for the night, I took my towel and wiped the sweat from my eyes. "Sorry I yelled," I began, turning back to him —

He was gone

Tom wasn't able to score a point on me the following week. As we fenced, I struck the way my teacher had shown me, in perfect cadence with the established rhythm, yet outside it, striking cleanly, devastating. Tom leapt back, whipping his mask off.

"Where'd you learn that?" he questioned. He turned and called Diana over from the bench where she'd been watching us.

"Did you see what he just did?" he asked her

"Yeah," Diana said. "Lucky shot."

"Nuh-uh." Tom rumbled. "That was a *feint in tempo*. Even fencers who've been at this as long as I have can't do it."

Diana squinted at me. "Then where'd you pick it up?

"Only person I ever knew that could do that with consistency was Phil Giscarde.

"Who?" I asked, avoiding their questions.

"Phil Giscarde," Tom began in his old-war-story voice. "Used to fence with us years back. He was damn good. Damn good teacher, too. He had a habit of taking beginners under his wing — and that's what finished him."

Both Diana and I had utterly puzzled faces. Tom continued. "He was practicing with one of his students when the student's blade snapped. The sharp, broken tip went right Phil's jacket, into his chest. The kid stepped back and drew the blade out — the last thing he should have done. Phil had a hole in his chest, and that blade was the only thing plugging it. He didn't stand a chance. Bled to death in seconds. We didn't even have time to call the paramedics. God, that was years ago."

I had to ask. "Did he have a real intricate, antique- guard and grip with his name engraved on it?"

"Yeah, it was his grandfather's before him — how do you know?"

Everyone else had already left. It was late; and with Tom's stories, the three of us had lost track of the tine. I felt a chill creep through me as I looked past Tom.

"He has it."

My instructor had arrived.

Seeing that foil, Tom was outraged. "Where'd you get that!" he yelled. Max — or Phil — whipped his weapon at Tom to command him silent. He gestured for me to take my place before him.

"Tom," I whispered, "when was Phil killed?"

"It was October. The day before my daughter's birthday — the seventh."

"Today," I said walking across the gym floor to my instructor.

My heart was pounding so hard 1 could hear it. I could feel the adrenalin and whatever else pumping, slamming its way through my veins. My breathing sharpened.

Relax, I told myself, *you can't do it if you're all tensed up.*

Giscarde saluted me solemnly, and we began.

His attack was relentless. I had time only to defend myself, to parry, to retreat, to guard and parry again.

This has to be done, I kept telling myself. *Whatever exorcism or laying to rest this takes, it's got to be done.* One thought, though, kept creeping into my head: *it could cost me my life.*

I realized for the first time that Giscarde's feet made no noise as he moved, no squeaks, no thumps, nothing. Faceless and silent, his body may not have been real, but his weapon definitely was, and that worried me.

He was forcing me further and further back, pressing his attack tighter and tighter. It almost seemed too fast to react to, but I was beginning to feel a rhythm to it. It was my only chance. *Still the teacher?* 1 wondered. Could he be making me use the maneuver he'd taught me? Why? Somehow, I knew that the first hit in this match would make all the difference. It had to be mine.

1 found my moment. My blade thrust in through his guard, jabbing into his chest. A clean touch, fair and skillful. One no fencer would mind losing to, not a stupid, unfortunate accident. I saw the phantom fall back, but only his weapon — that unusual, intricate, antique foil — clattered to the floor before my feet.

Standing there alone in the middle of the hushed gym, I didn't know what to do, or even what to feel. I was finally learning the sport, and 1 finally won. But doing so, I lost my teacher — a ghost who'd taught me more about fencing, I later realized, than anyone else.

THE LADY IN RED
Ed Farber

It was an innocent enough statement by my four-year-old daughter, but it was alarming to me.

"What lady do you mean?" I asked.

"The lady in the red gown, Mommy," she answered.

"Where did you see this lady?"

"Here, in my room. She sat on my bed and smiled at me. Then she was gone."

I looked at my sweet Margie. She returned my glance with that wide-eyed innocence that only children can muster. She did fib some, I knew, but I could usually tell. This didn't sound like a fib. It must have been a dream.

"Do you think it could have been a dream?" I asked.

"Oh, no," she answered. It wasn't at night, it was in the afternoon. I was playing with Patty by the window."

Patty was her favorite doll. Margie was lying in bed clutching her now.

"I saw her before, too," she said. "Walking down the stairs, once in the parlor at the piano, and in your bedroom. Does she live here, too?"

I didn't know how to answer her. It was inexplicable, and yet I had to tell her something.

"Perhaps," I said, forcing a smile, "she used to live here and was just visiting. Now it's bedtime, so let me tuck you and Patty in."

She seemed to accept my explanation and kissed me goodnight

I went down the stairs, but couldn't help looking around in the glow of the gas light on the wall. What exactly did she see? I wondered. Was it her imagination? Children have wonderful imaginations. I remembered my own pretend companion when I was five or six. But she was a little girl, not a lady in a red dress.

Steven was in the parlor sitting in the chair under the lamp next to the fireplace. He was reading the newspaper. We'd been married for five years, engaged before that for two. Just six weeks ago we had moved here, an older home on this block of Clara Avenue. A very nice neighborhood. We had a large lot and a carriage house in the back, one of four such homes in the area. The rest were flats and rather new.

"Steven," I began, "Margie just told me a very strange thing, that she has seen a lady on several occasions in the house. A lady dressed in a red gown."

He looked up over the newspaper. "You know how children make up things."

"I don't think she was making up a story, but I don't know what to make of it either."

"If the lady steals your jewelry then we do have a problem," Steven said chuckling and returned to his newspaper. I picked up my knitting, but I couldn't keep the thought of Margie and the lady in red from my mind.

The next day after Steven left for downtown (it was just a short walk to the new electric streetcar line on Easton Avenue) I bundled up Margie in her hat and coat and set out to visit my cousin Annabelle who happened to live in one of the other larger homes on the block similar to ours. In fact, it was Annabelle who had alerted us to the availability of the home we now occupied.

We had been living in cramped quarters in a second floor flat on Cass Avenue, closer in to downtown, and since I was pregnant again it was time for something larger. Steven had been promoted at the accounting firm and said we could afford a bigger home in a nicer neighborhood. We chose this older residence because of the space it provided. We did have to make repairs to the house, but when they were done, we had a beautiful, two-story home, plus an attic area with an additional two rooms, plenty of space for the large family that both Steven and I planned on having. And because the nearby, newly built flats had indoor plumbing, Steven insisted we have it installed as well! Steven, of course, was positive they would bring electric lines to the homes here, too, before long. And, no doubt, we would be getting one of those new automobiles that Mr. Henry Ford was making, as well. I had noticed that Steven was reading the automobile advertisements in the newspaper.

After Margie and Barbara, Annabelle's six year old, went off to play in Barbara's room, I told Annabelle about Margie's statement of the night before. She poured us both tea and then settled her ample frame in a chair opposite me.

"And you think she was imagining this?" she asked, smoothing a wisp of her red hair which she wore piled up in the popular Gibson Girl fashion.

"Well, yes. Yes, I do. What other explanation can there be?" I answered.

Annabelle smiled. "I think she may have seen a ghost."

"Are you serious?" I asked. Annabelle was my cousin and a lifelong friend, but even as a young girl she had been a little, well, quirky. And that hadn't changed in the years since. Just the other day she had told me she had joined the women's suffrage movement to gain the vote. Alfred, her husband, had been mortified. Steven said there wasn't a chance in a million that it would happen in our lifetime. And at the World's Fair, she organized a protest because it was said that some of the foreign tribesman they had brought to the fair were rounding up and eating stray dogs. I adored her, but could she really mean that about a ghost?

"Oh, yes," Annabelle answered my question, "I believe that ghosts walk among us and always have. Obviously Shakespeare did. He included them in his plays. And Mr. Dickens, too."

"But Annabelle, they were writing stories, fiction."

"Perhaps, but who's to say it's just fiction? I believe that ghosts are unhappy spirits who have yet to find peace."

"I really can't accept that," I said, but I was beginning to doubt my own stand.

"My dear, you always were kind of straight-laced." She smiled again. "More tea?"

"Annabelle, are you saying that the lady in red is a ghost—in my house?"

"It's possible. If it wasn't Margie's imagination, why not?"

"But neither Steven nor I have seen it. Why only Margie?"

"I don't know. Perhaps it's because children are more receptive to things. They haven't yet been taught not to see."

"Have you ever seen a ghost?" I asked despite myself.

"No, dear, I have not. But I wish I could."

"But why my house of all places?"

"It's an old house, oldest in the area. I hear it was the first home built around here, someone's country estate. This house was built in 1890. I moved in six years ago, just before they opened the World's Fair in 1904. At the time, your house and mine and two others were the only homes on the block. They were just beginning to build the newer homes and flats here. Your house predates my mine by many years, possibly as far back as 1855. Some poor soul could have died in your house many years ago and hasn't yet found peace."

"If Margie did see a ghost, why wasn't she afraid? Aren't ghosts supposed to be scary?"

"There may be malicious spirits about, but by Margie's own statement, the lady in red smiled at her. That doesn't seem to be very scary now, does it?"

Later, I mulled over my conversation with Annabelle. Spirits! Ghosts! It was all Annabelle's nonsense. I supposed she believed in witches, too. That would be just like Annabelle. At any rate, Margie didn't mention the lady again, much to my relief, and I was convinced it all stemmed from a 4-year-old's over-active imagination.

About a month later, Annabelle and Alfred came to our home for dinner. Afterward, the children went up to Margie's room to play, and the men went into the parlor to smoke their cigars.

"I have a gift for you," Annabelle said. She reached down for her knitting bag (I had wondered why she brought it instead of her usual handbag) and pulled out a large, wooden plaque and set on the table.

"It's an Ouija Board," she said, and next brought out a heart-shaped piece placing it on the board. It had very short legs giving it the look of a tiny table. I looked at the board closely. It had two rows of alphabet letters arranged in an arc near the top, under which were the numerals 1 through 9 followed by a zero. The word YES was printed in the top left corner and NO on the opposite side. Underneath the numerals was the word, GOODBYE. I had never seen such a board before and asked her what kind of game it was.

"A very mysterious game if you want to call it that. I first saw a board like this at the home of my friend, Mrs. Gusdorf, and when I participated in using it at one of Mrs. Gusdorf's gatherings, I immediately thought of you and decided to get one for you."

"Good gracious, why me?"

"Because of the lady in red."

I had almost put that episode out of my mind. "What does that have to do with this game?"

"The Ouija Board can be used to contact spirits, and since you apparently have one residing in this house, we can use it to talk to her. Now."

I looked at Annabelle as though she had lost her wits. She must have seen the expression on my face and quickly added, "Really, it seems to happen. I've seen it with my own eyes and have no explanation for how it works. But it does. Come on, Louise, let's give it a try."

She took my hand and placed my fingers on the little platform atop the board. She placed her fingers beside mine. "This is called a planchette. See how it comes to a point? It will move to the letters above and spell out answers to our questions. Or it can move to the words YES or NO at the top."

"It moves by itself?"

"Yes, we don't guide it, but it does move. I know it sounds impossible, but I have seen it work. I'll ask the first question," Annabelle said. "Is there a spirit listening to us?"

We waited but nothing happened. I felt absolutely foolish, my fingers resting lightly on the planchette.

"Spirit, are you there?" Annabelle asked. Again, nothing happened.

"Annabelle, this is nonsense. Nothing is going to happen," I said. Then the little wooden platform began to wobble beneath my fingertips. Very slowly, it began to move.

"Stop it, Annabelle. I know you're doing that."

"Shhh," Annabelle whispered. "I'm not doing it. It's moving by itself, I swear."

I stared in disbelief as the planchette moved up across the board to the word, YES.

"Is there any other spirit with you?" Annabelle asked.

The pointer moved across the board to the word NO.

"Are you a female?"

I was amazed when the planchette crossed back to the word YES. "What is your name?" she asked.

The pointer moved first to the letter N, next, to the letter A, and back to the N.

Nan. Her name was Nan. My fingers trembled on the platform. Could this possibly be happening?

Just at that moment, Alfred walked back into the dining room. "What are you two doing there," he said moving to the table.

Suddenly, the planchette moved quickly to the word GOODBYE.

I was stunned. Had we actually contacted the lady in red? If so, despite my reluctance to believe it all and a sense of fear, I wanted to know so much more. Why she was here? Why had only Margie seen her?

Alfred looked down at the board, and I quickly pulled my fingers from the planchette.

"Oh, I heard of those," he said. "Utter rot. Produced by some company to take money from those foolish enough to believe it. I hope the two of you didn't buy that piece of tomfoolery."

"I did," Annabelle said defiantly, "and you can just take your smelly cigar out of here."

"Women!" Alfred exclaimed and then marched back to the parlor, shaking his balding head.

"Let's try it again," Annabelle said.

"No. I don't want to," I said trying to stifle the fear I had felt. "I'll just put it away,"

That night I couldn't sleep. Steven lay snoring softly in our bed. I arose, donned my robe and walked into Margie's room. I sat on her bed and looked at the angelic face of my little girl. As I did, I felt a little movement in my belly; it was Margie's tiny brother or sister making its presence known. At the same time, I felt a strange warmth about me as if someone had wrapped a shawl around my shoulders. Then the gaslight which had been turned down to a dim flame suddenly flared up for a second and diminished once again. Is that her, I thought, the lady in red? Is that you...Nan? If so, I felt no fear as I had earlier in the evening with my fingers on the Ouija Board. Instead, I felt oddly comforted. I returned to bed and slept soundly.

I didn't see Cousin Annabelle for the rest of the week, nor was there any further mention from Margie of the lady in red or any indication to me that she was, well, haunting my house. I realized I had clearly crossed the line from skepticism to believing, but I really did not wish to pursue it and hoped that there would be no recurrences.

One Saturday morning, I took Margie with me on the trolley to go shopping downtown. The weather was turning colder, and both of us needed warmer coats. I was looking at a coat for me at the department store when Margie tugged on my arm.

"Mommy, it's her," she whispered.

"Who, dear?" I asked.

"The lady in red. The one I see at our house," she answered.

"Where is she?" Could a spirit follow us around, I wondered?

Margie pointed to a young woman standing at the nearby counter. She was attractive, fairly tall, wearing a navy blue dress in the latest ankle-length fashion and holding her coat folded over her arm. She looked to be around my age, with dark brown hair and eyes.

"Margie, she's not wearing a red dress."

"But that's her, Mommy. It's her face. I know it."

As if overhearing our whispered conversation, the woman looked at us and smiled. Impulsively, I stepped over to where she stood, Margie holding my hand.

"Pardon me, Miss, but my daughter thinks she knows you," I said. I don't know what possessed me, but I added quickly, "Is your name by any chance, Nan?"

She looked at both of us for a moment, and then smiled. "No, my name is Sarah. Sarah Bains. But my mother's name was Nan...short for Nancy. I don't think your daughter would have known her. She passed away many years ago." She touched a large, rather ornate locket that hung around her neck.

"I'm so sorry for interrupting your shopping like this. My name is Louise Thornton and this is my daughter, Margie, short for Margery," I added with a smile.

"Think nothing of it, she answered, "but I am intrigued." She looked down at Margie who had stared at her throughout our short conversation. "Margie, why do you think you know me? I am a school teacher so perhaps you have seen me at school?"

"I don't go to school, yet," Margie answered. "I saw you in our house."

The woman, Sarah, looked up at me quickly. "In your house? I don't understand."

"It's an odd story and I don't fully understand it myself," I answered. "Let's sit down here, and I'll try to explain."

We sat in a grouping of chairs near the dressing room, and I told Sarah about Margie seeing a lady in red on a number of occasions. I also talked about the Ouija Board session and how I came to know the name, Nan.

"I know it all sounds so strange, but there it is," I said at the end of my story.

Sarah sat silently for a moment absorbing the rather bizarre tale I had just told. "Where do you live?" she said finally. I gave her our address on Clara Avenue. Her eyes opened wide, and her hand touched the locket again. "That is the house where I was born," she said very softly.

Margie and I looked at each other in wonderment. What did it all mean? Could our household spirit be related to this young woman?

She began to explain, her voice almost a whisper. "My mother died at my birth in that house. I was taken to live with my aunt who, when I was old enough, brought me back and showed me the house where I was born. My father couldn't bear to live there after my mother died and sold it. I have never been inside. But in the years since, I have intentionally passed by it many times."

She reached up and unhooked the ornate gold locket which hung around her neck. "This is my mother." She opened the locket. Inside was a miniature portrait, and the likeness to Sarah was obvious.

"Look, Mommy, it's her and she's wearing that red dress!" Margie cried.

"I wonder," Sarah asked, "if I might visit you sometime and see the house. If what Margie has seen is the spirit of my mother, I would like to try and reach her."

"Let's all go back now," Margie said. And so we did.

After walking through the house and lingering for a long moment in my bedroom, Sarah touched my arm.

"Your Ouija Board. Could you show me how it works?"

Eager now, I nodded. "Let's go down to the dining room."

We left Margie to play in her room and went downstairs. I took the Ouija Board and planchette out and set them on the table. Quickly, I explained how to use it, and we began. I suggested that Sarah be the questioner, and we both placed our fingertips on the planchette.

Sarah began hesitantly, "Is someone present?" The planchette moved to the word YES. Sarah looked at me, a question in her eyes. "No," I said aloud, "I didn't move it. It moved by itself." Sarah stared at the board and then spoke again.

"What is your name?" As before, the planchette moved from letter to letter spelling out N-A-N.

I could see Sarah's fingers trembling.

"Are you the Nan who died in this house after childbirth twenty six years ago?"

The pointer moved back to the word YES. I looked at Sarah and she returned my glance. I could see she was trying to keep her emotions in check, as I was. She looked back at the board.

"Did you know that you had given birth to a daughter?"

After a moment's hesitation, the planchette moved slowly coming to rest at the word NO. I wondered if Nan could see the resemblance between mother and daughter for Sarah looked very much like the portrait in the locket.

"I am that child you gave birth to. I am your daughter," Sarah said softly.

The planchette wobbled under both our fingertips and moved to the letters, spelling out the word, N-A-M-E.

Sarah understood immediately and answered, "My name is Sarah Bains, daughter of Nancy and Raymond Bains."

We both watched as the planchette moved again quickly spelling out the word L-O-V-E. Tears were streaming down Sarah's face, and I realized that I, too, was tearful. The planchette began to move once more. It spelled out the word

P-E-A-C-E. That was puzzling to me until I realized it must refer to the way the lady in red was feeling at last. Once more, the planchette began to wobble. Very slowly, it moved and pointed to the word at the very bottom of the board, GOODBYE.

THE MORGAN'S BEND GUIDEBOOK TO OBSCURE TOURIST SITES
Nathan Feuerberg

When I was a young'un, I used to hear the howling at night. My granddaddy always referred to it as "the calling." Whenever we'd hear it he'd say, "That there's Greyback calling out to the people, so they know he's around protecting them." I believed him back then. I suppose I still want to believe him these days. I've heard other versions of the Greyback story and they certainty aren't as pretty as my granddaddy's.

One thing's for sure, he never got tired of telling it. On humid summer evenings, when the light was dwindling, he'd hang two lanterns from the eves, and have me sit next to him on the porch swing. We'd rock for a while and then he'd turn to me and ask, "I ever tell you the story of Greyback?" Even though I'd heard it a hundred times before, I'd always say, "No." Then he'd clear his throat and I'd rest my head on his shoulder and listen.

The Goat's Head Inn used to sit out on highway 154. That is before the place was sold off and turned into those white condos. Back then, it was the only inn and restaurant for miles. Melvin Griffin, the owner, got a good deal of business from folks passing through. Only problem was that they'd stop in to eat, but hardly anyone would stay overnight at the inn. So, he came up with the idea of telling them about Greyback in hopes that they'd want to stay in town a little longer. I'll tell you Griffin was a damn good storyteller too. One time, I was sitting in a booth, having myself a meatloaf sandwich, when a couple walked in, and even though I'd heard Griffin tell the tale a dozen times, I hung on his every word.

Griffin was standing there with his palms face down on the counter and the couple was sitting on stools across from him. The man was mouthing the names of the specials on the blackboard menu, while his wife was rummaging through her purse, saying "Now where'd I put my lipstick." They were obviously from other parts, because the man elbowed his wife and pointed to the blackboard where the special, 'Greyback Stew,' was described as 'A Tough Son-of-a-Bitch Stew."

"We'll just have two coffees," the man told Griffin. "I want to get back on the road before it gets dark."

Griffin moseyed on back to the percolator, filled two mugs, and brought them back to the couple.

"What exactly is a Greyback?" the woman asked.

"Greyback was a Great Dane, and bigger than most dogs of that breed. Some say he carried back a whole deer one time and laid it on the floor in front of his master. Now, I don't see how any dog could do that, but Greyback wasn't your average pup. He was a pure breed and came from a royal line."

The woman poured about five spoons of sugar in her coffee and then looked up at Griffin. "Can a dog really be of royal blood like a king or queen?"

"Well now, of course ol' Greyback weren't no king, but his line of ancestors had always been owned by them such folk. You know Lords and Barons and what not. Sir Clouston, his owner, was one such man. He owned every hill and dale in this here area. I'm a direct relation of his."

"A king who owns a tavern." The man chuckled, but quickly stopped when Griffin's stare turned grim.

"Well, what makes this dog so special?" the woman asked, trying to smooth over her husband's comment.

"You ever heard the expression, 'a dog is man's best friend?' Well, it's because of Greyback that people say that. He went far and beyond what a normal dog would do and died in doing so." Griffin took a deep breath. It wasn't the first time he'd told the story and he knew where to stop and start to keep his audience engaged. The tale could be rattled off in about two minutes, but if he didn't keep the mystery alive for at least twenty they'd dismiss it as soon as he was finished.

The couple sipped their coffee, waiting for Griffin to continue. When he'd cleared his throat, and was about to start up again, his seven-year-old daughter skipped in.

"Aren't you a sweet one," the woman said, reaching over to pat the girl on the head. "What's your name?"

"Faye."

"Your daddy must love having you around."

"Yep, he lets me choose any dessert out of the case if I help him." Faye pointed towards the end of the counter where a display case rotated plated pieces of pie and custard.

"You know the story of Greyback?" the woman asked.

Griffin leaned across the counter, put his finger to his lips, and whispered, "Hush, it ain't a story for children." This was an outright lie. Faye had heard the legend over a thousand times, but Griffin's tone made it sound legitimate. "You run along now you hear. I'm sure you got some dolls that need playing with." Faye darted out the double doors and into the kitchen. She'd acted her part. Whenever guests arrived, it was her job to come down and tell them about the pies in the display case. And this time it seemed to have worked. The woman ordered up a piece of rhubarb two seconds after Faye had left.

"Ah, so where was I?" Griffin asked, tossing the slice of pie in the toaster oven behind him.

"You were saying the dog did something." The man hadn't seemed too interested before, but now, he was pacing his sips of coffee so they could stay longer.

"So, one evening Sir Clouston came home after an afternoon of hunting. He was a damn sight angry because deep in the woods Greyback had turned around and ran homeward. Clouston had kept on for a bit, but without his prize dog, he hadn't caught anything. By the time he got to the house he was cursing like a sailor. He walked in and yelled, 'Greyback, get your skinny shanks over here.' The dog came a running into the living room and jumped up on his master looking for affection. Clouston probably would have forgiven him too, except there was something odd about the dog's snout. Taking a closer look, he saw that there was blood on it, like the dog had been eating something. Clouston shoved the dog off him and called out for his wife. 'Has Greyback been up in the chicken coop?' No one answered. In fact, it was incredibly quiet in the house. Usually when he'd get home his baby son would be screaming or his wife would be ranting but that evening there was nothing."

"Without thinking twice he started searching the house. He went into each room and then stopped when he got to the nursery. The crib lay toppled over on its side and there was blood splattered all over the place. Clouston's mouth hung open like a busted bear trap. It looked to him as if an animal had ripped someone apart. He moved the crib aside, looking for what was left of his baby. When he didn't find the corpse, he slowly turned towards the doorway where he found Greyback panting. With a closed fist, he lunged across the nursery and cracked the dog in the nose. The Great Dane whimpered, but he didn't run away. Clouston took up his rifle and aimed. 'You son of a bitch,' he said, pulling the trigger. The bullet went in right between the hound's eyes. As the dog fell he let out a tremendous howl like his sprit was being torn from inside him."

Griffin backed off letting it sink in. He enjoyed watching people's reactions. If he'd done his job right, his audience would always look appalled by the gruesome details by this point. Taking his time, he warmed up their coffee cups and brought them over their pie. The woman covered her mouth when she saw the slice oozing reddish-black goo.

"Now, don't get all worried," Griffin said, after snorting a laugh. "Greyback didn't actually eat the boy. Clouston went out back afterwards and found out what really happened. It seems that a wolf had attacked the family while he was gone. In his backyard, he found his wife half-dead still clutching their son, who was very much alive. Nearby was the corpse of the wolf. The animal had found Clouston's wife in the nursery, but she had escaped with the baby out the back door. Luckily, right then, Greyback had come running out of the woods and sprang on the wolf. And he didn't stop fighting until the wolf was dead."

The woman looked perplexed as though she hadn't quite understood. For a second, Griffin thought he may have told the story too quickly. However, a second later the woman asked, "That's it? That's how the story ends?"

"There is a bit more, but I don't know whether I believe it."

"Go on then."

"Well, Clouston never did get over what he had done. Even after his wife recovered and he'd buried ol' Greyback, he never felt all that well about killing his dog. So, one night he went out to Greyback's tombstone and begged the dog's spirit for forgiveness. Right when he'd finished he heard a loud howling sound come up out of the grave."

"Some say you can still hear Greyback at night up on the meadows howling so that folks know he's there protecting them. Maybe it's the wind or maybe it's his ghost." Griffin let a knowing grin clench his lips. "People do hear stuff up there. The calling as they say."

The man almost spilled his coffee while he tried to set his cup on the saucer. "So, his grave is here? In this town?"

"Yes Sir, about a fifteen minute walk over yonder." Griffin pointed to a trail outside the West bay windows.

"I'd be interested in seeing it," the man told his wife. "How about we stay here and make a fresh start in the morning." The man turned from his wife to Griffin. "Do you have any vacant rooms?"

Griffin slowly nodded his head. His story had done what it was supposed to. More than half the time after Griffin had related the tale, his listener would want to see the grave and then it'd be late and they'd wind up taking a room. He didn't think of it as tricking people. It was just a way to talk folks into doing what they already wanted to do. It's wasn't like he was lying. It was a story for Christ sakes. Hell, if he was lying then so was Joe Hall, who sold Greyback t-shirts out of his grocery store. For that matter, you could also include Lawrence Reiner, who made a pretty penny selling *The Morgan's Bend Guidebook to Obscure Tourist Sites* out at his gas station. It wasn't a big deal if it was true or not. Everyone knew in the back of their minds that it was just local lore. That is everyone except for little Faye.

There was no one in town who believed the legend more than her. She'd grown up hearing about two things, the gospel and her daddy's stories. At the age of seven, she was also sure of two things: angels lived high up in a town past the clouds, and Greyback had killed a wolf because Morgan's Bend was crawling with them. Griffin hadn't thought much about it the first time she'd told him. "So, she believes the legend, she'll grow out of it." But in a few years when she was eleven, she still believed the wolves were out there. That wouldn't have been a problem except for one thing. Faye refused to leave the house after dark. It didn't matter if her daddy was with her or not. Once the sun was down there was no getting her outside.

As you might think, Griffin worried about his daughter's condition considerably. How would his baby girl ever live a normal life if she was so frightened of the dark? He tried various things to change her mind. He told her the story was an old wives tale that had been handed down through the generations. There was no proof that any of it had ever happened. "Don't be silly," she said, "Greyback's grave is right past the old elm." He took her to see Tom Brenton, the county game warden. He told her wolves were not indigenous to the region and it was highly unlikely many, if any, lived in the hills. She didn't buy a word of it. "I've seen paw marks in the forest."

"Well honey, that could be any number of animals, even a dog."

"But it could also be a wolf?"

Nothing seemed to work. She was bent on believing that the story was true. Finally, Griffin decided there was only one thing he could do. He'd have to tell her the truth.

Sunday morning he called Faye into his office behind the kitchen and set her down in the worn armchair in the corner. On the bottom shelf of the bookcase sat a black shoebox. He handed it to his daughter and pulled up a stool in front of her. "Go on, open it."

Inside, Faye found a stack of yellowing photos. They showed a younger version of her dad and his buddies, Lawrence and Joe, in the meadows nearby. The first revealed an empty plot; the next was a candid shot of Lawrence and Joe setting a tombstone into the ground; and the last showed the three of them standing in front of Greyback's grave.

"The truth is there is no Greyback. We made it all up. The story's a Welsh legend Joe read in a book one time."

"I don't understand."

"Before you were born there was a fire in the mine, and all the miners who worked down there shipped out. Without them around, most of us didn't have any income coming in. So, some of us got to thinking, 'how can we get folks to come here?' After a long discussion, we decided that if people heard about something interesting hereabouts they might come to our town. And that's what we did. We set up a fake tourist site."

She placed the photos back in the box and closed the lid.

"So, now you know the truth," he continued. "There's no reason for you not to go out after dark."

Her nails were already short from biting them, but she moved her pinky to her lips and tore off the end. "If Greyback doesn't exist then what makes that howling sound at night?"

"Don't you get it?" Griffin took the shoebox and set it on his lap. "There's no ghost dog or wolves. It's all made up."

"Daddy, just because you made up Greyback doesn't mean this place isn't swarming with wolves."

Four winters passed, and Faye turned fifteen. But she still refused to go outside at night. Instead, she took up waitressing for her dad in the evenings. She even started telling Greyback's legend to the people that were passing through. I heard her run through it a couple of times. She didn't tell it from Clouston's point of view but rather from Clouston's wife's. I can't say that she did a better job than her father, but she did get a fair amount of tips.

One day in early May I was sitting in my booth waiting on my usual, a meatloaf sandwich, when Randy Quinn, his older brother, and some local boys, came strutting through the entrance. Faye was hopping about behind the counter. She'd twisted her ankle the week before, and the doctor had given her crutches, but she refused to use anything but her daddy's silver tipped cane to get around. It's a wonder she didn't spill my sandwich in my lap when she finally hopped out with it.

But as I was saying, Randy and his friends went straight up to the far end of the counter where the bottles of booze were on display and started salivating.

Faye blushed. She'd had a crush on Randy for over a year, but from what she could tell, he didn't know she existed. In the hallways at school, she'd tried to get his attention by ramming into him and dropping her books, but he never seemed to notice her scrounging around on the floor picking up papers. It was probably because he was eighteen and a senior, and she was only a sophomore.

"What can I get you?" she asked.

"Two quarts of Mad Dog 20/20," Randy's brother said, pointing to the top shelf.

Faye worked the cane as best she could and maneuvered herself in front of the cooler where they kept the bottles of beer and wine.

"Randy," his brother said, "you best help that girl get that bottle or this is the last time I buy you MD."

"I was about to." Randy shuffled past Faye, and grabbed two bottles. "Hey, I know you," he said, setting the booze on the counter. "What happened to your leg?"

"Gymnastic practice." She could feel his eyes moving up from her legs, over her belly, and then stopping on her breasts. Without thinking, she covered them with her arm.

"We're going over to Greyback's grave. Do you want to come along?"

"I'm sort of working."

Randy glanced across the dining room at me, the only customer, and then back at Faye. "Come on there's a great view. You can see the whole town from there."

"Well, there's my ankle and the dinner rush starts in about an hour."

"I'll have you back by then."

She looked up into his blue eyes. "Let me tell my dad."

It was a humid outside, especially muggy for spring. Faye hopped along with her cane in one hand and, Randy's shoulder in the other. His brother and friends had run ahead, but Randy had made sure to get one of the bottles from them and was taking nips from it every now and again.

"My ankle's killing me."

"We can stop for a minute. I'm in no hurry to get there."

They sat down on the grass. A tired elm hung its branches over them. Randy unscrewed the wine and handed it to Faye. "That should set you right."

She took a swig and tried not to cough. "Tastes like Hawaiian Punch."

"You know that stuffs going to be illegal next year. A couple of boys died after drinking it and the state's passing a law to stop kids from buying it."

"Yeah, I heard about that. This stuff supposed to make you go crazy."

Randy's hadn't been lying about the view. As the sun began to set, it left a warm glow over the town. Some of the houses had already turned on their lights. After Faye had drank a few more gulps they seemed to sparkle. She was about to point out how lovely she thought it was but before she had a chance Randy's mouth was on hers. It wasn't her first kiss, although it felt like it. The first had been Jimmy Wallace. Still, that had been more like a lip grazing than a full smooch. This was definitely a real kiss. Faye took it all in: the breeze fluttering over the hills, the sun dwindling, the warmth in her chest as Randy moved his hand down the front of her dress.

They went on as such for another twenty minutes before Faye opened her eyes and saw the last ray of sun disappearing behind the hills.

"I've got to get back," she told him.

"Just a little longer." His mouth made small bites on her neck, and his hand slowly crawled down her belly.

"No, I really have to go."

"Don't you like me?"

She pushed him away. "I do but, there's wolves out here."

"Don't worry about that." He held up his hip so she could see the knife pouch attached to his belt. "I've got my Bowie." His mouth latched on to her neck again as he pawed at her thigh.

"Please, just walk me home."

"I will. Just as soon as we're done here." He peered at her as if to say I've done enough sweet talking, it's time to get down to business.

She looked down to find his fingers creeping up her dress. She slapped them away like she'd just noticed a spider on her leg.

"Come on baby." In the faint light, his eyes seemed to change from blue to a milky yellow. This wasn't the boy she was infatuated with. This one panted and drooled like an animal. She searched the ground for her cane, but before she could pick it up, he pushed her onto her back. The ground felt rough against her shoulders. She screamed as he held her wrists down with one hand and lifted up her dress with the other.

Some say that the whole valley heard her scream. They say she howled like an animal caught in a trap; she called out from a primitive place deep inside her heart. I can't say one way or the other. All I know is that after she screamed, Randy was lifted up in the air and tossed aside.

Faye sat up gasping for air. There, about ten feet away, was a Great Dane, and next to him lying on the ground was Randy. The dog snarled at him and then, in a mighty leap, he dove and landed on Randy's chest. It's Greyback, she thought. He heard my cry. Randy reached down to his belt and pulled out the Bowie knife. Greyback snapped at the boy's face tearing off an ear as Randy thrust the knife into the animal's belly. For a moment, it was hard to tell who was in control. Fur flew up like dandelion fluff. Blood and pieces of flesh fell over the lawn. And then it was over. Randy lay dead and Greyback hovered over him with a piece of cheek in his mouth.

Faye's whole body trembled and her dress stuck to her skin like a damp hide. Greyback trotted over and licked her on the nose. She held his face in her hands and leaned her forehead against his snout. They stayed like that for a while, and then the Great Dane ran off into the darkness.

Of course, some folks tell it a little different from my granddaddy. They believe that Randy was murdered by Melvin Griffin. He heard her screaming and sprinted across the meadows. When he found the boy with his pants dangling from his knees he grabbed the boy, threw him off his daughter, and ripped him into pieces with his bare hands.

I can't say if either one of the stories is true. The Goat's Head Inn was sold off and Griffin left town after that. I've heard people say they think he moved with his daughter down to Camdenton, but no one seems to know for sure. I guess it doesn't matter in the end, because the version I want to be true is my granddaddy's. I need to believe there is something out there protecting me, especially on dark nights when I hear the calling.

SYLVAN SPRINGS
Robert Holt

Heart disease took my father last October, two weeks before his birthday; due to his service in the Korean War, he was laid to rest in Jefferson Barracks Cemetery in one of the quiet nooks near the Mississippi, where the acres upon acres of gravestones could be seen stretching out to the west as far as the eye could see. The burial was held on the thirteenth, and his eightieth birthday was on the twenty-third. On the day of the old man's birthday, the plan was for my brother and me to go to the cemetery for a last drink with him. My brother, living true to his nature, ditched me that morning due to a business engagement. So, with a heavy heart and somber mind, I drove from my suburbia home in Fenton to the National Cemetery, to pay respects to the hero of my youth and the father that I had always longed to know better.

I stopped off at the Wal-Mart at the Telegraph exit on 270 (or is it 255 at that stretch, I can never quite keep it straight), and bought a few cheap, plastic flowers. I hit the Steak n' Shake in the parking lot and then drove to Captain Z's liquor store near the turn on Sheridan Road that led to the cemetery's front gates. There I bought the Jack Daniels that the old man was so fond of and a shot glass shaped like a tit, to match the old man's humor.

It was after noon when I finally parked the car near the grave and walked over. I had imagined a heart-to-heart with the dirt that now represented my old man. I had foreseen myself crying as I poured the whisky into the soil, tear falling to mix in, and a feeling of love and peace washing over me. Another burial was taking place twenty yards away, and I found myself feeling awkward, embarrassed, and ashamed of my overly sentimental reaction. I stood silently and stoically and split the fifth with the always-thirsty dirt. I would suck one out of the tit glass, then I would pour one, and so it went for an hour. When I remembered the cooling burgers and fries, there was less than a shot left. I unceremoniously flicked the remaining bit onto the grave and hustled back to the car. I had to reverse it for several dozen yards to avoid the jam that the other burial caused. But I was soon pulling out onto Sheridan Road and feeling the heavy effects of the whisky. And there it was, sitting quietly off to the side of the cemetery like a beacon for the mourning drunk with cold food to eat, Sylvan Springs County Park.

I pulled into the park, grabbed my sack of food, and wandered out into the sparsely wooded fields. I sat at a picnic table and eagerly dove into my meal. The grease had mostly dissolved the bun, but the flavor was that classic diner fare that I had known from my childhood. I devoured it. After all the food was gone, I turned on the bench and rested against the table. My head lulled back on my neck, and I watched the squirrels and birds rustling amongst the treetops and the soft white clouds floating above them. I have no idea how long I remained in this drunken reverie before the rustling of the nearby brush, but I imagine now that it must have been several hours, as the sun was already making significant progress on its descent.

I stood up and looked at the place where I had heard the rustling and moved towards it with a mixture of curiosity and something else that I can't quite describe, but that I have taken to calling a pull (I have heard others describe a similar experience).

Honeysuckle grew in great masses in the brush, and as I got closer, I saw a small girl wearing an off-white dress and no shoes. We made eye contact for a second, and then she was gone. I could hear her stomping through leaves and sticks as she escaped from me. I don't know why I didn't let that be the end of it, but I didn't. I followed her into the thick growth, forcing my way on an old trail. My foot hit a stone that I never saw, and a moment later I felt myself falling. My hands grabbed at the honeysuckle to slow the fall, and it worked, but my fall was not to the flat ground but to the stone stairs that went down ahead of me. I landed hard on the cold stones and felt the skin ripping from my shin and elbow. I screamed in pain and rolled down a step before situating myself into a sitting position.

I found myself sitting on a deteriorating stone stairway leading down to a stone courtyard. In the distance, I heard kids laughing at me. They were at a nearby skate park, and when I looked, none were looking at me, but I saw the girl there standing with an older boys arm draped over her shoulder. I stood and called out to her. "Hey," I yelled, but when the girl turned, I saw that this girl was not the angelic grade-schooler but a teenaged punker with piercings covering her face. I turned away, embarrassed by my mistake, and the skaters went back to their delinquency or whatever.

I stood and slowly applied pressure to the leg that had taken the brunt of the fall. It held me, but throbbed with pain. I moved slowly down one uneven step at a time, until I reached the courtyard, surrounded by a stone wall with a shallow creek flowing through it. Several bridges with ornate and crumbling stone rails crossed the creek and I felt as if I had crossed into another world. St. Louis is not a city known for its antiquity, yet here I was, standing in ruins within the area that I had often referred to as my stomping grounds.

I moved with wonder around the courtyard, noticing the dedication in etched stone saying 1939. I crossed over a bridge and looked down into the clear flowing water. I followed the creek from side to side within the courtyard and saw that it seemed to start at a large rock at one end and vanished into a large stone archway at the other end. I went towards the stone and found that the water was bubbling from beneath it. It was only then that the name Sylvan Springs held any meaning to me. I bent down and touched the chilly water with my fingertips. I sucked the droplets off of them.

I heard more laughter from over the wall in the direction of the skate park. I straightened, and with a steady and even step, despite the pain, moved back towards the stairs that I had fallen down. As I moved up the steps, I heard more laughing, only this time it sounded as if it was coming from right behind me in the courtyard, but when I turned, I saw nobody, not even in the distant skate park. I pushed my way through the brush, to find my picnic table cleared of the litter that I had left upon it. I shrugged, assuming a park ranger or hippy had thrown out my trash. I walked down towards my car. My hand probed at my pockets. My wallet was there, but my keys and cell phone were missing. My heart started to beat a little faster, and I jogged in a semi-panic to my car. The doors were locked, but I could see through the window that my phone was there, sitting in the cup holder in the center console. My keys were not there. I cursed and punched the window without any real force.

Then I heard the laughter again. I turned with a fury but saw nothing but the Steak n' Shake bag blowing in the gentle breeze among the honeysuckle. I started jogging towards it, thinking that my keys were absentmindedly dropped into the bag. I caught up to it, just as it was threatening to free itself and blow out across the field. The instant I grabbed it, I knew that my keys were not in it. Nothing was it. I crumpled the bag into a tight ball and threw it into the brush. Then I heard the laughter again, only now it wasn't a mocking laugh but a vicious and angry laugh coming from the hidden stairway.

I ran in that direction. "This isn't funny, you little shits!" I watched my feet and stepped swiftly and carefully, but the laughter was far ahead of me. I continued my pursuit down the stairs and into the courtyard. I looked around furiously, but there was nobody there. I grunted in frustration and turned to go back up the stairs. Then the laughter started again. It came from the archway that the water disappeared into. I ran towards it and looked inside. The mouth was three feet high and the water was only inches deep. I yelled into it. "Come on out. I can wait here all night."

I sat down on the dirt with every intention of waiting until my tormenters came out. However, as the sun vanished and darkness settled over the park, my resolve began to fade. I started to get up, and then I saw movement. I thought at the time that my eyes had adjusted to the dark or that the girl saw me moving and thought that she could get away with moving. Regardless, I was certain that I saw her. Fueled by a fury that drove out conscious thought I stepped quickly into the creek and the cold water seeped into my loafers and drenched my socks. I crouched and began to stumble blindly into the darkness. I felt that I could hear her breathing before me. I stumbled further on, stretching my hands to the sides to touch the walls to ensure that she couldn't sneak by me. Then I saw her. She was laughing silently before me. I reached out and felt spider webs break around my hand. My mind instantly jumped on this. How could unbroken spider webs be here if she had just come this way? In the darkness of the tunnel, she spread out her arms and lunged at me. Her face was a distortion of cruelty and pain. I screamed and flung my arm around my face to block her attack. My legs straightened, and my head collided with the roof of the tunnel. There was a push; I swear that there was a push. And I fell backwards into the cold water.

As I began to scramble out of the tunnel, I felt a hand grab my foot and yank at it, causing me to fall face first into the water. I heard commotion above me and felt things beating at my back and squealing with delight. I crawled across the rocks and broken glass through the freezing water while being assaulted until I emerged into the dark night air. It was then that I saw the vast number of bats that were also escaping the tunnel. I stood there in the spring water shivering and panting looking into the darkness of the tunnel. The girl was there. She wasn't laughing, just looking and smiling. And then she was gone, not retreated into the tunnel, but vanished.

The laughter started to come from all around me now, and I was crying in terror as I looked from side to side. I climbed out of the creek and stumbled backwards towards the old stairway. I don't know why I didn't go around the brush and through the parking lot, but I didn't. I went back the way I came. And in one of those nonsensical actions, I saw my discarded bag and grabbed it off the step. As I did, something grabbed my foot. My knee crashed into stone, and my hands slapped at the stairs. The hand that still held the crumpled bag scraped into something metal. My other hand swiftly swung over to grab it, and I turned to throw it at whatever had tripped me.

Nothing was there.

As my heart calmed and I got up to continue my limping retreat I noticed that I held my keys in hand. I left quickly, and I took my trash with me.

Since that night, I have researched the park. There are no ghostly legends surrounding the World War Two Beverage Garden. No bodies have ever been found in the drainage pipe. However, the girl I saw vanish matched a missing person's bulletin from the Lemay area, missing since October twenty-third, Nineteen sixty-three.

A CHILD FOR A ROOM
C.V. Hunt

1

"I can't believe I let you talk me into this," Eve said. She pulled the lever on the passenger seat, leaned back, and rubbed her hands over pregnant belly.

I eyed the GPS again and looked at the clock. We passed through Salem at least twenty minutes ago. Our turn would be coming up soon. My eyes flicked to the rearview mirror to make sure the moving truck was still behind us.

Eve sighed. "At least the trees are pretty in the fall." She gazed out the car window at the changing foliage that lined the road. Eve twirled her fingers around the end of her messy, golden ponytail.

I said, "You know what I can't believe?" I thumbed over my shoulder. "Those Juggalos get paid for drive time."

"Juggalos?" She laughed and continued to stare out the window. "I don't think they're Juggalos, Shawn."

"They sure acted like a bunch of clowns," I grumbled. "Did you see their pants?"

She turned toward me. "You're the one who wanted to move two and a half hours from St. Louis."

"And your mother was the one who said hiring movers would only cost two-hundred bucks," I retorted.

"I don't why you'd think two-hundred dollars would cover the cost of moving everything we own to the middle of nowhere."

"We should have rented a U-Haul."

Eve pointed at her swollen belly. "Hello? Do you think the baby would have jumped out of the womb and helped us carry furniture?"

I sighed in defeat. "Yeah... you're right."

The hushed female voice of the GPS signaled that the turn was approaching.

"Tell me again why this is a good idea," Eve groaned. She rubbed her belly and stretched her legs.

I took a deep breath and exhaled slowly. "I don't want our kid growing up in the city. I grew up in the country and went to a small school. I want our kid to do the same. I don't want to have to worry about something happening to him walking to school or any of that crap."

"You could have at least picked a better house," she said.

Following the GPS instructions, I turned onto a gravel road. The moving truck followed us.

"There's nothing wrong with the house," I said.

Eve laughed.

I asked, "What?"

"You're only saying that because of your job."

"Hey, I would love this house even if I wasn't an architect." I gestured at our new home as it appeared on the right, nestled between a cluster of trees.

Eve groaned as I drove onto the gravel driveway. The house, in my mind, was awesome. I didn't know the history of the three-story structure and didn't know if I ever wanted to. It was apparent that it was originally a small two-story farmhouse, but a previous owner either wasn't satisfied with the amount of room it provided, or he was out of his mind. Rooms had been added to the house, but there wasn't any rhyme or reason to their placement. The third floor was completely lined with windows, giving it a sunroom appearance, and the first story wall facing the drive was painted a bright yellow. Each room added was built with different materials. Some of the house was sided with different shades of vinyl, while other areas had wooden shingles covering it. One room even looked like they'd used an old boat to build the outside structure. Someone had painstakingly hand painted what appeared to be a mixture of Egyptian hieroglyphics and Celtic symbols around the doors and windows. Overall, it looked like a giant tree house. I imagined the previous owner was an eccentric person who wanted to remain young at heart. I had to admit, I was in love with the house.

Eve gawked at the house and shook her head. "The place looks like it's going to fall in."

I parked the car and placed a hand on Eve's belly. "I would never buy anything that would put you or the baby in danger. This house is more structurally sound than the apartment we were living in."

She gave me a half-hearted smile.

"It passes every building code," I said. I leaned in and kissed her lightly on the nose. "Trust me... everything is going to be okay."

"If you say so."

"I say so."

2

The inside of the house was just as hodgepodge as the outside. Each room looked like the owner had hired a different person to decorate it without allowing them to see any of the other rooms. The kitchen had pastel blue cabinets, bright peach walls, and the door leading outside was lime green. Eve stood in the sunshine yellow living room connected to the kitchen and directed the movers. She rubbed her arms to chase a chill, then added a couple of logs to the fire I had started in the fireplace.

The afternoon sun shone through the bay window in the living room. The rays touched her hair as she walked around inspecting the room and holding her belly, and momentarily, her hair appeared to form a golden halo. I watched her for a moment, absorbing the moment, before I approached her.

My presence broke her from her trance. She looked at me and broke into a crooked, sly smile.

"What?" I asked.

"Nothing." Her grin grew. "You look really happy."

I laid my hand on her belly, kissed her, and wrapped my arms around her. Nuzzling in her hair I whispered, "I'm very happy. Are you happy?"

"Mmm. With a few coats of paint and new floors I will be."

We both chuckled. I pulled back from her and gave her a quick kiss. We were interrupted by the shuffling of feet. We turned to see the moving guys carrying the mattress. Both of them were red-face and sweaty.

"Where do you want this?" one of the moving guys panted.

"Third floor," Eve answered. "In the room with all the windows."

They both groaned and proceeded toward the open staircase.

I raised my eyebrows. "Third floor?"

"I like the room with the windows. It's like being outside... and it's the only room not hideously decorated."

"It's plain," I said.

"White walls and hardwood floors are plain?"

"It doesn't have character like the rest of the house."

She looked around the living room. "No. It doesn't. But it feels very Zen in there and I'd like to keep it that way."

"Whatever you want."

3

I placed the bacon on the broiler pan and popped it in the oven. Quietly, I unloaded another box of pots and pans on the counter until I found the large frying pan. I turned the burner on and fished in the fridge for the eggs. The fridge was loaded to the gills. Living in the country wasn't as convenient as the city. There wasn't a grocery on every corner. So after an exhausting first day of unpacking, Eve and I made it a point to stock the kitchen.

Eve shuffled into the kitchen as I set the carton of eggs on the counter. She ran a hand through her tangled hair and yawned. I scratched my chest as I watched her.

"Good morning," I said in a cheerful voice.

Eve growled and gave me the stink eye as she slid into a chair at the table.

"How do you want your eggs?" I held up the carton.

"Scrambled," she grumbled.

I proceeded to break the eggs into a bowl and whisk them. "How'd you sleep last night?"

"Terrible. I kept having vivid nightmares. This house is too dark. I think it messes with my subconscious or something."

"How so?" I poured the eggs into the pan.

"I don't know. Like... my whole dream was really dark and disorienting. Kinda like the house at night when the lights are off."

"There's no light pollution out here in the middle of nowhere."

"I know. I'm not used to it. I'm a city girl. Remember?"

"Yeah." I pulled the bacon from the oven and scrapped the eggs around in the pan. "I forgot about all the bugs. Did you get bit?"

"Bugs?" Eve's eyes danced around the kitchen nervously.

I chuckled as I finished the eggs. I prepared plates for the both of us and joined her at the table. Eve pounced on the food. I lifted my shirt to show her three angry red dots the size of peas on my chest.

Her eyes widened. "Oh, Shawn," she said with a mouthful of eggs. "You should see a doctor." Concern painted her features.

"They're just bug bites. They'll be gone in a couple of days. No big deal." I lowered my shirt and scratched.

"They look painful." She swatted my hand away from my chest. "Don't scratch them. They'll get infected."

"They're not painful. They just itch like hell."

"We'll pick up some cortisone cream today."

"No need to make a special trip."

We ate in silence for a bit. I absentmindedly scratched the bites. Eve seemed to be deep in thought.

I asked, "What was your dream about?"

Her brow scrunched as she chewed on some bacon. "I dreamed I was watching TV in the living room with the lights off. Just some movie, nothing in particular. Then suddenly, in the middle of the movie, a bunch of random pictures started flashing on the screen. I don't remember any of them except the last one. It was an old woman. Her whole face filled the screen and she just stared at me. I don't know why, but it felt like she was in the room with me. She looked angry. Then the screen went black like it was the end of the movie. Except there weren't any credits. The whole house was plunged into darkness. I felt a sharp pain on my left hand in the dream." She looked at her hand and rubbed it. "It felt so real," she whispered and looked at me. "There was a clawed hand growing from my wrist. I freaked out in the dream and was stumbling in the dark until I found our room. I woke you up, but it was still dark. I made you feel the clawed hand and you grabbed it and ripped it off. You threw it on the floor in the bedroom. With all the windows up there, we could barely make out its shadow in the moonlight. It popped up on its fingertips and started running toward us." She stopped and stared at her eggs.

"What happened after that?" I was enthralled with her story.

She looked up at me. "I woke up."

"Sounds like a bad horror movie."

"It was terrifying." She pushed her eggs around with her fork. "It felt real."

"It's probably because it's a new place." I scratched the bites on my chest. "Once you get settled you'll feel more at ease."

Eve nodded and pushed her plate away. "I'm not really hungry."

I patted her hand. "I'll make you a big lunch." I picked up our plates and put them in the sink. "You should get some more rest if you want. I have to get the computer set up so I can work. The cable guy will be here today to set up the TV and internet. I'm sure I have a million emails from the office to check."

She said, "Yeah. I'm still really tired. I think I'm going to lay down for a little bit."

4

Eve slept through the cable guy banging around. I tried to wake her for lunch, but she only grunted at me, rolled over, and fell back to sleep. After I unpacked some boxes and got my office set up, I decided to take a short stroll. The yard was lined with trees and I thought there might be some walking trails nearby.

I walked the perimeter of the yard and found a worn path at the back of the property. The path looked overgrown from nonuse, but I decided to explore it anyway. The ground was covered in fallen leaves. The sound of birds and the crunch of leaves beneath my feet were a great soundtrack to decompress to. After five minutes of walking I noticed a clearing a few yards ahead. As I got closer, I saw some irregular looking stones poking up through the foliage. When I was at the edge of the clearing, I realized what the stones were.

The open area was a small cemetery. I thought, why would someone would put a cemetery in the middle of the woods? I counted twelve worn headstones and approached the closest maker. There was no name or date on the stone. A single, unmistakable word was chiseled into the surface: Infant.

A tingle ran down my spine. The thought of a stillborn child made my stomach knot. I thought about how sad it was that the child wasn't even given a name. I moved on to the next marker. The word "Infant" was etched on it also. My throat tightened, and suddenly, I felt nauseous. My tongue felt thick and my mouth went dry. I hesitantly looked at the next stone: Infant.

My stomach dropped. I felt fear's icy fingers grip my chest. I broke out in a cold sweat. Panicked, I raced around the graveyard and checked each headstone. Every one echoed the same, single word: Infant.

I began to feel dizzy and started backing away from the clearing. I tried to calm myself by taking deep breathes.

I told myself these stones were pretty old. A child's survival rate a hundred years ago was much lower than today. This was probably a family cemetery... a family with really bad luck. I turned toward the trail, tripped on something, and fell.

Sitting up, I realized what I tripped over. Another stone. I counted the others again. I'd missed this one before because it was different from the others. It was flush with the ground and covered with dead leaves.

Something inside of me screamed to get the hell out of there, but something deeper told me I had to read this one. I crawled on my hands and knees to it and hesitantly brushed the debris from the marker. The stone felt unnaturally cold and contained one word: Mother.

The other stones freaked me out, but this one stabbed an icicle of terror straight into my heart. I got to my feet quickly and ran back to the house.

5

I opened the door to the kitchen and found Eve digging around in the cabinets.

She looked at me sleepy-eyed and said, "Where are the plates?"

"Right here." I opened the cabinet by her head.

"Where've you been?" She gave me a confused look. "You okay?"

"I was out walking through the woods." She studied my face, waiting for me to say something more. I said, "You should probably stay out of the woods. The whole place is swarming with poison ivy." I didn't like lying to her, but it was better if she didn't know about the cemetery. It spooked me enough. There was no reason to upset her. "Did you get enough rest?"

She opened the fridge and sighed. "Not really. I'm still keep having weird dreams about that old lady. I don't like it."

I hugged her from behind and kissed the top of her head. "Sorry, honey."

"Agh! Shawn!" She wiggled away from me. "I don't want your poison ivy cooties!" Eve rubbed her belly in a protective manner.

I held up my hands in surrender. "You're right. You're right. I'm sorry. I'll go take a shower. I feel a little beat anyway. A hot shower would be nice." I headed toward the stairs.

I looked back over my shoulder at Eve and watched her pull some leftovers out of the fridge. Outside the kitchen window, the long shadows of evening snaked through the back yard and I thought I saw someone standing by the tree line. I did a double take, but no one was there.

6

I lay on my side in bed and was halfway between sleep and awake. The house was quiet.

Eve whispered, "I can't sleep."

I opened my eyes, but I was too tired to roll over. I debated whether I should pretend I was already asleep, but figured she knew me well enough to know I was awake.

"It's probably because you've been sleeping all day," I mumbled into my pillow.

She sighed.

The sky was clear and the moonlight shone through the large windows of our room. There was no door to this room for privacy, but we wouldn't need one for a few more years anyway. A small landing was located outside the door and then a flight of stairs led to the second floor. Eve left the light on in the hallway of the second floor so that the house wasn't completely dark. From where I lay, I could see all the way down the stairs.

Eve sighed again.

This was her way of saying something was wrong and she wanted to talk. She couldn't just say she wanted to talk. She wanted me to ask her what was wrong and then she would talk my ear off. I was too tired for this. I knew she wanted to talk about what she hated about the house. At some point, I was bound to fall asleep and when I woke in the morning, she would be pissed at me. She'd accuse me of not caring, or that her story was too boring for me to pay attention. I opened my eyes wide, forcing myself to stay awake.

"Is something wrong?" I asked, rolling over onto my back.

"Well, these dreams... I keep dreaming about the same old woman."

I stifled a yawn, sought out her hand, and gave it a light squeeze. "It's okay," I said and closed my eyes. "You've had a rough couple of days. I'm sure you won't keep having—"

A loud humming sound interrupted me. I turned my head to look down the stairs — the direction of the noise. Eve was saying something to me, but the words were smothered, and I couldn't understand her. Slowly, a shadow emerged in the doorway at the bottom of the stairs. It pooled on the floor like an oily stain. I opened my mouth to say something to Eve, but I couldn't find my voice.

The shadow darkened and grew — rising up off the ground — until it formed a silhouette of a woman in a dress. Her outfit had a high neck and long sleeves. The skirt was as wide as the staircase and touched the ground. Her whole outfit was a dull black, but I couldn't make out her face.

Again, I tried to say something to Eve, but I couldn't breathe. I tried to turn my head toward Eve. My whole body felt cemented to the bed. I couldn't move.

The woman at the bottom of the stairs bent forward, placed her hands on the steps, and began to crawl toward us in jerky movements.

I panicked.

I wanted to jump up. I wanted to protect my wife. I tried with everything I had to move or scream at Eve to run, but my body and voice wouldn't respond.

When the figure reached the top of the stairs it righted itself, and suddenly, it was at the side of the bed. My muscles twitched weakly as I tried to move or speak. I tried to ask the woman what the hell she was doing in my house. The only thing I could manage was a pitiful whimper.

The woman raised her hand and pointed toward something beside me. Still struggling to move my body, my head turned slowly toward what she was pointing at.

Eve was asleep beside me. Her pregnant belly was covered by a thin sheet. The woman's hand was pointing in the direction of Eve's belly. The faceless woman began to lean over me. Her pointing hand quickly transformed into a clawed hand. In the blink of an eye, the clawed hand was on Eve's belly.

I shot up in bed and screamed, "Get out of my house!" I threw the blankets off and jumped out of bed.

Eve rolled over. Her voice was thick from sleep. "What's going on?"

The woman wasn't beside the bed anymore. I didn't see her anywhere in the room. I dodged to the wall and flipped on the light. There was no one in the room but me and Eve. I looked around the room quickly for a weapon, but there wasn't anything. The best thing I could find was one of Eve's high heel shoes. I grabbed the shoe off the floor and held it with the heel facing out. I scanned the room again.

"Shawn?" Eve sat up and squinted against the bright light. Her hair was a mess. "What are you doing?"

"There's someone in the house," I whispered.

I checked the closet.

Eve sobered out of sleep quickly. "What?" She sat up and pulled the covers over her belly in a defensive gesture.

"I saw a woman in here," I said, "and now she's gone." I felt like an idiot holding the shoe like it was some sort of deadly weapon that could defend the both of us.

Eve sighed, dropped her defensive pose, and lay back down. "Oh my god, Shawn. You just had a bad dream. Go back to sleep."

"It wasn't a dream. It was real."

She threw her arm over her eyes to block out the light, and then we heard a noise. The distinct sound of a crying baby emanated from somewhere in the house. Eve jumped out of bed in a flash and stared at me with terrified eyes. She clasped one hand over her mouth and the other hand held her belly.

"See?" I whispered. "There's someone in here. I'm going to check it out." I turned to head down the stairs.

Eve ran around the bed and grabbed my arm. "Where are you going? You can't leave me here alone," she hissed. "Call the police."

"My phone's downstairs charging. I'll check the house and grab my phone and come right back up."

"I'm coming with you."

"No you're not. What if it's someone dangerous?"

She looked around the room. "What if they're still up here? You said you saw them up here."

She was right. I saw the woman up here just a moment ago. Who knew where she went. I couldn't leave Eve and take a chance that I missed the intruder.

I sighed. "Okay. But you have to stay behind me." I turned again to descend the stairs.

"Oh, God," Eve whispered.

I stopped. "What's wrong?"

"You have a lot more bites on your back."

"We'll deal with that later."

We both cautiously made our way down the stairs toward the second floor.

7

The wind picked up outside as we descended the stairs and the crying grew fainter. The lights flickered on the second floor. Eve made whimpering noises and held the back of my shirt for reassurance.

"It's just the wind," I whispered. "It's probably blowing up against the house and making that noise."

"No." Eve sounded terrified. "That's a baby. And it's somewhere in this house."

I approached the level slowly, holding Eve's shoe posed for attack. I checked to make sure the intruder wasn't in the hallway. I waved my hand at Eve to follow. The crying sounded like it was coming from the first floor.

The wind howled in erratic busts outside. A flash of light appeared outside the hall windows and was followed by thunder. Rain began to pelt the house.

As we started down the hallway toward the open staircase leading to the first floor, the lights flickered and went out. Eve yelped behind me and started sobbing, almost mimicking the baby's cries from below. I stopped and took her in my arms to comfort her, still gripping the shoe tight.

"It's okay," I said.

Lightning flashed and illuminated the hallway for a second. Over Eve's shoulder, I saw the woman figure standing in the hallway ten feet from us.

"Jesus!" I said and jumped back, dragging Eve with me.

"What?" Eve's panicked voice was shrill.

Eve squirmed in my arms to see what I was looking at. Lightning illuminated the hallway again as she looked. The woman was there again, only five feet from us. Her arms extended toward us.

Eve screamed and broke free from my embrace. She ran for the open staircase leading to the first floor. I threw the shoe at the woman and followed Eve.

Once in the living room, Eve dashed toward my charging phone. The living room was cast in an eerie light. The logs in the fireplace had burned down to red coals. Eve sobbed uncontrollably as she fumbled with the buttons. I snatched up a fire poker. The baby's cries emanated from everywhere. I began searching the living room for the source of the cries.

Eve cursed, looked at the cell's screen, and threw the phone down. She began to wail.

"What's the matter?" I asked. "Call the police!"

"There's no cell phone signal!"

"What?"

I rushed over to her and scooped the phone of the floor. She was right. There were no bars illuminated to show a signal. The phone was in search mode. I hadn't used my phone since we'd moved in and all of my work was done online through e-mail.

Eve looked past me and screamed. The woman was in the living room and walking toward us.

"That's the woman from my dreams!" Eve cried.

"What are you doing in my house?" I held the fire poker above my head. "Don't make me use this thing, lady!"

In the dim lighting of the living room, I saw the old woman open her mouth. A swarm of black insects flew from her throat and swarmed me. The bugs began biting and I swung the poker to ward them off, but it was useless. Eve sobbed behind me. The child's crying turned into cooing. Then as suddenly as the insects had appeared, they were gone. I stared at the woman, panting from my exertion.

"Who are you?" I yelled. "What do you want?"

The woman's mouth did not move when I heard her words. "Another room or another sweet child." She pointed.

I reluctantly turned to look where the woman pointed. He finger pointed at Eve. I snapped my head back to the woman and started walking backwards to shield Eve.

"What does that mean?" Eve asked, hysterical.

"Screw you lady," I said. "You're not getting our baby."

The woman started walking toward us and said, "Then you will build me another room."

"Get out of my house!" Eve screamed.

I raised the fire poker again in a threatening manner as the woman got closer. "I swear to God, lady, I will bash your head in!"

The woman laughed and her body exploded into a million tiny flying insects. Eve gripped me tight. The insects swarmed around each other and flew toward the fireplace. The red coals grew brighter as the insects flew up the chimney. Eve and I barely moved as we absorbed the new silence of the house.

"Where are my car keys?" I said.

Eve snatched them off an end table.

"Let's go," I said.

8

"Are you guys going to build something else on this lot?" the contractor asked me.

I stared at the house as the wrecking ball positioned itself beside the house.

"No," I said.

The contractor gave me a quizzical look and asked, "What are you going to do with the lot? Sell it? This is a nice place. You could probably get a descent price for the place. Hell... I'd be interested."

The wrecking ball operator pulled the massive weight back.

I said, "It's not for sale."

The contractor said, "You just gonna visit the plot every once in a while?" He laughed.

"Aren't you a demolition man?" I snapped.

"Yeah."

"Then your job is to demolish this thing. Don't worry about what I have planned. If I want the lot to sit and rot that's my business."

The contractor held his hands up in a submissive gesture and walked off toward his crew. The wrecking ball was released. I heard a child's cry in the distance. And right before the ball hit the house I saw a silhouette of a woman move in the third floor window.

THE SPIRITS OF CALVARY AVENUE
Wendy Klein

"Hey, Annie. Did you know that this is where people say they see Hitchhiking Annie?" Joe asked as they rounded the corner onto Calvary Ave.

"Don't be a jerk," she said, punching him in the arm. "As soon as I turn eighteen, I'm leaving St. Louis for good, just so that people stop asking me if I was named after her."

"Well, were you?"

Annie punched him again, but this time it was a bit less fervent. She wished she hadn't let Joe choose the route for their morning run. Of course he would pick the only half-mile stretch of road she'd been taught to avoid. She ran her hand along the black, iron fence that surrounded Bellefontaine Cemetery. Across the street, an identical fence surrounded Calvary Cemetery, like two warring kingdoms setting up battlements to keep out the enemy.

Annie could feel Joe's gaze. "You were, weren't you?" he asked, laughing at the absurdity.

Annie sighed. Joe could read her in a way no one else had ever been able to. Normally, she appreciated this quirk, except on occasions like this where she'd rather have kept the truth to herself.

"My mom was one of the people, you know, back in the 1980s, who claimed to have seen Hitchhiking Annie. In fact, I'm pretty sure she was the last one to ever see her." Annie shrugged. "I guess it made quite the impression on her."

"Whoa," Joe said. "I feel like I've just met a celebrity." Annie shifted to punch him again, but he veered off the sidewalk to dodge the blow. A Chevy truck swerved to avoid hitting him, and the driver blared its horn and stuck a rude finger out the window.

"Geez, watch out," Annie said, pulling Joe back onto the sidewalk by his sleeve.

"You could pull off the look, you know," he said.

"What are you talking about?"

"Hitchhiking Annie. They say she's got dark hair, pale skin, wears a white dress . . ."

Annie snorted. She never wore dresses.

"We should totally dress you up like her for Greg's Halloween party this year. We could even come out here, stick your thumb out, see if anyone will pick you up . . ." Annie glanced over to see if Joe was serious. He sure looked serious.

"No. No way."

"C'mon," he said. "I'll dress up, too. We can do it together. It'd be fun."

They turned the corner towards North Broadway, and Annie took a final look back over her shoulder at Calvary Avenue. It looked so ordinary, so benignant, that she sighed and said, "Fine. I'll be the creepy Annie-ghost for the party. But no hitchhiking."

Joe grinned. "Yes! This is going to be awesome."

***

Their run took them back to Annie's house, where they pulled up two kitchen stools and chugged down their Gatorades.

"Good run?" Annie's mom asked as she entered the room.

"Awesome, Mrs. Lewis-Parker," Joe said. "Annie here was like the Roadrunner. Beep-beep!"

Mrs. Lewis-Parker laughed, a bright giggle that sounded like a bird chirping.

"Annie, you should ask her," Joe said, nudging her in the ribs.

"Ask me what?" Mrs. Lewis-Parker blew on her cup of coffee.

Annie shot Joe a scathing look, but he ignored her. "We want to know about your experience with the hitchhiking ghost."

Mrs. Lewis-Parker's coffee mug slipped from her hand and shattered across the floor.

"I'm sorry," Joe apologized as he stooped to scoop up the steaming pieces.

Annie knelt to help, too, but Mrs. Lewis-Parker grabbed her arm. "Don't you go near that road."

"Mom, you're scaring me," Annie said, trying to pull away from Mrs. Lewis-Parker's grasp. Pink-painted fingernails dug into her skin.

"Stay away from that road. Promise me."

"Okay, mom. I will. "

***

"Ta-da!" Joe said, swinging the door to Annie's room open.

"Joe!" she shrieked. "You can't just barge into a girl's room without knocking."

Joe looked Annie up and down, taking in the white party dress with thick shoulder straps, straight neckline, and skirt that puffed out at the bottom. As he studied her, she twisted the string of pearls she'd found on the bottom of her mom's jewelry box.

"Wow, you look great!" Joe said. His own attire was a bit of a hodgepodge, consisting of long, brown trousers, suspenders over a white shirt, and a newsboy cap.

"What are you supposed to be?"

Joe shrugged. "Your date."

Annie rolled her eyes. "I just need to grab some shoes and then we can go. Do you know how to get to Greg's from here?"

"Yeah. The Red Devil's in the shop, so we'll have to walk," he said, referring to his candy-apple Chrysler that seemed to spend more time in the shop than it did on the road. Annie frowned, hoping it wasn't going to be too far, as she was going to be wearing a pair of her mother's heels. "Don't worry," he said, seeing her hesitation. "I know a shortcut."

Fifteen minutes later, Annie stopped short in the middle of the sidewalk. "I'm not going down there."

"Are you kidding?" Joe asked. "You were just complaining about your blisters, and now you want to walk all the way around Bellefontaine, when his house is just on the other side of Florissant Avenue? That would add another two miles!"

"I told my mom I wouldn't go on Calvary Avenue. You were there — you saw how she freaked out about it."

"C'mon, Annie," Joe said. "It's just a road. So something creeped her out way back when. You don't have to buy into her superstitions, you know. Plus, I'm here. It's not like you're on your own in the middle of the night or anything. I'll be right here next to you."

Annie swallowed and, with a slight nod, wrapped her hand around Joe's. He was right, after all, the road did look perfectly normal – cheerful, in fact, with its orange and yellow-leafed trees shading the well-worn path that ran beside the road.

They had just rounded the first of the road's curves when Joe stopped short. "Hey, what's that?" On the road's shoulder, just past the curb, something was glowing. Annie dragged her feet, but Joe was undeterred. "I just want to see what it is."

Even standing directly beside it, neither could tell what the glowing light was. It hovered in midair, with a greenish tint and a slight hum. "Joe, let's go," Annie said, tugging at his arm. "This isn't right. We should never have come down this way."

"It's okay, Annie." He shrugged her off and reached out to the light. "I just want to see – "

And he was gone.

***

Headlights flashed around the corner. The grill and bumper of a long, green Hudson station wagon swerved around Joe, bleating its horn as it barely missed him. Joe stumbled back to the curb, watching as a 1940 Lincoln Continental passed by on the other side of the road. "Is there a classic car show going on that I didn't hear about?" he asked with a chuckle, trying to lighten the mood. Annie would be freaking about how he almost got hit by a car. "Annie?"

He looked around, but she was gone.

"Annie?"

***

Annie hadn't even thought twice before throwing herself forward to the spot where Joe had disappeared. In a flash, the world had gone dark, and she found herself standing alone on the side of the road. The sun had set and the only light was from a streetlight, which cast eerie shadows over the surrounding cemeteries.

"Joe?" *He must be here somewhere.* "Joe?"

A long-hooded car pulled up beside her. "Need a ride, miss?"

She shook her head. "No, I'm fine. Thanks."

116

Ten minutes later, she was beginning to think she should have taken the offer. Though she walked at a brisk pace, she never seemed to get any closer to the street light. It always seemed just a few yards away.

"Come on, Joe, this isn't funny," she shouted, though logically, she knew this was something beyond one of Joe's clever pranks. Wrapping someone's car in cellophane was more his style. This, whatever this was, seemed to defy the rules of physics, and Annie knew for a fact that Joe had only gotten a D+ in science.

"Don't panic," she told herself. Crossing the road to the Calvary Cemetery side, she found a particular headstone – a white cross that stood so close to the iron fence that she could slip her hands between the bars and touch it. The letters "IHS" were visible, even in the dim light. She counted the thick fence posts that separated the headstone from the street light. Five. Five fence posts.

Holding her shoes in one hand, she took a deep breath and sprinted. One. Two. Three. Four. Five. The street light still seemed just as distant. Six. Seven. Eight. Nine. Ten. She slowed to a halt. There beside her, within reach of her fingers, was the cross headstone with "IHS" engraved on it. She counted the fence posts until the street light. Five.

"You look like you could use a ride, miss." Annie had been in such deep thought, she hadn't even seen the dark, vintage car pull up beside her. A woman with hair in curlers smiled gently at her and Annie – on the verge of tears – just nodded.

The car was roomy and clean. It must have been professionally restored, because although it was an older car – from the 1940s, maybe – it looked clean and new. "What's your name, sugar?"

"Annie," she responded automatically. She was too busy watching out the window to listen to the woman prattle on.

"Now, I know it's not my place to ask, and you probably don't want to listen to a bunch of gobbledy-gook from an old fuddy-duddy like me, but if you need a listening ear or a cryin' shoulder, I'd be glad to help."

"I'm fine," Annie said, sighing with relief as the car passed first one streetlight, then another. The road straightened out. Finally, progress! "Really, I think I'll be fine. My car just broke down," she improvised.

Up ahead, she could see the headlights crossing Florissant Avenue. Her heart thrummed in anticipation. "Almost there," she whispered.

"What was that, hon?" the woman asked. Then, the woman, and the car around her, faded from sight.

***

Joe was getting better at dodging vehicles. By his fourth jump through the strange, glowing light, he had figured out that these orbs somehow brought him to different eras in time. Being the car buff he was, he could quickly distinguish when he was by watching the makes and models of the passing traffic. So far he'd been somewhere in the early 1940s, in the late 1970s, and the early 1950s.

The fourth jump brought him right in front of the hood of a red 1967 Pontiac Firebird. The car swerved, nearly crashing with a green 1961 Dodge Dart. *Late 60s, maybe early 70s,* Joe thought as he stumbled onto the sidewalk. He'd been traipsing along the side of the road for hours, jumping into the green orbs when they appeared in hopes that he'd be able to find his way back to his present, back to Annie. So far, no such luck.

Far off in the distance, a green light hovered. With a resigned sigh, Joe wiped used his newsboy cap to wipe the sweat from his brow, and took off running towards the orb.

***

Five cars later, and still no luck. It seemed the only way Annie could progress along the road at all was by hitching a ride in a vehicle, but each time, as soon as it reached the end of Calvary Avenue, the car and its passengers would drift away like smoke. There had to be some trick to it.

Annie stuck out her thumb and when the clunky old Toyota pulled up, she swung herself in without even waiting for the driver to stick her head out and offer. "My car broke down," she lied. "Can I have a ride? Just down a couple blocks."

The girl in the driver's seat looked at her curiously. She appeared to be about the same age as Annie, with pale skin and dark hair pulled back in a ponytail

"I like your necklace," the driver said. Something in her voice sounded familiar to Annie. "Is it a family heirloom?"

Annie ran her fingers across the string of pearls. "Thanks. They're my mom's. She said she's had them since she was my age. I always figured some old boyfriend gave them to her before she met my dad, because she never wanted to talk about where she got them from."

The girl laughed, and Annie jolted in her seat. She'd know that laugh anywhere — that bright giggle that sounded like a bird chirping could only belong to one person. Annie stared.

"What?" the girl asked.

"Is your name Evaline?"

The girl's head jerked towards her. "Yeah, how did you know?"

Suddenly, a form appeared, centered in the headlights of the speeding car. Annie saw the startled face, all too familiar to her, and gasped. "Watch out!"

Evaline looked back to the road and — catching the briefest glimpse of the boy standing there — jerked the wheel to the left, but it was too late. Annie's scream was the last sound Joe heard.

***

Evaline Lewis woke up in the hospital. A young policeman with the nametag OFFICER LAWRENCE PARKER sat beside her bed.

"Evaline Lewis?"

Evaline just nodded.

"You've been in a car accident. You had quite the shock, but I think you'll be okay."

"What about the others?" Evaline asked. The image of the frightened boy's face, the sound of the girl in white's screams — it was too much for her to handle.

Officer Parker shook his head and frowned. "There was no one else," he said. "From the skid marks, it seemed you must have swerved for an animal. Deer, maybe, at this time of year."

"But, the girl in my car. I'd picked up a hitchhiker."

"You must be confused, miss," Officer Parker said. "You had quite a bump to the head, so it's understandable. There was no one else in your car, no other cars, and nothing on the road aside from the skid marks. Your car was totaled, but I did see these in the front seat, and thought you might like to have them back right away. Family heirlooms?"

He held up the string of pearls that the hitchhiking girl had worn. Evaline gasped and, misreading her surprise, Officer Parker smiled. "Here, let me help you put them on." He reached around her neck and fastened the clasp. "Beautiful," he said with a smile that somehow dissipated the chill in her bones.

***

Twenty years later, Evaline Lewis-Parker, waiting anxiously for her daughter to get home from a Halloween party, discovered that her pearls were missing.

She crumpled to the floor and wept.

***

The door behind her creaked open and a hand fell onto her shoulder. She looked up through bleary eyes.

"Annie!"

"I'm sorry I took the pearls, Mom," Annie said, dropping the shimmering string into her mother's outstretched hand. Joe looked on from the doorway, his clothes smudged and his face streaked with concern. "We took the shortcut down Calvary Avenue. I'm sorry. I . . . I didn't know."

"You're okay." Relief flooded through Evaline, overflowing and gushing from her eyes. She stood and wrapped her arms around her daughter, her beautiful daughter who hadn't died that day on the roadside. Annie didn't squirm out of the hug like she normally would have.

"And Joe! But how . . . ?"

"The car didn't hit me, Mrs. Lewis-Parker," Joe said. "When I saw the wreck, I ran to help. You were both unconscious, but the moment I touched Annie, we returned here, to the present. We're okay. We're all okay."

A few miles away, a green orb pulsed once, then faded out of existence.

APPROVAL OF A GHOST
John Kujawski

There was a time when I wasn't sure if she approved of my evil deeds. I would go about my day, taking part in whatever horrific task I could think of, and the most I'd usually get from the woman was a slight smile, if that. Of course, it was always, always a weird subject for me to think about. Not everyone can say that they've lost sleep at night pondering the feelings of a woman that was no longer alive.

It was obvious to me that she was a ghost. I can't say that she really scared me, though. It was actually kind of a nice event when I first caught a glimpse of her. I was only seven years old at the time. The memory has always haunted me and it's become one of the many recurring dreams I have at night.

Everything started with a trip to the park. It was a secluded location just outside of downtown St. Louis. My babysitter took me there one afternoon. She happened to be the babysitter that I liked. She was the beautiful one with the long hair. She didn't mind the trips, because the park was never very crowded. It was a nice place and it had three main sections. There was a pond, a playground, and then a path that someone could walk on that led to a bathroom and a public telephone. I never used the path much though, and we went straight to the playground as usual that day.

It was nice being at the playground at first, because no one else was there. I had the swings to myself, and the merry-go-round. My babysitter had a nice bench to sit on so she could read an adult book she found at the grocery store. All was good, until about twenty minutes into the outing when some chubby kid showed up. He didn't have his parents with him and I guess they just dropped him off. He had this green t-shirt on and his stomach was rolling out from the bottom of it. He kept drooling, too. Anyway, he got on the merry-go-round and he was just sitting there. It was like he was waiting for someone to give him a push, and the last thing I wanted to do was make friends. So, when my babysitter wasn't looking, I ran over and pushed the kid off the merry-go-round. He hit the ground with a splat. I mean, it was like I had squashed him. He just laid on the ground crying, and of course my babysitter went to see if he was okay because she was a sweet girl who loved kids. That was when I saw her, though.

She was sitting across the playground on one of the swings. She had kind of a faint image. It wasn't totally clear. It's still hard to explain, but she looked beautiful and had long hair just like my babysitter. She was only there for a minute, staring at me with her glowing green eyes and I could have sworn she smiled, even if it was just for a moment. Then she vanished.

From that day forward, I was excited by my discovery of the ghost and I knew that I liked her. I just wasn't sure if she liked me, and I couldn't think of a way that would even make it possible for me to find out. I just decided to give her the name Anna. It was like she was my imaginary friend, but I knew she was real. I figured she was in her twenties. She was an adult. I just didn't know if she wanted to scold me for my behavior or not.

Of course, my behavior stayed the same for the rest of the year. My favorite moment came when I was at the park on a class trip. There were a whole bunch of us together and the teachers just let us run wild. I don't know why. Anyway, I was hanging out by the pond with a few friends, and we noticed that someone had left a bike down by the water. I guess they were planning on coming back to get it so they could ride it on the path, but the thing was just propped up with a kickstand, and there was no chain on it. I guess there really was no place to chain it up but it was still careless of someone to leave it there.

My first thought was to pop the tires. I thought that would be neat but they were the really thin kind and I wasn't sure how satisfying that would be. I went with my second idea and grabbed the bike by the handlebars, rolled it down to the water, and then pushed it into the pond. Everyone was laughing. My friends were almost in tears because it was so funny. I did feel a bit bad, though, because the ducks had to swim around the thing and I didn't want to cause them any grief. Aside from that, I was pretty happy. When I was looking at the water and at what I had done to the bike, that's when Anna appeared again.

She didn't show up quite like she did last time. It was more like I could see her reflection in the water. I could see her beautiful hair and her face reflected in the sun, and once again I could have sworn that she smiled.

I don't even know why I worried about it so much, but I knew that sometimes smiles could be deceiving. I suppose I feared that she was just grinning at the thought that I'd get what was coming to me some day. It was a concern I had when I went to bed that night, and something that was always on my mind, really, throughout the rest of my childhood.

By the time I was twelve, I was able to ride my own bike to the park. Often, I wouldn't see her, even when there was no one around. There were times when I didn't even look. Every now and then, I was sure I'd caught a glimpse of her. Usually it was when I was letting off some steam. Oftentimes, I'd be throwing rocks at trees and stuff, and once I threw one at the telephone outside the white building that had the bathroom in it. I would always see her face, even if it was just for a second. I always knew she was there, haunting the park, watching me.

The bad part was that she did haunt me. She haunted my entire life. Every day at school, I'd be sitting in the cafeteria or the library, wondering what she thought of me. I never cared about the girls at school. My concern was for Anna.

That smile of Anna's became a source of obsession for me. I had seen teachers smile as they were writing notes home to my parents or they'd smile when I was sitting in detention. I just wasn't sure if Anna had that same smile. It drove me crazy.

I knew I was crazy, too. I was crazy in all sorts of ways. That was another thought on my mind that I'd been fixated with. I just wanted to meet my equal, though, even if it was just a ghost.

Anyway, nothing haunted me quite like the time I finally went to the park after dark. I knew I had to at some point, and it all went down one night when I was fifteen years old. I rode my bike to the park, just like usual. It was pitch black outside, though, and I knew wasn't supposed to be there, but I figured it was a good chance to see Anna. My guess was that a ghost would love the night.

Luckily, I had a good way of dealing with the dark. I had a large flashlight with me that I had just put batteries in and it was a damn good one. I had a steady beam of light as I rode around the grass on my bike. The first thing I did was head to the playground, but I didn't see Anna there. I thought she might appear on the swings, but she was nowhere to be found. The next place I went to was the pond.

The pond is where it happened. It was where all my concerns were answered. Sure, when I rode my bike down to the water, I didn't see Anna. I could hear breathing though, like some old man struggling with the Missouri humidity that was such a strong part of the summer. Whoever it was sounded awful. It was like they were sick, but sure enough, when I got to the water, there was some man sleeping on the ground a few feet away from where the ducks were sleeping. I didn't want to scare the ducks. I didn't want to wake the ducks up, either, but I had to. I had to do it to get a reaction from Anna so I would know how she felt.

These little things I had done to get Anna to notice me in the past had just been pranks. I knew it was time for the real thing. I managed to ride my bike right up to the sleeping man and he didn't budge. His breathing had become snoring, more or less. He had long grey hair and a sleeveless white shirt on. I got off my bike and walked over to him. Right away, I started kicking him.

He woke up pretty quick, but I was kicking him really fast. He really didn't have any place to go. He was coughing and making all sorts of sounds. I know I kicked him the ribs at least once. I just hoped Anna was watching, but I didn't see her. After a long series of kicks, it was pretty clear that it was over for my victim. He wasn't moving. He wasn't breathing. I had killed him.

I just didn't see Anna, though. It was horrible. I stayed in one spot for a while. I felt so bad that I had scared the ducks off. They were at the other end of the pond and it was a terrible feeling. I realized I had forgotten to bring them any bread to eat, which made me feel worse.

Finally, I got back on my bike and rode off. There was no sign of Anna. I wondered if that was a message that she was unhappy with me. All I could think to do then was to ride over to the phone booth and head into the building where the bathroom was located. I knew I had to drink some water from the sink.

When I arrived at the phone, though, that was when things became clear to me. That was when I discovered how Anna felt and how she thought and what kind of woman she had been when she was alive. I had the answer to the very thing that had haunted me most of my life.

I didn't even realize it at first, but the phone was ringing. I let it go for a minute and then I picked it up, thinking I'd see Anna in the distance somewhere, but I never did. I didn't even hear anything at first, when I answered the call. It was just the sound of wind coming through the phone. Then I heard it loud and clear, though. It was better than a smile and it was a sound I understood. It was pure. It was wicked. It was evil like me. It was the sound of a woman laughing.

FIRE ON THE RIVER
Rebecca Lacy

The Flyway, which follows the Mississippi river basin, is one of the greatest avian highways in the world. Twice a year, millions of birds stop along the river during their arduous migrations. It was to study this treasure that I spent 1989 in St. Louis, Missouri.

My research took me to the banks of the river, trudging through swampy sloughs and hiking the sandy banks, documenting the myriad of species. To the uninitiated, this may seem like a dull pursuit, and I readily admit that it is difficult to describe the spectacle that awaits the patient observer. To me, it was a moving experience to see flocks of pelicans, which were once on the brink of extinction, gracefully skimming the water. And there is nothing mundane about seeing a stand of trees, still bare of leafs, looking as though they are in full foliage because they are so crowded with red-winged blackbirds. It is almost supernatural – like a scene that Hitchcock would have created. These encounters with nature were priceless to me, and I wanted to experience it as fully as possible.

I soon came to realize that if I wanted an accurate picture of the number and habits of the birds I needed to go where they go. That journey would take me to a realm that has no earthly explanation.

It began with an exploration of the numerous sand bars and small islands that dot the Mississippi river, which can only be accessed by boat. During migrations, they become the Motel 6s for the avian set. So, I bought a cheap skiff that I used to make regular visits to the islands. Perhaps my little boat wasn't the best choice of craft for such a mighty force as the Mississippi

River, but I was young and adventurous – maybe even reckless in spite of my scientist's disposition.

Eventually I found one island that seemed to be most hospitable to both the birds and me. I often stayed there for several days at a time noting the comings and goings of the migrants. After a while, I began to feel more at home on the river among the birds than I did in the city surrounded by people.

When I wasn't busy with work, I would get lost in contemplation as I stared out at the river. I came to see it as a living thing, full of mysteries and changing moods. Some days it seemed to be playful, the ripples and eddies its laughter and pranks. Other days, it was dark and mournful, and everything around seemed hushed in acknowledgement of its temper.

During the summer, avian traffic subsided, but I continued to visit the island out of habit. I felt increasingly as though I was a resident of the past, separated by the great river from society and modern conveniences. Most people would laugh at my preference for the sultry night air, filled with the sounds of nature, over air-conditioned comfort.

As summer faded into fall the birds that I had greeted earlier in the year on their northbound migration began to arrive as they made their way to their winter homes. It was as though I was welcoming favored guests back to my humble inn. Unfortunately, it wasn't long before were gone again, which signaled that it was almost time for me to abandon my place on the river. I was going to miss that timeless peace that I had found there.

I gave myself the first two weeks of October on the island – ostensibly to finish the bird observation – but in truth it was just an excuse to linger for a few more days. With temperatures in the 90s, my last day on the island had been more like summer than fall. However, when the sun set, the air became pleasantly cool, and I sat on the bank watching the river make its lazy journey south under the brilliant night sky. I felt blessedly alone – I didn't even notice the lights and sounds of traffic from St. Louis. It was as though I had slipped back in time to quieter, slower paced era.

Almost on cue, a delightful sight came into view. It was an old time riverboat. She looked like a beautiful ghost paddling up the Mississippi, glowing a silvery white in the moonlight. It was close enough that I could hear laughter mixed with the sounds of a band playing Old Susanna, and the paddlewheel churning the water. It was a wonderful scene that fit perfectly into my musings of life on the river in bygone days.

I continued to watch the boat's slow progression up the river, imagining what it must have been like to travel in such fashion before more efficient modes of transportation had rendered the riverboat obsolete. I could well imagine the genteel surroundings – velvet banquets, polished brass fittings, gas fueled wall sconces and crystal chandeliers, and liveried waiters serving elegantly dressed passengers. The romanticized picture that I painted in my mind was nothing like the modern tourist attraction that I supposed the this boat to be.

My pleasant reverie ended abruptly when there was a terrible explosion, with flames and debris shooting high into the air. To my horror, the boat quickly became engulfed in fire; pandemonium erupted as people tried to flee the inferno. From my vantage point, I could see their silhouettes as they jumped into the river to escape the blaze. I looked to see if lifeboats were being lowered, but there were none.

The hellish scene had momentarily made me unable to breathe, such was my inability to grasp what I was seeing unfold before me. As I regained my faculties, I ran to my skiff. I didn't know what aid I could render, but I was determined to do what I could. As I motored close to the burning vessel, I could see a woman on deck. She appeared to be wearing period dress from the 1800's, and I fleetingly thought that this must have been some kind of costume party. The woman stood at the railing, trying to work up the courage to jump overboard. I yelled for her to jump, saying that I would pick her up in my boat. She stood there frozen until some embers landed on her voluminous skirt, catching them on fire. With no other option left, she leaped overboard. I motored closer to where she had entered the river, but couldn't see her. I called to her, turning in every direction, desperately looking for some sign of her. Finally, I saw her head come up above the water, but only for a second. I jumped into the river, holding on to my bowline so that the swift current wouldn't carry me away from my boat. Repeatedly, I dove where I had seen her, but she was gone. I knew that she was lost; her heavy skirts had once again betrayed her, weighing her down as the river carried her to Ophelia's death.

I returned to my skiff and sat stunned by this close encounter with mortality until the cries from others in the water drew me back to reality. A man was floundering a short distance away so I made my way to him. He thrashed his arms in an attempt to keep this head above water, but I could see that he was quickly losing the fight. I threw him my line, and pulled him, coughing and sputtering, onto the skiff, nearly upsetting it in the process. I decided it would be best to take my half-drowned passenger back to the island before any further rescue attempts.

I helped the man to shore, but he was weak from coughing up a lungful of river water, and he collapsed after walking only a few feet. He had sustained serious injuries and would need medical attention quickly if he was to survive. I scanned the horizon and was surprised that there were no other vessels to be seen. Surely someone had witnessed the explosion and alerted the authorities, but there was no sign of rescue boats that I could see. It looked like I was the only aid available to these folks, and I wasn't equipped to do much.

There were a few other survivors who had found their way to the island. Some had collapsed on the bank, too tired or hurt to go any further. Others had made their way to my campfire. The flickering flames illuminating the scene look like something out of Dante's Inferno. As I stood taking in this tableau, a man ran to me, grabbing me with burned hands, begging for me to help find his wife, Nellie. I left him there and quickly returned to the river, both of us knowing that there was little hope that I would be able to reunite him with his beloved wife.

When one is in the midst of a terrible tragedy, time plays tricks with the mind. Minutes can seem like hours and hours can speed by like a few brief moments. For me, it felt as though it had been hours since the explosion, yet it had happened only minutes before. The boat continued to burn, and I could still hear pleas for help. I was able to locate several more survivors as I tried to ignore the bodies of those who had already perished.

I found three men who had been lucky enough to have run up against a snag that prevented them from floating downriver. As I approached they all made a desperate grab for the boat at once, threatening to overturn it. I pushed them away with my oar, and commanded that only one at a time could climb aboard. Once they were loaded, I ferried them to the island.

I made several searches, circling the burning boat, and running down river for a ways searching for survivors. All told, there were thirty-seven people who made it to the island. Of those, 3 had died. I didn't know how many people had been on the riverboat, but judging by its size, I anticipated that many lives had been lost. One bright spot in the midst of the horror was that I found Nellie. How she survived was nothing short of a miracle. She had floated downriver clinging to a piece of debris and was able to make her way onto a sandbar. I have never witnessed such joy as what I saw in her husband's face when they were reunited.

When the last of the survivors were on land, I turned to watch as the wreck sank, sending up a great hissing cloud of steam as the flames met the water. Not a trace of the boat was left. No one would think that this was the scene of a tragedy if it weren't for the moans of the wounded, which bore evidence to the contrary.

I made a quick survey of the injuries, and realized just how unequipped I was to help. I had nothing except a simple first aid kit, a couple blankets and my sleeping bag. That wasn't going to be enough to keep some of these people alive. We needed help, but there was no sign of anyone coming to our aid. We were on our own.

I considered going for assistance, but I had used most of my fuel rescuing survivors. I was certain that there wasn't enough. If I took off across the river and ran out of gas, I would have a difficult time rowing against the current, and could end up miles downriver. Thus, I decided that would be my last resort, and I prayed that before I had to make that decision, rescuers would arrive. Truth be told, however, my hope for assistance was fading.

As we waited for help to arrive, I joined several of the passengers in offering what care and comfort we could to those most seriously injured. I have never felt as impotent as I did that night. There was one man who lay near the river's edge. He was badly burned and I feared that he wouldn't survive unless help arrived soon. Like the other passengers, he wore a costume that looked to be from the mid-nineteenth century. He bore insignia that suggested he was playing the part of some type of officer, and I wondered again about what type of party they were having before tragedy struck the ill-fated boat.

I knelt beside him to offer a sip of water. After a couple swallows, he beckoned for me to come nearer so that I could hear his whisper.

"I am Captain of the Acionna. It's my fault," he said with an anguish that encompassed more than just his injuries.

I tried to quiet him so that he could save his strength, but he was determined to be heard. "I...I should have known."

In spite of my admonition to rest, he continued, "The boiler. More steam."

I didn't understand his cryptic message, but before he could offer additional information, he passed out. I hoped that he would remain that way until he could be treated since it was the only way that he could escape what had to have been excruciating pain. However, it was only moments later that he regained consciousness. Evidently he had something weighing heavily on his heart. He motioned for me to take something out of his pocket. It was a cross that appeared to have been carved out of onyx. I placed it over his heart, and this seemed to give him comfort, but there remained something he needed to say.

"The boiler," he began again in a whisper that had grown weaker. The look in his eyes told me that he knew he only had moments to live, and needed for me to hear his confession.

"Shouldn't have pushed the boiler . . . too dangerous . . . I wanted the bonus . . . Caused explosion . . . Forgive me."

I assured him that he was forgiven. With that, a kind of peace settled over him and he closed his eyes. Moments later, he passed from this life.

I continued to replay the man's last words, trying to piece together a picture of what had happened. According to the captain, he had wanted to make better time in order to earn a bonus, and had given the order to stoke up the boiler. That was a dangerous proposition on steamboats that navigated the river in the 1800s because the boilers were made out of inferior materials, and often exploded under pressure. What I didn't understand was how that could happen with a modern piece of equipment powered by diesel not steam. Finally, I chalked it up to the confused ramblings of a dying man. Surely, once the investigation was complete, there would be a logical explanation.

Moments after the captain died, a woman passenger informed me that two other survivors were getting worse and desperately needed medical attention. I could no longer delude myself into believing that help was on the way. I was their only hope, and so I left in my small boat, hoping that there was adequate fuel to get me safely back to St. Louis.

The motor stopped just as the sky was beginning to show the promise of a new day, and I was still several hundred yards from the riverbank. I rowed with all my strength, fighting the current with each stroke. When I finally reached the shore, I ran toward the nearest place that I felt would be open at that hour: a hotel located two blocks away. I ran so hard, my breath felt like knives piercing my lungs.

I must have looked like a crazy man as I ran into the hotel because the security guard intercepted me, blocking my entrance. "Whoa! Where are you going in such a hurry?" he demanded.

I conveyed my story to him as briefly as possible aware that every moment I spent talking with him was a moment medical assistance was being delayed. When he made no move to call for help, I became angry, and pushing him aside, I started for the front desk. Before I could take more than a couple steps, however, the guard grabbed hold of my arm, saying, "Buddy, I don't know what you been smokin', but there wasn't no riverboat accident."

I opened my mouth to argue, but his next words startled me into silence.

"Every year when October 13th falls on a Friday, one of you damned fool kids comes running in here yelling about a riverboat wreck. It usually happens earlier in my shift, so I had started to think that this year would be different, but no such luck 'cause here you are. Do you really think that people're so stupid that we will fall for a load of malarkey like that?"

I was angry that this Neanderthal refused to listen to me when there were wounded people desperate for help on the island. I felt like punching the smug SOB right in the mouth. Thankfully, wisdom prevailed.

"I wish the Acionna had picked someplace else to blow up. Then you damn kids could make someone else's life hell with your stupid pranks."

Keying in on one word, I exclaimed, "Yes it was the Acionna that wrecked last night." Perhaps I was making progress after all.

"Buddy, you must be drunk. The Acionna blew up on October 13, 1848. I don't see where you kids find so much fun in making up stories about it. Have some common decency, why dontcha? A lot of people died that night. You should show some respect."

His words suddenly had me doubting my sanity. I shook off his hand that still had hold of my arm, and slowly walked away as he muttered something about 'damned fool kids.'

I couldn't understand what had happened out there on the river. It had all seemed so clear to me. My mind tried to sort through the bits and pieces, trying to construct something that made sense.

I wandered aimlessly for what seemed like hours, my mind in disarray. Perhaps the entire event had been a hallucination. But how? Eventually, my wanderings led me to the door of the Riverfront Historical Society. Surly I would find some answers there.

After a short time it became apparent that the only answers I would gain was the confirmation that the Acionna had, in fact, been destroyed on the night of Friday 13 October 1848, just as the security guard had told me. The cause was a boiler explosion.

There were several pictures of the Acionna in the archives along with photographs of several of the more prominent passengers, some of whom had survived the accident, others who had perished. The woman I had seen drown was identified as Mrs. Theodore (Margaret) Rene of New Orleans.

One article said that Mrs. Rene had succumbed to the fire, but I knew differently. I would never forget her face as she submerged just out of my reach.

There was a wedding photograph of the man and wife I had helped to reunite. They were Myron and Nellie Strom, newlyweds from Memphis on their honeymoon. It was like a slap in the face to see their picture. I recognized these people! I had talked to them – touched them. Yet, the newspaper clippings made it clear that that was impossible. I tried to come up with a rational explanation – perhaps it was a bizarre reenactment – but even that didn't make sense. Thus, I continued looking through the archives in search of something that could help explain what I had experienced.

I came across a photograph of the Captain of the Acionna. His name was John Sebastian Coffman, and he hailed from St. Charles, Missouri. He was a well-respected man who left his widow to care for their seven children. The article made no mention of the bonus nor did it indicate his culpability in the accident. However, it did mention that the boat's builder was hoping that that trip would demonstrate the crafts speed in order to increase sales.

Interviews with several of the survivors told of the events that night. The boat was scheduled to dock in Hannibal the following morning, but they were running ahead of schedule by several hours. Some of the passengers who were interviewed attributed their survival to the fact that the explosion happened before they had retired, so they were on deck and able to escape the fire by jumping overboard. Several said that they were able to reach a nearby island with the aid of an unnamed local.

I left the Historical Society and walked to my apartment. I was so tired both physically and emotionally that I didn't even consider going back to the island to reclaim by gear. I didn't know how I would ever be able to, but I knew I would have to find a way to do so soon or I would lose valuable research.

Several days later, I worked up the courage to return and I found my camp in order – there was nothing to suggest that anything unusual had occurred. I'm not sure what I had hoped for or expected, but the ordinary nature of the scene was somehow unnerving.

I packed up my gear with a heavy heart, the whole time thinking that I must have experienced some type of psychotic break. How else could any of this could be explained?

Before I left the island for the last time I went to the place where I believed that I had sat with Captain Coffman as he lay dying, once again trying to make sense of it all. I mindlessly stirred the sand with a stick as I contemplated what these events meant for my future. I'm a scientist, and if I was unable to distinguish fantasy from reality, there was no place for me in the scientific community. Of that I was certain.

It was while I was wrestling with these thoughts that my stick stirred up something in the sand. I picked it up thinking it a piece of driftwood. Just as I was about to toss it into the river, I saw that it was Captain Coffman's cross, which I had placed over his heart.

I knew then that what I had witnessed on that awful night was not a result of my imagination or a psychotic break. It had been real – or at least it was the ghosts of reality.

THE LEGEND OF AVILLA'S JOHNNY REB
M.J. Logan

Take Route 66 across the Kansas border into Joplin Missouri, and then it's just a short ride down back roads that seem to lead into doom itself – a town what used to be Avilla, and still is if you can find it. Local folk will tell you the whole place is haunted by shadow folk, and when you ride in, chances are good you'll catch one in the corner of your eye, and when you look, it'll be gone.

Avilla's shadow folk – dark ghostly spirits of the netherworld – are mostly harmless spirits with no desire to bother the living. They just exist in their sorry state, forever trapped within the confines of their souls and whatever forces hold them there. Leave them be and they won't bother you. Bother them and perhaps you'll wake up changed; how you won't know afore it happens. Then you live with it forever, as found out 16-year-old Miss Annabee from parts unknown, even to this very day.

Miss Annabee thought to taunt the shadow lady with the fancy hat and followed her about at dusk one evening, speaking unkind things about supposed ladies who'd wear a hat of such nature, and what of the poor bird gave up the feathers for such nonsense.

Then there she was, inches from Annabee's face and those eyes, those deep black pools of liquid inky blackness were mirrors into Annabee's soul and what Annabee saw weren't pretty. Not a word did the shadow speak, not a word did the girl utter. Unable to do naught but stare into the reflection of her own sinful self until she was struck dumb and faint. The shadow hat lady soaked up the dark that oozed up from the corners and the cracks and the hidden places as darkness crept up on the street and faded with the light.

Smelling salts brought the lass around, so say some, but maybe not all for when Annabee rose the next morning after a night of nightmares and ill dreams where long-legged worms chased corpses without feet through the street, one look in the mirror and she fainted away again and could not be roused. The doctor was called to administer a shot. A shot of whiskey maybe, or perhaps Laudanum for that was the cure-all of the day. A little opium in a bottle of shine whiskey would set the worst of pain aright, but did little for the hurt in the brain except numb it beyond thinking.

When the young pretender of a lady finally sat up in bed, she lifted the once golden-red locks that graced her head and bemoaned their loss. Hair of the finest sort that turned other young ladies of the time green with envy and brought young men to walk close just to gaze upon her hair and her fine skin and emerald green eyes. Many said those green eyes matched the fine golden-red hair and milky clear skin just so, or until that morning anyway, for once the morning was done, no young men would be coming to court or flirt or admire. Beauty might be skin deep, but when that beauty turned into the reflection of one's soul, the scar runs deep.

Annabee's mother cried for a day and a fortnight about her daughters dull gray hair, pasty white skin, and black, limpid eyes that made her look dead like a fish from the Great and Mighty Mississippi River and hauled across the state in the back of a pickup truck without the benefit gutting or ice. Annabee fell into a remorseful state and all but gave up living for a time. No sooner had her mother's hysterics subsided when Annabee fled the town of Avilla on a stolen horse, her mother close behind in a surrey to save the girl from whatever bent of destruction she set upon herself.

The story is true, they say, those rumors. What part of the rumor is fact, one cannot tell after the passage of time when all has gone to shadow and decay. But a look back in time can reveal much.

The town was founded in 1858 by village landowners and merchants, and as the civil war rose up around them, they formed a militia to act in the town's defense. Later it served as a garrison for the Union Army for a time, which is perhaps what brought the evil in the first place.

No one knew the young soldier that came trudging into town one day, wearing the confederate gray. He was unarmed, badly scratched and unfed. His true name remains unknown to this day, except to one now gone to time, but the town folk all called him Johnny Reb. When questioned, he told the sheriff his unit was wiped out and that he'd given up rejoining his regiment.

He only wanted to go home and marry his girl and be done with wars of all kinds.

Being good and God-fearing folk, and not having had much to do with the war at that point, the townfolk speculated on the visitor and what ill he might have planned or if he even had a girl. Those 'Rebs' as they were called, were known to be bushwhackers. Sneaky sly folk who crept on ya in the middle o' the night and were as like to draw a knife across your throat as they were to shoot ya.

He was given the best bed in the jail, a double helping of Mrs. Sheriff's fried southern chicken and biscuits with gravy, and two bottles of beer because whiskey wasn't allowed in the jail (though the sheriff had a bottle in his bottom drawer, beneath a fine collection of teeth from jail fights and a few miscellaneous weapons that held down the extra stack of wanted posters.)

The lights were down when the soldier called the deputy over; most of the town was asleep and those that weren't wished they were.

Through the bars, quick as lightning, the soldier's arm struck, grabbed the deputy by the throat and throttled him with one hand, yanked him hard against the bars and knocked him out. It was all waiting then and he watched as he squeezed the life out of the deputy, then let go to see him crumple to the ground, nothing left to remember him by 'cept a cheap felt hat and a scar on his nose. He made quick work with the keys, and let himself out onto the silent street.

On the edge of town, not that it was big town, it was in fact quite small in those days and still is, he gave a low whistle and was shortly surrounded by other men in gray.

Johnny Reb and his regiment raided the town of Avilla, and took no prisoners. Men, women, and children of an age old enough to bear arms were left behind to bleed into the streets and turn the mud red. And as the bushwhackers left town, Johnny Reb paused to light a tobacca twist and look back and laugh at the poor folk as they lay dead or dying in the streets, and hear the lamenting cries of the children left behind.

A single gunshot rang out and Johnny saw the flash from the gun's muzzle from atop the hotel and Saloon. It surprised him because all the town folk were dead, and he wondered in that long moment who had survived. What was done was done, and though Johnny had a scant portion of a second to consider these things, all thoughts were ended when the bullet entered the top of his head and scrambled his brains like they was eggs in the hotel dining room.

Horns sounded in the street, and the pursuit was on. The militia had returned from patrol just in time to chase the rebels out of town. Several were caught, and the deeds done to them are not worth mentioning in such fine company, but let it be known that before the sun rose at dawn and chased the shadows back into the cracks, there was plenty of talking done.

They were stood, the four of them, on a makeshift bench, nooses about their necks and the militia leader simply kicked it over. Their last sight was Johnny Reb laying in a pool of bloody mud.

Graves were dug for the four, but Johnny was left to rot and feed the crows and magpies. The maggots and flies had their share, and by the time fall turned into winter, naught was left of Johnny but bones and a mournful restless spirit.

Rumor says, and the trouble with rumors is that somewhere there is a grain of truth, but who knows what that truth is, that when Johnny's skull was found, they put a cord through the bullet hole and out the spine where a knot was made. A loop in the other end and it was hung in the tree he died under and where his companions paid their price for the evil deed done. Hung to warn others, hung to insult him, hung to ward off rebel bushwhacking soldiers with evil intentions.

To hear some tell it, when the railroad came though it missed the town and that kept Avilla a sleepy little burg, what was left anyway. That and the shadow folk who didn't bother most people, if they were left alone. Still, who wants to wake up from bad dreams to find a sad, ghastly shadow sitting on their bed? Gradually, the dead town died more, until all that was left were the buildings and the shadow folk, and the curiosity seekers that came to see.

Word reached Johnny Reb's girl that he died in a battle, and that his body was not recovered. Determined to put his soul at rest, she went to Avilla and made discreet queries. Queries that revealed the truth of the matter and told of a Johnny Reb who hadn't been an honorable soldier and had killed unarmed women and men, and even children in the black of night; a Rotten Johnny Reb who sneaked up and bushwhacked the whole town.

Nevertheless, a Christian burial is deserved for all sinners and she wanted it, but the town refused to let it happen. Determined, the girl bought a funeral dress and hat for herself and a pine box for the rebel soldier, intending to take him home. They say the hat was the finest in town, a black silk affair with swirls of netting inset with pearls and tiny sparkle stones, and the long tail feathers from a Black Ibis, shipped all the way from India.

One evening when the town lights were down, she took her hired man and a carriage and the pine box and set out to find the persimmon tree he had died under.

She happened upon the tree as the new moon was rising, a dark disk in a dark sky surrounded by stars. It was as described; old and gnarled with sour, rotting fruit. Beneath the tree lay the skeleton of Johnny Reb, the man responsible for killing the town and leaving it in despair.

Even so, the stark bones made a chilling sight in the guttering lantern and a chill bore the young woman across the road to gather her wits and feelings. There would be time for mourning later when the deed was done and her once fiancée buried in proper Christian ground and prayed over.

The hired man was instructed to put the bones in the box and be quick about it. He hurried as he had no desire to be there any longer than necessary to collect his fee and be on his way. All was done in a minute or two, except the skull was nowhere to be found. He searched and looked and hunted, all to the plaintive worrying of the lass across the road.

A chill descended on the site and he pulled his cap down over his ears. Fog swirled in from nowhere and he was struck by fear and compelled to look up.

There! In front of his face, just inches away, hung the bone-white skull of Johnny Reb! A wide toothy grin and eye sockets of liquid ink stared into his. The hired man turned screaming for the road, tripped on the carriage tack and startled the horses who dragged him and the coffin full of bones away.

One can only imagine the poor girl in her grief and fright, crossing the road to see what terror the skull foisted upon the man, and found herself staring into the soul of her beloved. A low moan and perhaps she tried to look away, but failing that, she embraced the darkness and evil. Joined with the soul and spirit of the ruthless rebel soldier and let him take her.

They buried the girl in the same coffin she had commissioned for her fiancée, along with his bones. Some of the town folk called it immoral to place them together, unmarried as they were. Others said it served her right for digging up spirits that she ought not have bothered.

They found her hired man with the carriage and the horses; he an indescribable mass of flesh and blood after miles of dragging behind the horses under the carriage. Now just one more shadow person to haunt the streets and hide in the cracks and crevices that make up the dark places.

Rotten Johnny Reb. Rumor says, and what smidgen of that rumor is truth, one cannot say, that on dark moonless nights, the unsuspecting that stumble on the tree first find the skull, and then they find the evil, and then they join the shadow people, and the town's population grows.

If ya find the tree and find the skull, ye must cut the skull down quick they say, afore that malevolent ghost cuts you down to join the shadow folk that ooze from the dark places in the town of Avilla, Missouri.

THREE TRUE STORIES
Conny Manero

RATTLING WINDOWS

I was alone in the house. Around 10:30 p.m. I made my rounds, checking if all the doors and windows were locked, then switched off the lights.

"Goodnight Pitou, goodnight Husky," I kissed the cats, who were curled up at each end of the sofa, and asked them, "are you coming with me? No? Well, you know where to find me should you change your mind."

In bed I snuggled up under the duvet with the latest novel of Maeve Binchy, planning on reading for half an hour or so and then going to sleep. Somewhere in the middle of page three, there was suddenly a rattling noise from the kitchen window. It was very loud and very aggressive. My first thought was that there was an earthquake; but I couldn't feel any trembling.

While I sat there, still holding Maeve's book, and with shivers running up and down my spine, Pitou and Husky came flying into the bedroom and hurled themselves on my bed. Side by side they sat there, looking at me, with eyes like cannon balls.

When all remained quiet, and the cats had settled down, I went back to my book. I was on page seven when there was that rattling again! This time I dove under the duvet, pulled it up to my chin and lay there, holding my breath, eyes going from side to side, waiting for what was to happen next.

When I peered over the duvet at Pitou and Husky, they didn't trust the situation either. They were still curled up, but their heads were raised and their ears were flat.

"If this happens one more time, I'm out a here," I thought. I waited, the seconds ticking away on my **alarm clock.** Just as I thought that I would be able to go to sleep there was that rattling again! So loud, and so aggressive, that I thought the glass was going to burst.

I jumped out of bed, pulled on my dressing gown, grabbed my keys and flew out the door.

In the short distance to my friend and neighbor's house, I didn't feel the cold and I was totally unaware of the sharp gravel beneath my bare feet.

"A rattling window scares you?" Joan said when I stood shivering in her living room.

"It didn't just rattle," I told her. "It was more than that. I've never heard anything so loud and so violent."

I slept that night and the following two nights in Joan's spare room. I knew this couldn't go on though. What must the neighbors think if they say me coming home every morning at the crack of dawn? Not the mention that I was deserting Pitou and Husky.

Not that they were particularly bothered by the ghost or whatever was playing with the window. When I came home in the morning, they were peacefully asleep on my bed. But, they jumped to attention when they saw me, and then weaved around my legs until they got their breakfast.

When I mentioned this experience at work, a colleague asked if I had any family members or close friends who has passed away.

"My grandmother," I said. "She died about three months ago."

Sharon thoughtfully tapped her finger against her bottom lip and continued, "Aren't you going through a divorce?"

"Yes," I admitted.

"Must be hard," Sharon said, "maybe your grandmother is letting you know that she's there for you."

"If she is, I wish she wasn't," I said. "She's scaring the living daylight out of me."

"Then tell her," Sharon said. "Tell her she's scaring you and ask her to go away and leave you alone."

"You want me to talk to a ghost?" I asked her.

"You don't have to do it out loud," she said. "You can just think it. It makes no difference."

Three weeks later my son Dieter, came home from a European vacation and I asked Joan and her son Brendan over for a little celebration. While Joan and I were in the living room catching up on the latest news, Brendan moved with Dieter to his room to play computer games.

Suddenly the kitchen window started rattling again. So loud and so aggressive, that for a moment, it overpowered all other sounds. Dieter and Brendan came running into the living room. Joan sat as pale as a sheet of paper on the sofa, holding her coffee cup with a trembling hand.

"What was that?" all three of them demanded.

"That," I said with a hint of triumph, "was the kitchen window rattling. You laughed with me when I told you about this," I turned to Joan. She wasn't laughing now.

"That is the scariest thing I've ever heard," she said, hand on heart.

"You think this is scary," I said. "There are four of us here now and it's broad daylight. Imagine this when you're on your own in the middle of the night."

While they pulled themselves together, I went into the kitchen and said – in my mind – grandma if this is you, please leave us alone. You're scaring us!

The kitchen window never made another sound.

SPENDING THE NIGHT AT DIANE'S

It was late, it was raining and I had at least a thirty-five minute drive ahead of me to get home. When my friend Diane said that I could spend the night in her house, I eagerly accepted.

Diane lived with her mother in a spacious country house. The obviously old furniture in the guestroom was not quite what I had expected in the otherwise modern home.

"It's my grandmother's furniture," Diane explained. "When grandma passed away, my mom decided to keep her stuff for the spare room. The mattress is new though and the sheets are fresh, so you should be quite comfortable."

A few minutes after I had turned out the light I heard the door opening and softly closing. I was about to ask Diane if she had forgotten something when I heard her moving through the room, every so carefully as to not to disturb me.

I heard her by the vanity table, opening and closing drawers. Not wanting to make Diane feel bad for waking me up, I pretended to be asleep. But I smiled as I heard her rummaging; apparently she could not find what she was looking for.

Suddenly I felt her sitting down on the bed. I stiffened as my body tilted towards the extra weight. Enough was enough. Diane and I were good friends, but we were not THAT close. So I reached up and switched on the light. There was nobody there.

Had I dreamed this? Had I fallen asleep while Diane was in my room and had she left unnoticed?

"Did you find what you were looking for last night?" I asked her over breakfast.

"Huh?" Diane said, not understanding.

"Last night," I explained, "you were in my room, going through the drawers of the vanity table. I heard you but I did not want to say anything. I didn't want you to think you woke me up."

"Girl, I was not in your room," she said with a shake of her head. "I fell asleep the moment my head touched the pillow."

THE LADY IN THE ROSE GARDEN

She was standing in the rose garden, wearing a bright red and blue sari, with intricate gold embroidery. Her long dark hair was hanging in a plait down her back, a white dog at her feet. She was there one moment and gone the next.

I came down from my apartment on the 11t floor with the elevator and paused in the lobby to tuck my shirt in my pants. While doing so, I glanced out the floor to ceiling lobby windows and that's when I saw her . . . the Indian woman in the sari.

I didn't think anything of it, as plenty of Indian women live in my building. It was only when I got outside and the woman was nowhere to be seen that she had my full attention.

She couldn't have gone far. From the lobby to the front door of the building had taken me a matter of seconds. Where could she have gone? I looked to my right, I looked to my left, I scanned the whole area, but the woman seemed to vanish.

Passing the rose garden, I continued to look for her in all directions. So mystified was I with her that, even after leaving the building grounds, I continued to look for her. I kept turning around, examining every inch of the front garden, but there was no sign of her.

Where could she have gone in the mere seconds it took me to get from the lobby to the front door? I suppose, if she lived on the ground floor, she could have climbed on one of the balconies, but someone I didn't see that happening. If she had worn jeans and a T-shirt, yes, but not in the sari she was wearing.

Some time later, I found out that one of my neighbors and her dog had died in a car accident on their way to the vet.

AFTER THE RAID
Sean McLachlan

The bushwhackers had left. Helena Schmidt had lain weeping over her father's body in the front yard until the neighbors came. They took their time, eager to help but not wanting to run into the Confederate raiders who had shot her father. When they finally did arrive, they made sympathetic noises. The men carried Lars Schmidt up the three steps of the porch, through the front door, and into the dining room where they laid him out on the table, wrapping him in a sheet until the coroner could be called. The women had led Helena away.

That had been in the morning. Now it was night. The coroner had come, declared the obvious, made it official by filling out a form, and took her father's body to the church until it could be buried. The men had all gone back to their shops and fields. The women Helena had to send away. Several offered to stay the night. Those who had rooms left vacant by their sons going off to war offered them to her. It took some time to make them understand that she wanted to stay in her own house and that she wanted to be alone. They left shaking their heads.

"Lars was such a quiet soul," they said. "Never spoke out against anybody. Why would the rebels want to kill him?"

Yes, why? Father never concerned himself about politics. While a Unionist and an abolitionist, he was not outspoken with his views. Being lame in one leg, he wasn't part of Columbia's Union militia. He lived a life of quiet study, interacting with the public only through his photographic studio.

There had been six of them. They wore Union uniforms and flourished Union passes but Helena was suspicious from the start. They were too young, too cocky, too well-armed. They posed for a photograph and then gunned Father down.

As Helena sat benumbed in the study, her gaze wandered over her father's library—hundreds of books in half a dozen languages on all matters of the occult. Spiritism, theosophy, Gnostic cosmology, Hermeticism, geomancy.

Was this why they targeted him? The house stood close to the edge of town. It was dangerous for the bushwhackers to come here, and while they often targeted German civilians, they could have easily gone after those who lived in more isolated farms and vineyards. They hadn't wanted to kill a German; they had wanted to kill Lars Schmidt, and the only thing that distinguished him was his study of the occult. Yet few knew of this.

They hadn't touched her. "Cavaliers of the brush" these bandits called themselves, teenaged boys who read too many Arthurian romances and felt they were being chivalrous if they gunned an innocent man down in front of his daughter's eyes but didn't hurt the girl.

One of them had tried, though, when she called down the curse.

It was that wild-looking one, the one who had examined Father's library with knowing eyes. He knew that the words she'd used were a real curse and not some countrywoman's mumbo-jumbo. He'd leveled his pistol at her and got punched by one of the others.

"We don't make war on womenfolk!" the other one had said.

"Oh, but you have," she whispered as she sat in her father's study. "And I will make war on you."

What the wild looking one didn't know was that she had no Power. Sometimes it is passed through the bloodline and sometimes it is not. Father had it, but his only child was a normal woman.

So the curse was nothing but words and spite. All it could do was make them nervous, not make them suffer. And they needed to suffer. She needed to make the curse real. The local militia captain had promised he would hunt them down but even if he was successful, that wasn't enough. Death wasn't enough. Father had told her enough about death for her to know that it was nothing to fear.

Being raised by an occultist she knew many things that others only guessed at. Life lessons had a deeper meaning. When she was eight and Father caught her filching penny sweets from the local shop he didn't smack her bottom. Instead, he sat her down and explained why that was wrong.

"All spirits have a frequency, child, like the tones on a musical scale. Those that are more pure have a higher frequency, and inhabit a bright place they share with all the greatest spirits of the ages. Those who steal, who kill, who live lives of greed and vituperation, those have low frequencies. They inhabit a dark place trapped with dirty spirits of their own kind."

"Is Mother in the bright place?" she had asked. Mother had died the year before.

"Yes, child," Father replied with a smile. "When I speak with her she tells me the most amazing things. We must live purely, so that when we pass from this world to the next we will be with her forever."

Helena had walked back to the store alone and tearfully confessed to the shopkeeper, returning the candy and doing chores to pay for those she'd already eaten.

Now Helena sat alone in Father's study. He and Mother were together in that place. Of that she was sure. He had always been a good man, a pure man. Honest and kind.

So why kill him? That's the question that burned in her mind. Did he know something the rebels wanted to hide?

Helena sat alone for a long time, her thoughts numb and her eyes unfocused.

She felt him before she saw him. One moment she was alone and the next she knew he was there.

She looked up. Something was materializing in the corner of the room.

Helena wasn't afraid. It was Father, so why should she be?

The faint outline of the portly man whom she had admired and loved all her life grew clearer. When he spoke, his lips didn't move and he made no sound anyone but she could have heard.

Don't cry, Helena.

Helena tried not to.

"Are. . .are you with Mother? Are you in the bright place?" she managed to ask.

She slipped back to what she had called it as a child. She knew the occult terms for it—the Aetherial Plane, Goloka, Jannah, and many others—but seeing Father reduced to a shade made her feel like when she was seven years old and Mother died.

It's more beautiful than I ever imagined.

"But what do I do now?"

Live well, as I taught you. And when your time comes, you will join us.

"Those boys, those bushwhackers. They need to be punished! You never hurt anyone, why should they kill you?"

Her father shook his head.

They killed me because I chose a different path than they did. One of them comports with foul spirits and those spirits wanted me removed. They will be punished in the end.

"No, they need to be punished now! Not just death, not just going to the dark place. They need worse."

Have you forgotten all my lessons? That is not my way and it shouldn't be yours either.

"You have Power. You could come back and put them in a far lower place."

Again, Father shook his head.

No. I would sink closer to their level. I would no longer be with your mother. And even if it were not for that, I wouldn't do such a thing. Goodness is its own reward, even though goodness gives more rewards than its own nature.

Helena felt rage rise up in her, the same rage she'd felt when Father toppled to the ground with a bullet in his chest and she'd spat the curse at his murderers.

"Hunt them! Drag them down!"

No. I will go now and come back when you are calmer. I love you.

"Wait, don't go! I'm sorry. Stay a little longer," she pleaded.

But he was already fading.

Helena sat there fuming, her grief cut with anger. Father had always been too soft, too forgiving. When they'd seen Archibald Keyes whipping his slave by the side of the road, Helena had wanted to intervene, but Father had just snapped the reins to their buggy horse and sped past. "He'll suffer enough in the Afterlife, child."

It had been the same when the Sisters of the Union had invited her to join in their fundraising efforts back in '61 and Father had forbidden it. "We want no part in this war, child, those who take up arms against their brothers pay for it in the Afterlife."

The Afterlife, the Afterlife, all he ever talked about was the spirit world. But she lived in this world, alone in a hostile country with no relations on this side of the Atlantic.

Father said not to get involved in the war. Now the war had killed him and he was still saying not to get involved. Well, she was going to get involved, and in a more effective way than the Sisters of the Union with their bake sales and knitting bees.

But how? She couldn't don Union blue and go fight like the men did, and she didn't have the Power to make that curse on the bushwhackers effective.

Unless. . .

She walked out of her father's study and down a narrow corridor. One door opened into the photographic studio, where those evil boys had preened and posed for a tintype before gunning her father down. Opposite was the darkroom. The sharp smell of chemicals stung her nostrils. She blinked away tears. That smell always reminded her of Father.

At the end of the corridor hung a curtain of heavy black silk. She parted it and entered a small, windowless room. Striking a match, she lit the red candle that sat on a small gilt table next to the doorway.

This was her father's secret study, the one visitors didn't get to see.

The room was barely ten feet to a side, with paneled oak walls and a smooth floor of slate. Drawn in chalk in the center of the floor was a large pentagram surrounded by magical sigils. Facing it was a simple triangle. It was here that Father spoke to the various denizens of the spirit world—the dead and those things that had never lived. He would stand inside the pentagram for protection and would make the creatures appear in the triangle. Despite the popular fairy tales, he would not summon demons to go wreak havoc on the world. There were those who did such things, but Father steered clear of them.

"Their spirits are even lower than the unclean things they call from the Beyond," he would say.

No, he summoned the shades of great men and women from bygone ages, and ethereal beings that had no name in any human language. He would stand there protected by his pentagram—for the wall between this world and the next had to be kept firm even if the beings he spoke with were beneficent—and the spirit would appear trapped in the triangle. For long hours through the night, he would speak to them and learn the secrets of the universe.

Helena looked longingly at the chalk designs. If only she had the Power, she could summon some fell being to strike down those boys, and to hell with the consequences. She had the knowledge. She had read many of Father's books and listened attentively when he spoke of his rituals, but without the Power, it would be like a man struck blind trying to paint a sunset he remembered from childhood.

She turned to a low shelf standing to one side, stuffed with a few books and various items Father used in his rituals — a little gold bell, a flute made from the bone of a giant lizard that had lived in a bygone age, an astrolabe that measured the angles of stars that no uninitiated eye could see, and an ancient brass bowl.

This last item caught her attention. It was the pride of Father's collection, a relic of ancient Chaldea. Father had instructed her in its use. Unlike everything else, this required no Power or even knowledge to use. She picked it up lovingly and examined the strange script that ran in a spiral around the inside of the bowl.

She set it down and filled it with water from a crystal decanter. Bringing the candle closer, she peered into the water.

For a moment, nothing happened. Then the water clouded as if she had mixed it with milk. The writing on the interior of the bowl wavered and faded from view. The surface of the liquid grew still and flat as a mirror and began to emit a pale light. Two figures materialized into view on its surface—her parents.

Helena smiled and they smiled back. Grief tugged at her again, mingled with relief to see them finally together again after being separated by the Veil for fifteen years.

She had looked through this bowl many times since Mother's death. Strange to think how she had grown from a girl to a young woman and Mother had remained ageless. Now Father would be the same way. They would watch as she grew older, become a mother perhaps, and grow into an old woman, while they remained beyond Time.

Helena smiled again and pointed to her Father. She held up his pocket watch, pointed at it and then at him.

"Next time I wish to see you alone," she said, enunciating the words. The device could not transmit sound, but hopefully Father would understand her gestures and read her lips. He nodded.

For a moment, parents and daughter stared at each other through the Veil, and then the image clouded over. The water cleared to as it was before.

Helena sighed. She poured the water back in the decanter and set to work. She had much to do. Time was of the essence, for if Father decided to materialize again before she reached him through the bowl, all would be lost.

Little did he know that his upbringing gave her all the knowledge she needed to defy his wishes.

While Father's passion had been the Hidden World, he had provided for his family well in the material one. He had built up a thriving photography business. He was one of the first men to open a daguerreotype studio in St. Louis back in the 1850s. When cheaper and easier tintypes were introduced late in the decade, competition became fierce in the city. He had sold the business, upped stakes, and moved to the outskirts of Columbia.

Once again, he was among the first. Father proved an excellent technician and his photographs always gave satisfaction. Helena had talent for painting the photographs, adding rosy cheeks to the babies or coloring in a man's favorite hat.

Helena had learned all aspects of the business. While the public wouldn't accept the idea of a woman taking their likeness, she often did the developing in the back room and arranged the lighting in the studio, giving the subjects just the right light at just the right angle.

It was this last skill that she needed now. She bustled around the house, collecting mirrors, ropes, and lamps.

Within an hour, she had finished. Father's secret studio looked much different now. The bowl stood at the center of the summoning triangle. Above it hung two mirrors suspended by ropes from a hook she had hammered into the ceiling. One mirror hung parallel to the floor, reflecting the triangle and the bowl's interior. One was set behind the bowl and at an angle, so that it reflected the pentagram and the black crepe she had hung behind it. Lines of writing limned in fresh white paint ran down two edges of the crepe, with a space in between where Helena could stand.

With trembling hands, Helena bent under the mirror and poured the contents of the decanter into the bowl. She rushed over to the pentagram and stood in the center.

From her vantage point, the angled mirror behind the bowl showed her the interior of the bowl. She nodded in satisfaction. She had set it perfectly.

She stood, nervous, waiting.

The water clouded over. Father's face appeared. He smiled as he saw her reflection, thinking that he was looking directly at his daughter's face.

Then he looked around with a growing expression of horror.

One mirror reflected the bowl in which he had appeared, and the triangle around it. Father's head jerked to one side, and Helena knew he was looking at the other mirror's reflection.

It showed Helena standing in the middle of the pentagram. To either side he read his daughter's terrible command, her terrible mistake.

I LACK THE POWER TO SUMMON A DEMON TO DO THIS DEED, SO I SUMMON YOU. BY THE POWER OF THE PENTAGRAM AND TRIANGLE, I COMMAND YOU. TAKE VENGEANCE ON THOSE WHO STRUCK YOU DOWN. CAST THEM TO THE LOWEST DARKNESS. YOU ARE BOUND BY THE MAGICAL SIGILS YOU YOURSELF DREW. YOU ARE UNDER

COMPULSION. THE STAIN IS ON ME, NOT YOU. I AM SORRY FATHER.

Lars Schmidt's face contorted in despair. His image smeared, his wailing mouth stretching out in a silent scream.

And then he was gone.

Helena collapsed. The summoning had worked. Father would have to do the right thing now, and being forced into it, he would not lose his place in the Light.

Helena, on the other hand, had stained her soul forever.

She wept for the second time that day, knowing that now death really was goodbye.

AFTER HOURS
Schevus Osborne

We heard the staff member's footsteps and saw a flashlight beam dart past the entrance of our hideout. My younger brother, Mike, began to giggle, caught up in the emotions surrounding what we were trying to do. I quickly clamped my hand over his mouth. All it would take was for that flashlight to spear down into our alcove in the caves, and our plan would be ruined. Thankfully, the beam and the footsteps passed without incident. The City Museum staffer had not been diligent enough in her duties to scour the caves for stragglers after the museum closed.

We waited for quite some time after the staffer passed. Mike got bored and started playing games on his phone. Eventually, the lights in the caves were turned off, and his phone was the only illumination we had. It was well after 1:00 AM. The staff must have finally been closing up and heading home. I made Mike wait another fifteen minutes before we dared to edge out of the deep chamber we had stowed away in.

Despite my best efforts to avoid it, my stiff legs caused me to stumble and I stepped right in the small pool of water that filled the depression at the bottom of our cave. The cool water splashed loudly and soaked through my right shoe, chilling my foot and making the hairs on my leg stand on end.

'Smooth.' Mike said as he helped me up and out of the chamber, 'What do you want to do now?'

I pulled out a small penlight, and motioned up into the pitch-black shaft. The light caught the sculpted concrete above strangely, briefly flashing over monstrous faces carved in the stone. 'Let's do the slide. It should be a blast in the dark,' I said, starting the climb up through the winding caves.

Remembering he had one, Mike pulled out his flashlight as well. Having been to the museum often, we made swift progress and soon found ourselves climbing the spiral stairs to the top of the ten-story slide. Mike was in too much of a hurry ahead of me and tripped, banging his knee on the steps. He grunted in pain. The sound echoed around the empty slide shaft in a way that was never possible with the hustle and bustle of the crowds that frequented the museum. He righted himself, cursing, and before we knew it, we were at the top of the slide.

'You want to go first?' Mike asked.

'Nah, you first clumsy. I don't want you getting impatient and crashing into me at the bottom.'

Mike shrugged and fixed his grip on his flashlight as he scooted up to the lip of the slide. With a push, he was gone. The staccato ringing of his body passing over the welds of the slide also echoed loudly around the chamber. Suddenly, that echo was fractured by a startled scream from Mike. It continued all the way to the bottom.

'What's wrong Mike?' I shouted down into the darkness. I couldn't see his flashlight beam, but he had finally stopped screaming. No answer came from below.

'Mike? Are you alright?' I tried again. Still nothing. I shrugged and figured he was just playing a prank on me, as he did so often. Sitting down at the lip of the slide, I braced my flashlight facing down ahead of me and pushed off. The slide juddered my body as it always did. I held onto my knees, keeping my feet up to go as fast as possible. My flashlight strobed through the metal cage covering the top of the slide.

After a few revolutions down the tight spiral, I briefly saw two small hands clutching the side of the slide from the outside edge. Before I could even react to what I had seen, I sped past. As I reached the bottom I found Mike cowering in a corner, his flashlight turned off. I quickly turned and scanned up the exterior of the slide.

I saw the profile of a young girl clinging onto it several stories up. 'Hold on!' I shouted, but I wasn't sure what I could do to help. After a few more seconds, the girl lost her grip and plummeted down the slide shaft. Her arms and legs pinwheeled wildly as she fell. Without thinking, I raced forward to catch her.

My arms did nothing to stop her fall as the girl passed right through them and disappeared into the floor. I caught one final expression on her face before she disappeared. I expected it to be a look of sheer terror, but instead found a sad smile and an appreciative glint in her eyes.

After she was gone, my arms were chilled to the bone with a bitter numbness I had never felt before. I shook them violently to try to dispel the feeling as I struggled to come to terms with what had just happened.

I had just tried to save a ghost. No other explanation made sense.

'What happened to you?' I asked Mike, kneeling down in front of him.

Mike took a while to answer, and when he did, I could barely hear his whispered response. 'I knocked a boy off the slide. When I reached the bottom, he was just lying there. He turned to look at me before he disappeared.' A mask of complete and total fear covered his features as he looked up at me. 'I'll never forget that face. Pure hatred, like he wanted me dead.'

'Well let's get the hell out of here then!' I urged Mike, dragging him up and toward the exit of the caves. As we hurried along, with only my flashlight to guide our way, I expected another apparition to pop out from every dark opening. My nerves were tingling with adrenaline and my heart pounded in my chest, to the point where I could hear nothing else but its steady drumming.

When we arrived at the exit of the caves and my heart sank. The door was locked, apparently from the outside. 'What now?' Mike asked.

'There's another way out upstairs,' I said. 'Let's head there.'

We made our way quickly through the maze of ramps and obstacles up to the second floor. My flashlight lit up the fish tank that sat in the wall of the World Aquarium. I saw a young boy's face behind me, glaring in the reflection. I spun around, but no one was there. Mike tried the door, with no luck.

It was also locked.

I began to panic, gasping for air and shining the flashlight in a jagged pattern around us, with my back to the aquarium. Out of the darkness, a faint illumination materialized into the shape of a boy. He stepped toward us slowly, and I understood what Mike meant. His eyes burned with an unrelenting malice. His mouth was twisted into a scowl that had no place on the face of such a young child.

Suddenly, a lock clicked in the door and it slowly opened. Before I realized what I was doing, I was dragging Mike through it. As we sprinted toward the stairs that would take us out of the building, I turned and saw the ghost girl standing in the doorway. She had the same slight smile on her face as a pair of hands grabbed her from behind and pulled her away into the darkness.

The door slammed shut.

At the stairs, I stopped for a moment, listening. A slow funeral dirge had started playing on the old piano upstairs. Its mournful notes filled me with a renewed sense of dread, as I realized there was no one else in the building to be playing it. I pulled Mike violently down the stairs toward the main entrance. I wanted nothing more than to get out of there and away from the madness. We flew into the doors of the entrance and crashed painfully backward.

For a brief moment, I was certain whatever was with us in the museum had barred this exit as well. My light played over the door. There! I reached up and unlatched a bolt lock at the top of one door and it swung open.

Outside, the noises of a busy Washington Avenue filled my ears. Cars, horns, people. Real people. Relief flooded through my body as we reached my car. Looking back at the building rising high into the cloudy night sky, I was certain I could see two human shapes glowing softly in an upper story window.

THE BANSHEE OF BALLWIN
Caryn Pine

Every single day I had to live in a nightmare. Every time I closed my eyes, I saw you. I was crumbling into nothing and you were the only person I could turn to, but you were gone. I wanted to scream, claw out my own eyes so I wouldn't have to see what happened to you. They kept telling me to move on, but how could I move on when I knew that you were dead because of me? You disappeared, but I was stuck facing what I did to you.

How was I supposed to know that you would actually do it though? It was just a dumb dare. I didn't think anything bad would happen. Maybe you would just get a little scared, but that was it. I didn't want to lose you.

"So," I said, "you have to stay in The Banshee's house all night."

The Banshee's house was a few streets away from mine and it had been empty for years. It was owned by Emma McCarthy, a young woman who used to be beautiful. When I was five, I would always see her in her garden, her blonde hair tied back. She looked so perfect doing the simplest things, but then she stopped going gardening. She stopped going out where there would be crowds. She was slowly losing her mind, becoming more tired looking. She aged ten years in six months. I didn't understand what was happening to her.

When I was eight, Emma disappeared. Her body was found hanging in the basement, with scratches etched into her skin. Everyone had always said that her house was haunted and that she lived with demons. Whatever occupied her house must have gotten sick of her and drove her mad. People always said that it was such a pity that we lost her when she was so young and now they're going to say the same thing about you.

I never thought that the ghost story was true, but people loved it, always wanting to go inside and figure out exactly what happened to her. It seemed like everyone around me thought that she started to haunt the house with the rest of her demons, so it eventually became known as The Banshee's house.

You must have believed in the story because your entire body shook when I gave you that dare. Your blonde hair looked as if it was turning white, just like your face. I didn't know that blood could leave a person's head so fast. You tried to compose yourself, but you couldn't hide any of your fear and I didn't know why until it was too late.

"You don't have to do it. It's fine." You wouldn't listen. You could never say no to a dare, no matter how stupid. Cliff jumping? No big deal. You would run with the bulls if you had money to go to Spain. Your bravery was amazing and I always wanted to be more like you. I had never seen you so vulnerable before. You always looked so strong and I wanted to see you falter a little. It was selfish, but you were always so perfect. I just wanted to see a little imperfection. I didn't want anything terrible to happen though. I should have known it wouldn't go well, but I ignored anything telling me how bad it could have gone. I just wanted a few seconds of vulnerability.

"N-no. I'll do it. Just keep your phone with you." You knew that something was going to happen, didn't you? Why else would I need my phone? Was I ignoring how scared you were just because I was selfish? How bad of a friend was I?

You turned away from me and began to walk down the dark road, your body still shaking. If you were so freaked out, why did you even say yes Kasey? Why didn't call me sooner? Why did you go?

You called at midnight. I thought it was a joke; you were just playing a cruel trick. You wanted me to be as scared as you were. Well, you got me Kasey; I was terrified. Your screams surrounded me and filled my ears. They made me feel hollow. You didn't sound real anymore. You didn't sound like you.

Tears were running down my face before I was out the door. I wouldn't let my legs stop moving. I had to find you. I just needed to get there and everything would be okay. If I was there, you would be fine. You would be sitting on the porch laughing at me for believing that anything bad could happen to you.

The sprint to the house seemed to take forever. My only source of light was the occasional street lamp. All of the house lights were off; everyone was sleeping like everything was normal while I was racing a demon to save you. No matter how fast I moved though, I wouldn't be able to get to you in time. When you called Kasey, you were already so far gone.

Emma's house was so ordinary looking, other than the needed paint job. The white house resembled the rest on the street, except for its dirty history. It was marked by a huge tree that seemed to be reaching towards the house right in the middle of the yard. It was like it was pointing me where to go so I could see what happened to you. The tree mocked my horror by guiding me to you.

I opened the door quickly, not wanting to waste any time because I thought you could still be alive. There was a large staircase in the corner of the main room and I walked towards it. You were waiting for me at the top of the stairs while some of your blood was waiting for me at the bottom.

I started screaming when I saw what had happened to you. Your stomach was ripped open like you were some sick science project and deep claw marks were carved into your once beautiful face. Your leg was on an angle that a contortionist would have been proud of. You looked completely broken. I wanted to throw up when I saw you drenched in your own blood, organs ready to leave you, but I was empty. Nothing was coming out of me except for my tears.

Whatever did it to you was gone, but I was there with you, not knowing what to do. I wanted it to come back for me so I wouldn't be alone with my guilt, but I wasn't that lucky. I was stuck knowing that I killed you. I was the reason that something tore into your flesh and threw you around. Why didn't it come back for me?

The Banshee and her friends didn't want me though. They only wanted you. As I stayed with you, holding you, sobbing over you, they left me alone. Completely alone. Maybe that's what they wanted. They wanted another lonely soul in Ballwin, just the person that Emma became. Taking you from me was the best way for them to do that. I was going to go crazy, just like she did. Maybe I would even die in the house just like she did. Like you did.

I was holding you trying to keep you with me, but I couldn't do anything. You were gone, but your blood stayed with me. I refused to wash you off of me for hours. I needed you with me Kasey.

My parents didn't know what to do. I wouldn't talk to anyone and I would hardly move. Everyone eventually left me alone. I was a lost cause. I was broken and no one could fix me.

Well, one person could.

But you're dead.

HITCHHIKER ANNIE
Marie Robinson

The whipping winds tugged at the corners of his eyes and mouth and pinched his cheeks like an obnoxious relative, but it was better than dying of suffocation, which was sure to happen if he rolled the windows of the car up. The weather in St. Louis loved to tease — cool and cloudy one moment and hot and balmy the next. Even though the sun was down the humidity was palpable, eager to wrap its sticky hands around his throat. The only way to banish it was to open the windows and let the air blast past as he flew down the highway.

Sadly, his exit was swiftly approaching and soon he would again be at the mercy of the stale, oppressive air. He frowned as he decreased his speed, ascending the off-ramp. As the film of sweat wrapped around his face like a cobweb he almost didn't notice the figure on the side of the road.

He only saw her for a split second — a pretty young thing with sad eyes and a hooked thump jutted out at her side; it was enough to make him screech to a stop. He eyed her from the rearview mirror, beads of sweat gathered on his skin only to slide down the slopes of his body.

She slowly turned, dropping her arm to her side. She began a slow, calculated pace towards the car.

"*She's probably frightened,*" he reassured himself. Still, her menacing approach unsettled him.

He took the opportunity to examine her. She had dark brown hair that hung heavy at either side of her face. Her skin was wan and almost had a dull glow to it, which he thought surely was a trick performed by the fog that floated about the road. The girl — she couldn't have been more than seventeen — was thin and wore a long white dress. The only color she had about her was a smear of red lipstick.

She leaned inside the open window, her thin wrists folded over one another. When she didn't speak, he cleared his throat.

"You all right, miss?" He could only imagine the way he looked, water pouring down his face, hair sticking in sick clumps to his forehead. Her skin was pristine—smooth and white like porcelain. It was so unblemished it almost seemed as if she wasn't exactly solid.

"I'm having trouble with my car," she said in a strange, velvety voice. She sounded much older, and much more somber than her apparent age.

He looked over his shoulder through the back window. He instinctively squinted in hopes of penetrating the eerie haze but it was no use, the fog was impenetrable. Still, he didn't recall passing a vehicle — broken down or otherwise. He had only seen the slight, lustrous figure of the girl.

"Where is it?" He asked. He jumped, every muscle in his body jolted, including his heart. Even though he hadn't heard a sound, the girl had somehow slipped inside the car and was seated in the passenger seat beside him when he turned around to face her. She still fixed him with unblinking eyes.

"Would you like a ride?" He choked the words out after he swallowed a pathetic yelp that leapt to escape his throat. His heart fluttered in his chest.

"My name is Annie," the girl said in the same calm, cold voice. He had forgotten the heat that hung in the air like the mist until he found his skin pricking with chills.

"*Why should I be frightened of a little girl?*" A small voice whispered within him. As he forced a jagged smile, he could feel his lips flicker as if it tried to flee. His fingers knotted themselves around the steering wheel. "Where to, Annie?"

Her demanding gaze still held him, and it felt as if a heavy weight bore down on him. He struggled not to crumble beneath it. She dragged a hand from her lap and pointed a long finger straight through the windshield before she finally looked away.

A sigh hissed from his lips when he was released from her grip. He pulled away from the curb and barreled through the fog. He dared not look over at the girl, even out of the corner of his eye; he focused all his attention on the cloaked road.

Several silent moments passed like an eternity, and he felt if he didn't speak, he might go mad.

"Don't forget to tell me where we are going, Annie." He chanced a glance at her, though it took him every ounce of courage to do so. Terror ripped through his chest like a knife when he found the passenger seat empty.

He braced himself as he stomped on the brake pedal,; his tires wailed as if begging him not to stop. His chest heaved. When he pried his hands from the wheel, he realized they were quaking furiously. He fumbled with the door handle until he toppled out of the car.

He called her name as he looked about the empty street. He spotted her walking away from the car toward the side of the road. She stepped in her slow, even pace as the fog gathered around her, slowly devouring her.

When he could no longer tell her apart from the haze he rounded the car and ran on teetering legs. The fog refused to part and he was forced to dart blindly until he ran into black iron bars. He stepped back to view a wrought iron gate. Etched into a stone pillar at one side were the words, "Bellefontaine Cemetery."

He looked back through the bars to find a long, pale face peering at him. He felt his blood run cold, freezing in his veins; he was sure he would faint but her burning glare held him. She floated at his eye-level, their noses nearly touching through the gate.

She grinned before she vanished into the fog, parting her scarlet lips to whisper, "Thanks for the ride."

REUNITED
J. T. Seate

The dilapidated house resided on the outskirts of a small Missouri town, long unused, dying if not already dead. And yet, the house could still hypnotize Alicia. There had always been something abnormal about the place in which she grew up. Even before she and her sister were old enough to hear stories about ghosts and goblins, Alicia felt things she could not explain. And now, after so many years, she had returned to the timeworn old house that still held secrets.

With its slanting angles and sloped roofs, the two-story structure stood against the horizon like a cardboard cutout in front of the sky's diminishing light. Alicia stood for a moment to receive whatever silent message the house might be sending. Brooding and bleak in the wash of twilight, the house looked back at her as if holding its breath to see what Alicia intended.

Most of its paint had peeled and gone gray. Spider webs of cracked glass crawled along its windowpanes. A remaining shutter hung askew from a broken hinge. Some of the gutters around the eaves drooped loosely, bent and rusted, having long since lost their ability to catch water. Alicia could make out the shell of an abandoned vehicle and bleached lumber scattered in haphazard piles, all looking as forlorn as the house. Back in the day, her father planted two saplings now gown to maturity, but overgrown and untended. Some of their branches hung from the trunks like dislocated arms, a dismal sight at best. She found little comfort in this creepy place where Death had once been its occupation.

Although the wooden porch drooped in places, it still cloaked the front of the house, just as Alicia remembered. She envisioned her mother sitting on the porch, her rocking chair creaking back and forth, a book face down in her lap, her hands folded atop it, daydreaming about what her life was or what it might have been while rustling wisps of her hair gently blew to and fro like the lace curtains from an open window.

Most surprising was the faint sound of wind chimes which had been removed from the porch even before she had left, taken down after Molly's disappearance. Alicia remembered sitting next to her sister Molly on freshly painted steps. At ages six and eight, the little girls looked equally shiny and new dressed in brightly colored Easter dresses. Molly held a doll that Alicia coveted. Alicia thought it prettier than any of her own, but that's the way it seemed to be; Molly first and Alicia second. The recollections flipped past like pages of a storybook. Molly had allowed Alicia to play with her things, but that did not matter because it was Molly her parents had given them to. Molly, the favored child.

The reverie of porch scenes faded as Alicia observed the old house's façade once more. If its silhouette was not intimidating enough, the knowledge that the cavernous dwelling once served as a funeral home before Alicia's family had come and gone was. She used to feel the presence of those other than her family members even before she learned about the house's former use.

As a young girl, Alicia had never gone into the basement alone to stoke the coal furnace. The basement was where bodies had been transformed into presentable corpses suitable for public viewing in the parlor above. It was bad enough knowing her mother or father or older sister were down in that dark shadowy place in the company of the ugly, leviathan of a furnace. To Alicia, it was a monster with a hungry mouth that swallowed its dinner of coal or split-wood ravenously. Its scary metal tentacles crawled up to the heating ducts that led to the elevated floors. On cold nights as she lay in her bed, she could her it beckoning like a siren from the depths of the earth with its blasts of warm air humming an unpleasant, insistent lullaby.

More unpleasant than the visions conjured from beyond the house were the ones Alicia would face once she entered. This time her presence was not déjà vu. She was actually here. The time had come for her to find out if the spirits of the dear departed, which might include her own family, had somehow been captured within the walls of this lonely place.

She approached the house with apprehension, the final member of the family had returned at long last. She entered the front door with the red paint darkened to the color of dried blood. Except for the starkness of its tomblike emptiness, rooms devoid of furniture, the place had changed little. Varnished tongue-and-groove wainscoting and patterned wallpaper was now dulled to a smoke-smudged, oily tan. None of the latches on cabinets quite closed anymore, a sorrowful sight to be sure. The dank, musty smell of neglect was strong, but Alicia adjusted to the sights and smells quickly. Within seconds she found her bearings and the place began to produce a dreamlike calm.

She was alone again in the house where she was born. Well, not quite alone. There were plenty of phantoms for company. In spite of the whispering voices in the corners, she passed through the first floor rooms to the stairway that led up to the second floor. She climbed the stairs and glided to the room that belonged to her sister. Although empty, Alicia could easily imagine the way it had once been. Every edge and corner was sharp and clear, filled with pretty things she herself had admired, a shrine to the dead princess.

Alicia again fell into a reverie. Although Molly liked to pull on Alicia's braids once in a while, she had treated her younger sister nicely enough. They had kept few secrets from each other, but still, Alicia often felt helpless, unable to connect as Molly began blossoming into a young woman. Molly was not only changing physically, but mentally as well. She had teenage friends of her own beyond the world of sisters, but she was still the first at her father's knee and at her mother's side.

Alicia remembered pulling the traditional younger sister routine when Molly was asked to a dance. "I don't ever want to go out with a stupid boy," she had declared at the dinner table over a steaming bowl of tomato soup. She had wanted to dump it on Molly's head. She would not have looked so prissy then. And as time passed, Alicia hadn't gone out on many dates. Still, she had wanted to be like Molly. She thought that might solicit the affection her parents seemed to shower on her sister, but the household was never the same after the family loss.

Molly had been seventeen and Alicia fifteen at the time of the event. It was a mystery never solved. Molly was the apple of her parent's eye one day and nonexistent the next. The wooded and watery areas in and around the town of Bedford were searched. Investigators investigated, but all efforts failed to uncover a body. There had never been any closure, a concept that seemed laughable to Alicia. At least, no one had ever spoken about heaven having a new angel.

On some level, people believe the worst thing their minds can imagine: a young girl in the bloom of life, taken by some loony, they theorized. It happened somewhere all the time. Alicia's parents had visions of Molly carried off by a cruel and heartless man who defiled, killed, and buried her in some unknown place never to be found, but they hadn't known the half of it. Alicia had busied herself in her mother's garden during that terrible time so as not to dwell on the thick sadness within the house any more than necessary.

The family dynamic became as fragile as spun glass. No more perfect Molly, only Alicia, who could hear her mother's heartbroken sobs from behind a closed door. Her father would go days without saying a word. They would sometimes wander out of a room like an unfinished sentence and Alicia would sit with her whole being in knots searching for a way to be the new number one daughter.

About the time her mother started spending large chunks of time on the porch looking wistfully into space, her father took to crawling instead a whiskey bottle, each thinking about how their lives had unraveled. The light had gone out in her parent's eyes and nothing Alicia could do would rekindle them, although she kept trying to be as special as Molly had been. No matter how hard Alicia tried, she continued to feel inferior, forcing her even further from normalcy. It was clear she would never be Molly's equal in beauty or charm. Molly had been special where Alicia was strange, hearing voices, and seeing things out of the corner of her eye.

The parents never healed from the shock of Molly's disappearance and kept vigil the rest of their lives hoping she would magically return. "The pain of discovery would be more bearable than the pain of uncertainty," her mother stated.

Alicia was not uncertain. When it came to ghosts, she had been aware of them since Molly and her first sat on either side of the Ouija board. The game's planchette practically flew around when they asked their questions. It had certainly been right about which of them would die first. After Molly's "disappearance," Alicia thought she saw her now and then hiding in a corner, watching, or standing like a marble statue near a window gazing with sightless eyes upon a world taken from her. Although startling, Alicia never screamed or said anything to anyone about these visions because she wanted to believe it was her mind playing tricks rather than black magic. Still, from the time Molly was gone and ever after, Alicia looked at the house's windows differently, as if they were looking inward, keeping an eye on what she might do next.

Alicia remained with her folks until she was out of school, old enough to find a job in another part of the country, and escape this home filled with its unhappy memories. The worst of it was not when the furnace hummed with fire or belched out its hot air. It was when her father burned trash and newspapers that produced bits of ash and char she could see floating above the roof, dancing and fluttering in the air like a horrible reminder.

In the years to follow, Alicia's were marked by depression and the bitter knowledge that loneliness would forever be her lot. She chose a path without the comforts and pitfalls of a husband or children. This led to a rather aimless, unfocused life lacking the ability to find contentment, joy or warmth. Generosity and selflessness were never in her character. Others told her she sometimes looked haunted. Maybe those people were able to see beyond her exterior into her soul. She talked to her parents by phone but rarely visited. When she did see them, the gray in their hair and the sad wrinkles on their faces was too much to bear. The old house with its history and its memories were best left to those without her predilection for seeing and hearing strange things.

Breaking through her reverie of the past, Alicia left her sister's room and went down the hallway to the room that had been hers. She tried to recall the hopes and fears she had experienced within its confines while the murmurs of others could be heard in the walls. She was free of the problems of the world now, but still not free of the house's scrutiny.

There was another part of the house calling to her—the underground room where the evil monster lived. She reluctantly made her way downstairs to the basement door that held her worst fears. It also held the secret that no one knew except her and the monster in the space suitable for embalming and destroying. She halfway expected to find the furnace glowing and groaning as it shoved hot air through its tentacles, but it was dark and quiet, as neglected as the rest of the old house.

The secret.

Yes, the secret shared with this despicable mass of metal. Molly never ran away. She had been home the whole time, first in the furnace as charred bones and later, as separated bones, buried around the property, bone by bone.

Alicia had killed her sister and stuffed her body in the furnace. Scenes from the fatal day flickered across Alicia's consciousness like an old silent movie. At fifteen years of age, she was tired of being the black sheep and getting only the leftovers of affection. For the rest of her life, she would have had to live up to the standard of her parent's sweet Molly who could seemingly do no wrong. Alicia had gone into the basement with her sister and knocked her out with iron tongs. It had been like clubbing a baby seal.

171

She covered Molly's mouth in case she should come to while Alicia stuffed her into the large mouth of the giant beast. Realizing she was alone in the room that once held untold dead bodies; she worked quickly at stoking the furnace with more coal and leaving her sister to melt away in the conflagration. Although she shut off the flue in hopes the odor would not escape through the pipes and fill the house with the smell of cooking flesh, the intensity of the heat must have made quick work of Molly. In the aftermath, it was a good thing Alicia had shown an interest in gardening. It gave her a reason to spend so much time there.

Initially, Alicia escaped the torment of her actions. She never feared Molly's dead spirit or any of the others that whispered in the walls because she did not believe the dead could harm the living. Never had she thought much about what she may have deprived her sister. But what about now, when Alicia was no longer anyone, as dead as the rest of the spirits she sensed all around her? She quickly realized, as she had feared, this was a new playing field when the others were equal to whatever it was she herself had become. Once again, the sound of the wind chimes. Once more, the voices in the walls became louder.

Molly was back. Alicia was sure of it now. They were all back, and she would have to confront them. She had to face what she had done, the act which had prevented her from the chance of a happy existence. If she wanted to leave, would the house let her? She did not believe it would. Moreover, she felt the house itself had come alive with her entry, and it needed to be fed.

It was a reunion of sorts, here where spirits resided, and since Alicia was no longer alive, time had become meaningless. She was again at the crime scene, and the monster in the basement suddenly belched and began to spring back to life. Would she be forced to relive the day she disposed of her sister, the only escape for body and soul through the heating ducts? Or would Alicia be thrown into the fiery furnace and enter hell's kingdom this time around? All her later years without anyone to confide in had represented a hell worse than those she had spent with the favored sister. All the birthdays Alicia had seen that Molly never did. The rivers of hot tears Molly never shed over triumphs and tragedies. Alicia remembered the little eight-year-old Molly in a yellow pinafore and the seventeen-year-old Molly in a felt skirt. The ghosts that outlasted all others were the ones that never got the chance to fully live. Alicia's guilt at long last surfaced

She floated up the stairs to the main floor where the windows still watched. The moaning sounds in the walls continued, but now they sounded almost gleeful. Alicia remembered the irony of it all now, how her return had come about. She too had passed from a physical existence in a conflagration, trapped in a burning house somewhere, dying in the most horrible of ways. How apropos for the final curtain of her life?

There were no more hallucinations. On this plane of existence, what she could see and hear was as real as she. Voices in the walls and around the corners became more distinct—chanting, troubled voices. Alicia saw the first of them. It wasn't Molly as she might have expected, but another wraith up from the basement. Its hair stood on end and a long, white burial garment trailed to the floor. Her expression was one of betrayal. Who knew how many revenants dwelled within the passages of time while the old house had stood as a witness. How many had been offended by what one now among them had done, all drawn to this place where they had died or been prepared for the hereafter. If alive, Alicia would have screamed, knowing she might have to answer to them all, one by one.

And finally, rising up from the dark basement was another phantom. The cacophony of voices raging through the old house faded into insignificance as a more dominant presence took over. Alicia felt fear certainly, but extreme sadness washed over her as well. Above the blouse and felt skirt, Molly's death ensemble, a face was shiny like candle wax. It possessed layer upon layer of emotions—truth and falsehood, youth and age—all going back to that moment, all those years ago, when Molly was betrayed by her sister. Slowly and relentlessly, she floated toward Alicia. It was time for the younger sister to fulfill her mission.

"I'm sorry for what I did, Molly," Alicia's spirit expressed.

Too late to be sorry, sister. Much too late was the unspoken response that floated along the aching joints of the old house.

Molly's clothes began to change. They turned from an array of colors to the ashy gray of char. A miserable history from deep within the house began to rise up through the floor like the smell of rot. A heavy moan of dread to accompany the house's moans escaped Alicia for that was the only sound she had the ability to make. Molly's arms stretched forward to embrace her sister with hands, face, and body now as charred as the clothes that had burned off of her.

The dead are patient, but the time had come—that moment when a being turns a flashlight on their soul and inspects it for will and courage. Alicia knew she had arrived at this place for a reckoning as had many others even though they had been physically gone for years. *Her* death had brought her back where so many dark spirits remained, especially the spirit of the girl she had betrayed. The structure felt like a great maw that had swallowed her whole as Molly had, at last, found her.

If anyone had been within a hundred yards of the old house that day, they would have smelled the electric stench of ozone and burnt flesh. It was a place where anything horrible was possible. Absolutely anything.

****

From the *Bedford Bulletin*, October 30th, 2013

Old Landmark Burns to Ground

A long vacant farmhouse at Whistle Stop cutoff along Route 6 burned to the ground last evening. "A thorough search for possible vagrants will be conducted," Sheriff Loomis told the *Bulletin*. "No cause has been determined for the fire, but an arsonist expert from St. Louis will arrive in a day or two." Loomis suspects a lightning strike. The weather bureau could not confirm a storm pattern in the area, however. The property had a colorful history and will be missed by those who believed it to be haunted. "Sorry, Bedfordites," the sheriff stated. "You'll have to find your ghosts somewhere else unless ghosts don't need an old house to brood in."

THE HOUSE ON THE MOUNTAIN
Jacqueline Seewald

Maybe if her parents had lived longer instead of getting killed in a yachting accident when Jess was only three, things might have been different. As it was, she was shuffled around from one uncaring relative to another, neglected and unloved. She was pretty much a lost soul until she met Bob.

The night they met, Jess attended a party in St. Louis. The young woman throwing the party had gone to the same small, private college as Jess. They were only casual acquaintances. Jess had no close friends. In fact, she was surprised to be invited.

One of the guests was a much acclaimed professor and well-known author whose latest book, *Legends of the Ozarks*, had won book awards for scholarly research. Jess admired the handsome bearded man dressed in Harris Tweed jacket and corduroy jeans. His mane of tawny hair gave him a leonine aspect. Jess couldn't take her eyes from him. The man had such magnetic charm. He spoke with a soft Southern accent surrounded by a coterie of admirers. Jess, usually shy and inhibited, actually spoke to Bob after their hostess introduced them.

"I want to buy a copy of your book," Jess said, then felt embarrassed by her expression of brash eagerness.

However, Bob looked pleased.

"You needn't go to the expense," he replied in that mesmerizing mellifluous voice. "My books are available at most libraries."

"Oh, Jess, can buy an entire bookstore of your work," Dinah, their hostess said.

Jess flushed. Dinah on observing her discomfort, placed her hand on Jess's arm.

"Darling, I'm sorry, but everyone knows you inherited wealth, gobs and oodles of money. I didn't think it was any kind of secret."

Bob threw her a speculative look, one golden brow cocked.

Jess fought for composure. "It's not the kind of thing I like strangers to know about me, at least not immediately."

"Sorry, darling. Oh, well, Bob doesn't care about that anyway, do you? I mean intellectuals are above crass material considerations." Dinah, so sophisticated and svelte, represented everything that Jess was not.

Dinah moved on, leaving Jess and Bob alone in a corner.

To Jess's immense surprise and gratitude, Bob made a joke of the whole thing, putting her at ease.

Bob spent the rest of the evening chatting with Jess. She could hardly believe it! He really appeared to care about what she thought and had to say.

"Are you teaching in St. Louis?" she asked him.

"I've had an offer at the university, but at the moment, I'm only here on a book tour. However, I could be persuaded to stay for a while. I'm on sabbatical. Time is not a problem." He took her hand in his. "I would like to get to know you better, much better."

It was on their honeymoon that Bob took Jess to the Ozarks.

"I was born in the mountains," Bob told her. "I love the music, the history, and the people. There's such a rich cultural heritage. I want to introduce you to it."

Jess was so happy. This wonderful, handsome, intelligent man wanted to make her part of his life. All at once she'd become a princess in a fairy tale.

Bob suggested to Jess that they visit a number of battlefields of the Civil War. "My next book will be a history of battles fought in Missouri. I thought we might visit some of them."

Jess didn't object. She loved American history and the history of Missouri in particular. But she found the battlefields eerie and depressing. She sensed the presence of the dead, as if their troubled spirits still hovered. She shuddered and clung to Bob who seemed to be enjoying the experiences, oblivious to the sadness.

"This is so grim. Do you hear them whispering to us?"

Bob raised a patrician brow. "What are you talking about?"

"The ghosts of the soldiers who died here. The dead aren't at peace."

Bob shrugged. "Darlin', I think you have an overactive imagination."

Jess didn't reply. Before her parents went away for the last time, she had cried and begged them to stay, saying she was afraid that they wouldn't come back. They had laughed, of the opinion that she was just expressing childish fears. But after they died, her nanny crossed herself and said that Jess was a sensitive, someone who had paranormal insights. Jess never had another incident of that ability and so forgot about it. She told herself that her nanny had been foolishly superstitious. But the experience on the battleground made her wonder. The ghosts were there. They'd connected with her. Jess knew it wasn't her imagination. She shuddered.

"I'm going to take you to my family home. It's on a mountaintop. I know you're going to love it as much as I do. The house has atmosphere."

"Will I meet your family?" she asked.

"Afraid not. My parents are both deceased, one of the many things we have in common. Actually, the house is in rather bad disrepair." He gave her an apologetic smile, betraying a dimple in his right cheek. "I thought you might enjoy fixing it up with me. It's in a wonderfully rural location. The house has character. It's truly unique. It could be our getaway spot when things become too hectic in the city. What do you think?"

It was impossible for Jess to refuse her wonderful husband anything. "Of course, we can fix it up. I'd love to live in a house that has family history."

But when Jess finally got to see the place, she wasn't quite certain. They had been driving upward on narrow, winding mountain roads for some time. The road they traveled was sinuous like a snake. The house rose up on top of the mountain. Paint peeled from the white clapboard shingles. The house sat surrounded by huge old trees that hovered over it with a dark and malevolent aura. Jess shivered although the day was not cold.

"You used to live here?" Jess asked in disbelief.

"Well, not exactly," her husband said with an easy shrug. "You see, my mother had an aversion to the old place. It all had to do with a ghost story, about an apparition that both haunted and cursed the house. If you've read my book, you know that there are tons of such legends in the Ozarks."

"Has any member of your family actually lived here?" Jess asked.

"Certainly. The house itself is nearly two hundred years old. It originally was owned by a very wealthy family. But as the years went by, they lost their money. Apparently, the last of the Wentworths was a gambler and a drunkard. He lost the house in a card game to my ancestor who was reputably a moon shiner during the Prohibition era. I've done a bit of research on the subject. Shall we go inside?"

Reluctantly, Jess followed her husband into the house. She could see that it had been well built, had once been a handsome mansion in fact, and could probably be restored. She resolved that she would pay for the restoration as a wedding gift to her new husband. What was the good of having money after all if you couldn't use it to give pleasure to loved ones? When she told Bob of her decision, he seemed more than pleased. He kissed her tenderly on the lips and then squeezed her hand.

"It will be wonderful living here," he said. "You'll see."

Jess was less than convinced but decided to withhold judgment for the time being. The old house obviously meant a great deal to her husband and she badly wanted to please him.

Still she'd sensed both evil and death hovering about the old place and it frightened her.

They drove back down the mountain and arranged for motel accommodations. The next few days were busy ones. They got estimates from home repair and construction companies. They arranged for plumbers and electricians to visit the property.

Jess bought a second car so that they could both come and go as they chose.

Work was commencing well and they were both at the house together, looking at what needed to be done. The restoration was going to be costly, Jess realized. But Bob seemed so pleased. Well, she could well afford it, Jess reminded herself. What good was money if it wasn't used to bring happiness to the man she loved? This was the mantra she constantly repeated.

Bob's cell phone rang. He looked at the number and frowned. "I need to take this call. You don't mind if I step outside?" he asked.

"Of course not," she replied but she was bothered. For some reason, the phone call troubled her. What could require privacy?

Jess walked around the downstairs. She hadn't even been upstairs as yet because the contractors told them that the stairs were not safe to use. It appeared they were rickety and the wood might have rotted out.

She hadn't been to the cellar either. Apparently there was a dirt floor, and all manner of creepy, crawly things lurked there. No, this really wasn't a very appealing house. But she had to believe that once the work was done here things would be different.

Bob returned with a concerned look. "Darling, I'm going to have to leave for a few days. Something's come up that I must take care of immediately."

What could possibly be so urgent, Jess wondered. When she voiced her question, Bob merely shrugged. His face colored faintly as in embarrassment.

"I don't have time to get into it right now. I'll be back as soon as I can. You've got your car here. When the carpenters come today, you can supervise, can't you?"

"I'd rather not be alone here. The house is more than a little creepy."

Bob put his arms around her. "I know, but that's only temporary. Our changes will make this a real home, an outstanding showplace. I'll be back as soon as possible. Honor bright." He gave her a warmly persuasive kiss and hug. And then he left her alone in the house.

Jess walked around the place for a time feeling a sense of dread, though not certain why. There was something eerie here, a sense of otherness.

Finally, she decided to go out to the car and eat some of the lunch that she'd packed. As she sat in the SUV, Jess studied the old house. It was quite large and might have once been grand, but a deep darkness seemed to enshroud it, a sadness. Maybe she just imagined it. She hoped that was the case.

Jess glanced at her watch. The construction people were supposed to have already arrived. Where were they? She located the business card in her handbag and then tried to dial it on her cell. But there was no signal. She stepped out of the car and tried another location, meeting with the same problem. Jess let out a deep sigh.

She was growing chilly and walked back into the house. Here she was greeted by the sound of a young woman singing. Jess blinked. She hadn't brought an Ipod with her. Was there someone in the house?

Jess began to look around, but the voice hovered and didn't seem to have a specific location.

"Who's here? Who's singing?"

"Just me," a voice said.

There was a sudden coldness in the room. An insubstantial form appeared, a girl dressed in a long, gauzy white dress, her hair long and golden, her eyes of the palest blue, like a frozen lake in winter. Her form came to rest in front of Jess who let out an involuntary gasp, eyes opening wide.

"Oh, hush now! I didn't mean to scare you none. I've been watching you and your man. And I'm worried for you."

"Who are you? What are you?" Jess stammered.

"I was Melinda Gray of Willardsville."

"What are you doing in this house Melinda?" The coldness caused her to shake.

"Haunting it for all eternity," the young woman replied.

Jess found it hard to breathe. "I must be having a mental breakdown," she said. "I'm imagining ghosts." She sat down hard on a dusty, old wooden chair that nearly collapsed under her.

"Oh, I'm here all right."

"Why?"

"Because I can't have no peace until I get buried right and proper."

"I don't understand," Jess said.

"I reckon it's been some time since my husband Caleb murdered me. You wear funny looking clothes. Did I just go and shock you? Sorry."

"You were murdered by your husband?" Jess tried to grasp the ghost's words.

"I was indeed. You see my daddy was a rich man. He was right impressed with Caleb. My husband was a gentleman, an aristocratic gentleman, unlike my papa who was in the mercantile trade. My daddy agreed that I would marry Caleb and in return, Caleb would get a generous dowry. I loved my tall, handsome husband and was happy for the match. Trouble was, Caleb had a ladylove. He wanted her and Daddy's money as well. He just didn't want me. And so one day when we were out for a walk, he smashed the back of my head with a large rock. While I was still dazed from the blow, he dragged me along and then he threw me into the old, dry well yonder. When I fully come back to my senses, I started screaming. But it were no use. He plugged up the well. The sides were smooth rock so I couldn't get out. I died there after some days. It was a slow awful death. I cried and cursed my husband. My bones still lie in that place. I want to be with my family in our family plot in Willardsville. Can't know any peace until I do."

"What happened to your husband?"

"Oh, he made up some story about how I run off on him. But, of course, I never left here. I cursed him and his house for all eternity. That's why nothing good can ever come of this place."

"Why have you come to me?" Jess asked, still wondering if she were delusional.

"Because I fear for you. I think your man is like mine was."

"Bob loves me."

"I felt the same way, thought the same thing," the apparition said. "But my husband was a false lover, faithless and untrue. Your man didn't tell you where he was really going, did he?"

Jess recalled her conversation with Bob. He had been evasive, she conceded. No, she didn't want to think this way. She should not doubt Bob. He loved her just as she loved him.

"I think I'd better go. The workers don't seem to be coming today after all."

"You watch after yourself!" the ghost called out.

Jess opened the creaking front door and found herself faced with a rainstorm. The wind howled and practically blew her down. She somehow managed to make it to the shelter of her car. But when she started the engine, it wouldn't turn over. How could that be? This was a reliable, new automobile? It made no sense.

Surely ghosts didn't tamper with cars? She tried her cell phone again but still got no signal.

Jess pulled herself out of the car, frustrated and frightened. What was going on? As she turned to go once more back to the house that she'd begun to hate, Dinah Hendricks suddenly appeared. Was her mind playing more tricks? She blinked twice. No, Dinah was really there.

"Dinah, is that you? What are you doing here?"

"I just came up to see how the progress is going on your house."

"How did you know that I was here?" Now she was completely confused.

"Bob and I have been very good friends for a long time. As a matter of face, he once asked me to marry him. Don't look upset. I turned him down, naturally. He had no money. You know what college professors earn. And I am high maintenance. But then I had the brilliant idea of introducing him to you, Jess, dearest. You should thank me. I encouraged him to marry you. And when you're dead, he'll inherit all of your lovely money and finally be a splendid catch." Dinah raised a Glock automatic.

Jess's heart beat so rapidly she thought she'd surely expire from fear. "You don't want to kill me. The workers will be here any minute. You'll be caught."

"Actually, I phoned, told them I was you, and explained that they should come tomorrow instead."

"You planned this with Bob?" Jess's eyes opened wide in horror.

"Of course not. He's a total straight arrow. He took his vows seriously. But he and I remain very close friends. I keep in touch. Today I called and told him how I needed his help in the city desperately. I got him out of here so I could manage matters. And now, I'm afraid you will have to die. Nothing personal, darling. Just a matter of necessity. So do start walking toward those large pine trees."

"I don't think so," Jess said.

"Oh, bother. Then I will have to shoot you right here."

As Dinah raised her weapon, Jess tried to move but her feet felt like gelatin and she merely wobbled. The wind howled louder like a banshee. The storm strengthened.

Something appeared before them. "You're not going to kill her. I won't let you! They'll be more innocent folk murdered in this place."

Startled, Dinah raised her weapon and shot at the specter.

Jess saw her chance and rushed toward Dinah knocking the other woman to the ground. They fought for control of the gun. With adrenaline pumping, Jess somehow managed to wrestle the weapon away.

"Stay on the ground," she warned as she pointed the gun at Dinah.

Hand trembling, she tried the cell phone again. This time, the signal came through and she dialed for assistance.

Looking toward the closed up stone well, Jess made a solemn promise. "I'll be back, Melinda," she said. "I vow your remains will be buried with your family, and I'll tear down this house of grief."

DAUGHTERS OF THE DEAD
Rosemary Shomaker

Interstate 55's Exit 49 looked like a good place to leave the highway. A quaint town with river frontage, according to the map, was just the place to stretch my legs. After several hours on the road, I needed a driving break on this dreary February afternoon. Main Street delivered me to 120-foot-long observation deck with an expansive view of the Mississippi River. I could see a pristine brick path along the river, and I relished in the easy, although cold, walk that awaited me. I parked and marched briskly from the observation deck to a boat launch, noting the cannons, benches, and interpretive plaques along this path. On my return trip, I glanced at a mounted panel showing tousled boats amidst high waves. I pressed the "audio description" button and settled back on a bench to hear a narrative while the watery sun sank toward the horizon to close out the day. The audio's bland male-voiced introduction set the stage for an early 1800's account by Laurel and Lily Anderson.

"Andrew's cries awakened us that night," an elderly woman's voice began in a calm recitation. "Through a slight parting in the curtains separating our corner from their sleeping area, I saw father stroke his son's head while mother tried to nurse Andrew in bed, but he rejected that comfort. Lily, you stirred but dug deeper under the covers that December night. The new moon cast no light through the grease papered high window, but the shimmery light from the star-filled sky danced off of mother's right hand catching the creamy opalescence of her prized bracelet and ring as she tended Andrew.

"The advancing winter season usually meant that father boarded the windows, including the tiny window near the ceiling, to secure the home's warmth, but mother had asked that the roof aperture remain unblocked to allow in the sunny day and starry night light from the big Missouri sky. She

183

beseeched him to leave an opening so she could have the company of the Great Comet when she saw to Andrew's needs in the night."

A livelier woman's voice chimed in, "Ah, yes, Sister. Travelers told us news of the comet — that it had entered the skies as far back as March — but we in New Madrid saw it not until the end of August, and then only at dusk or dawn."

"Lily, this is my part of the story. Please wait your turn," the earlier voice directed. "Mother first viewed the Great Comet the morning of August 28th after laboring from the past morning to birth Andrew. She now rested with her infant boy and held the comet as a sign of celebration.

"Andrew's health maintained. By October when the comet was a spectacular blaze in the night sky, mother relaxed, feeling that this baby would survive, and that he had the glory of the heavens protecting him. Yet I stray from my story. Let me return to the night in the cabin," the voice I associated with Laurel said. "While you slid back to your dreams Lily, the light and the shimmer of mother's jewelry as well as Andrew's crying quickened my mind. I thought of my parent's special love that created and sustained you, Andrew, and me. The gold and opal ring and bracelet materially marked this love, and mother seldom removed these ornaments. In my mind, I heard father's proud recounting: 'My darling Elise,' he'd say in his fine deep voice, 'so sure was I of you when we began courting that I knew these family heirlooms would be yours. They were given in payment to my clockmaker forbearers and were said to be from the Habsburg Court. To mark my proposal, I gave you these jewels, and they adorned your breathtaking beauty. The opals glow like your smooth ivory skin heated by the warm blush of your vigor. The soft rose, blue, and light green of the jewels are as the ethereal colors invisible in the air until unmasked on the perfect canvas of your pale blonde hair.' Reminiscing those romantic words were the last pleasant thoughts of my life.

"Thunder-like commotion sounded. Giant rumbles assaulted my ears. My throat quavered at strong vibrations that I feared would rend the cabin. Cups and bowls clattered from shelves, and pots launched from the sideboard to the hearth. Andrew yelped twice more and then was unnervingly quiet. The shaking continued, and you, Lily, awoke.

"We piled into mother and father's bed. After several minutes, the quaking stopped. By then Father had donned his trousers and boots and had ventured out the door, rifle in hand. Our home bordered the western edge of town, just shy the smithy and village stable.

"He returned quickly saying, 'The ground quakes. My own father told me of earth shakings in Connecticut more than twenty years ago. I was but a tyke then. I don't myself remember.'

'What shall we do, Thomas?' asked mother.

'Stay close. Pray our walls stand,' he said quietly.

"Andrew remained silent but awake all night, his eyes huge. Twice more the ground shook that night as we huddled in one bed, and Andrew's small arms plied the air as if he sought balance.

"At the cusp of day as we were in various stages of sleep and wakefulness, a roaring again filled the air. Loud thudding nearby amplified the din of the ground shaking — chimney stones were dislodging, Father presumed. Mother sprang from the bed, her jewelry flickering like milky lightning as a section of wall behind their bed crashed outward. She shoved Andrew into my hands, his tiny arms pinwheeling. She pulled me upright while looping a fabric bag across my shoulder and loaded it with cloth squares, soft wool, and weed batting. Mother had my shoes under her arm as well, and these she slung around my neck to hang down my back by their laces as she covered me with a shawl and pushed me out the door into the street.

'Go! Go! This trembling threatens us all,' mother said."

At this pause — if I followed correctly, Laurel Anderson's persona — the voice representing Lily picked up the story.

"By the time you were in the street, father had lifted me from the bed, set me on the table, put my shoes and coat on me, and handed me blankets to carry. He turned to grab his tool satchel, rifle, dried meat and a lantern, and then pulled me out the door into a dark December morning. The air was chokingly gritty and grey.

"I turned to see mother swing her sewing bag bulging with fabric across her chest and then scoop apples and load flour, oil, salt and potatoes into a sack. This she slung onto her back and followed us into the street.

"I was unsteady on my feet as though still half asleep. Mother had hold of my arm now, and she pulled me painfully, scaring me. My disorientation and tottering, as well as mother's roughness, I later realized was due to the rolling ground and mother's quick moves to avoid gullies and chasms.

"Father had met our neighbor Mr. Fletcher in the street. Both men gathered their families and marched, all the while yelling to others in the street to head north away from town to the clearing past the smithy."

Lily stopped her account, breathless at the recollection.

Laurel continued, "I was behind you and mother, and I was afraid. I had no one to stabilize me, and I had to protect Andrew. The ground was shaking, and the choking dusty air smelled of ash, iron, and minerals. I felt sand stinging my skin, and I shielded my eyes and covered Andrew's face with his light blanket.

"In the clearing mother spread a heavy cloth, and we collapsed. Father and Mr. Fletcher went back to help James Smith lead the horses from the village stable into a paddock. Still the earth shook. Trees fell. Cabin walls fell. People arriving from near the river spoke of watery turmoil, high waves, and the destruction of boats and the town pier.

"The comet, peeking just above the horizon in the breaking dawn, stood witness. I see this all now with eyes older than my eight years," Laurel declared.

Lily concurred. "I was but six years old. I believe we age with each memory of the events, Sister. By the time Pastor Morton came to the clearing carrying old Mrs. Denhart, the men had started fires, more for comfort than for warmth since the air was eerily warm. Mother handed out blankets and heavy cloth, and families set up tent shelters."

"It was here that I put on my shoes," Laurel added. "I don't know how we got through those first weeks. As children, we did not know the details."

***

I leaned forward on the bench, wanting to hear more.

"The settlers of New Madrid had many boy children but few girls," interjected the flat male voice, breaking the narrative's dramatic pace.

"The sight of tow-headed petite Laurel and Lily Anderson in neat homespun jumpers, their pigtails tied with colorful cloth strips, made neighbors, tradesmen, and shopkeepers smile. Mr. and Mrs. Ruddel, their own children grown and living in St. Louis, were kind and doting on Laurel and Lily when they came to the mercantile. Mr. Smith sweating at his forge with his oldest two sons gladly took a break whenever Lily dipped him water and handed him a kerchief to dry his face. The old banker's wife Mrs. Biggs served Laurel tea when she delivered the curtains, dresses, and shirts she commissioned from Mrs. Anderson. Miss Guerin the schoolteacher appreciated the cheerfulness, eagerness, and manners Laurel and Lily brought to a classroom of impish and bored boys. The Anderson girls were the daughters of the town."

Here the direct firm voice portraying Laurel Anderson resumed, "The ground continued to shake, often violently, after December 16th. Even the

186

mildest of shudders alarmed most everyone as they looked about with trepidation, interrupted in their work on salvaging belonging and repairing homes, buildings, and boats. Quakes happened for weeks throughout the day and night — more than thirty each day. Some families left town.

"We stayed believing in the potential of our river town as a commerce hub situated for growth and prosperity. Mother optimistically said the small quakes were settling New Madrid, stabilizing the town's firmament. Her optimism bolstered the town.

"Mr. Fletcher and father combined efforts to weather the winter. They began repairs to our home so both families could do daily chores and eat in our cabin. They fortified the standing half of the Fletcher home to serve as sleeping quarters for us all.

"The quakes continued into January. The incessant tremblers kept nerves on edge. The warm winter, instead of being a blessing, bespoke a lack of normalcy visually evident by the landscape of snapped trees, wide gullies, sand and tar beds, and a changed river course.

"The tremors all day on January 22nd unsettled me. I could not sleep that night, all of us quartered in the Fletcher house, our family sleeping in a row — Lily, mom, Andrew, dad and me. Spastic rapid flickers of pale color in the mother's gems frightened me as her arm moved randomly in the dark, yet I was mesmerized by the silvery opals. The Great Comet ruled the sky less and less but had appeared at twilight. Through an unchinked gap in the wall, I could see the waxing moon.

"Daily activities were muted in the morning as we went about tasks after arising and moving to our cabin. Nearby father and Mr. Fletcher salvaged boards and logs from crumbling structures. Mid-morning the roaring of a fierce earth tremblor drove us out of the house.

'Go! Go! With blankets! To the clearing. Cover your faces,' Mother said, clutching Andrew."

Lily picked up the narration, "You and I were first in the street, and you dragged me choking through that awful, sand and dirt strewn air. The thuds of falling trees, the cracking of breaking boards, the tumbling of roofs and collapsing log walls silenced me with horror. Trees fell, crevasses opened before us, and sand and black ash filled the air as we fled town. The stink in the air was horrible.

"At the clearing, you shook and shook, even with blankets around you, although once again the air was unseasonably warm. You said nothing but your eyes were wide, pupils white-rimmed like a frightened horse.

"We walked around the clearing many times without finding mother, father, or Andrew. Pastor Morton saw our fear and prayed with us but would not let us return to our dilapidated house. Mr. Chisholm the barber, druggist, and quasi-doctor pulled us to a tent in the clearing and bade us lay down our exhausted heads. You sat as commanded by this gruff old man but ran from the tent when adults dispersed. I followed you. At our collapsed house, Mr. Skinner and a soldier barred your way. You pointed, but I could already see the glimmers of milky opals on a grey lifeless arm.

"Survivors cared for us over the next few weeks, I expect. I don't remember. The ground continued to shake, but that mattered not. My body felt empty, and you also appeared as a depleted vessel. The unremarkable sky held no grandeur, the Great Comet having disappeared. Kind people collected what they could from our ruined home and left several bags of belongings, including Andrew's swaddling and mother's sewing bags, with us.

"Mr. Chisholm busy with the business of doctoring and body disposal told us that day that father and the Fletchers as well as mother and Andrew were dead. He took mother's opal bracelet from his pocket and put it on your wrist. Her ring he fit on my thumb. He had us stay with him. Mrs. Saffray his housekeeper fed us, but each day he had us help him care for the injured and run his errands. Sadly and silently, we did this.

"The New Madrid settlers, fearing the ravage of the river and the danger of collapsing buildings, set up a camp quite a distance northwest of town. In the late afternoon, Mr. Chisholm allowed us time alone, and we'd sit on the banks of the changed river until dark, waiting for the stars to shine on the water and populate the lonely sky. He'd collect us at day's end for a cart ride back to camp. From town he could see us on the bluff, our opals catching sunset's rays directly or reflected off the river.

"On February seventh many survivors gathered in our ravaged town to welcome our native brethren. They came by land instead of canoe, the changing waterway courses rendering river travel unsafe. Ostensibly they brought food to trade, and but they really wanted to share their experiences of the quakes. Destruction marred their villages, and their pain and fear mirrored our own.

"You and I stayed behind some men but peered at the natives, especially at three basket-carrying serene women our mother' age. The meeting began soberly yet soon brimmed with hand clasping and excited pantomime. The persistent mild tremors were forgotten, or perhaps they had halted. The camaraderie eased our collective pain, and this Friday night we shared, ate, and slept at the old town center near the river in a show of wholeness and defiance together with our wild brethren. Mr. Chisholm wholeheartedly participated and conferred with the native leaders. Mrs. Saffrey brought food and bedding. Finding us well cared for by the tribal women, she added blankets to their soft animal skins for our comfort.

"I believed the crashing and whirring I heard and the sting of water I felt in the night's darkness to be a nightmare, but in a wakeful moment of horror under the waning quarter moon I understood the immediacy of the river's churning volumes and the earth's cleaving beneath my feet. The riverbank gave away, tall waves plucked us from our covers, and our lives ended in the river as we gagged on mouthfuls of silt, unable to breathe in the bubbling, thrashing water."

***

After a mournful pause the voice I now knew as Laurel said, "By peering into the Mississippi River from this northwest bank perhaps you can imagine our frontier-era town, now at the river's bottom. Earthquake inundation and unceasing river erosion destroyed it. Today's New Madrid it is a modest town of about 3,000 people — more than seven times the size of 1811 town. Boggy and marshy still, the land around the river's oxbow at New Madrid carries the dank odors and sharp mineral scents synonymous with the defilement and destruction of the winter of 1811-1812."

I marveled at the effectiveness of the audio interpretation. I rose from the bench and moved down the gentle bank closer to the dark water, resolving to learn more about Missouri's early history.

Lily spoke, "From Interstate 55 east to New Madrid and southeast to Reelfoot Lake an odd phenomenon is apparent. Silvery orbs tinged with the dark purple of pooled blood float over the area. Sprits or swamp gas? Mr. Fletcher. Mr. and Mrs. Ruddel. Miss Guerin. Mrs. Biggs. Mr. and Mrs. Anderson. Baby Andrew. You decide.

"Amidst the silver hovering lights, two ivory white oval shapes float. Their creamy iridescence and regular shape unconsciously draw your attention. They warn you of the capriciousness of this place and of the terrifying power of what lies beneath.

"So we leave you now, two orbs blinking in the twilight — mine the shining of an opal ring, Laurel's the glow of a lovely opal bracelet. We are the daughters of the dead. Our end came at the hands of New Madrid's epic trio of earthquakes."

My mouth agape, I saw small balls of whitish light over the river, and I witnessed two shimmering ivory shapes fade away. I backed up to the bench and lowered myself, needing to sit down. Curiously impactful tourism ploy for a small town, I marveled. I thought of activating the audio once more but decided against it. Oddly, I no longer noticed a historical sign near the bench. Confused and yearning for a strong cup of coffee, I walked to my car, got in, and locked the door. Upon ignition, my dashboard screen flashed the date: February 7, 2013.

CIRCLES IN THE DARK
Tommy B. Smith

It was in a small, isolated house in eastern rural Missouri, some distance off of Hillsboro Hematite Road and hundreds of miles from home, that Michelle Shore lay unconscious. Circles filled her dreams until she began to stir. Uneasily, she opened her eyes.

She was lying on a dirty floor. Besides that and the musty smell which filled her nostrils, the first thing she noticed was that the flashlight was beside her, still on, the only reason she could see anything at all.

Pressing a hand against her pounding head, she sat up. By the look of it, she was in what might have been some kind of bedroom, but it didn't have a bed anymore and was now strewn with trash and filth.

A mark across the wall caught her attention: a large, shakily drawn circle in red.

Michelle reached out, her fingers curling around the flashlight. She picked it up to aim it at the red circle.

It, along with the rest of her surroundings, confused her. Her mind worked to recall anything it could while the insistent throbbing in her skull vied to distract her. Not only did her head hurt, but the rest of her hurt as well, and her stomach was queasy. The foul smell of this place probably didn't help matters in the case of the latter. It took a few more minutes of sitting on the floor, feeling miserable and inhaling the forlorn bedroom's mildewy odor, before memories began to sprinkle down on the congested avenues of her mind.

Suddenly, she remembered the girl. When Michelle had first entered this bedroom, she saw the girl sitting against a wall of the room — right over *there*, Michelle recalled, looking over to one now-empty corner.

The girl, who Michelle guessed to be in her mid-teens, was dressed in dirty clothes. Her arms were wrapped around her knees. Her round eyes, ringed with black bags of fatigue, stared at Michelle from the instant she opened the door and shone in the flashlight.

Michelle's head pounded with renewed intensity, scattering the memory. She pressed her fingers against her temples, closed her eyes, and waited for it to desist. After several seconds, the hammering relented minimally.

With a slow shake of her head, Michelle climbed to her feet, and was hit by a momentary wave of dizziness. After a moment, the dizziness passed, for which she was grateful. She walked out of the bedroom.

She stood in a dark hallway with two doors on each side. At its opposite end, the hallway stretched into darkness.

She pointed the flashlight into that darkness and could make out the outline of a chair and a table. *The kitchen,* she thought, and her memory soon affirmed it. *Of course. That was how I got in here — I came through the front door and crossed through the kitchen.*

The door right across from her was open. Through it, she saw a dirt-caked toilet and a broken mirror with only a few shards remaining. In the corner of the bathroom was a small bathtub that was as dirty as the toilet.

She stepped in and flipped the light switch, which accomplished nothing — the place had no electricity.

While she glanced into the broken pieces that remained of the mirror, thoughts of the unusual girl returned to Michelle's mind, along with the image of her blinking in the flashlight's beam and pulling back against the wall.

Michelle had almost dropped the flashlight at that instant, but caught it just in time. "I'm sorry," she had muttered, and averted the beam. "I — I didn't know anyone would be here!"

The flashlight caught the large circle painted on the wall. This drew Michelle's attention from the girl for a few seconds, until the girl murmured something that Michelle couldn't quite understand and lowered her head to her knees to look down at the scummy floor.

"I mean, I was hoping someone would be here," Michelle added, "but the place looks abandoned. You see, I'm looking for a friend of mine that I haven't seen in a long time —"

The girl raised her head and lanced black eyes into Michelle. Michelle gulped and stepped back.

"I'm sorry if this light is bothering you," Michelle said, "but I can't see in here without it." Michelle looked around, nervous for the girl's direct stare. "Do you *live* in this place?"

"Who are you?" the girl asked at last in a voice that was faint but husky, as if she was almost hoarse.

"My name is Michelle."

Michelle didn't feel comfortable saying much more, but the girl kept looking at her. Thinking on it for a moment, she realized that if the girl did live here, Michelle was the one intruding — she probably owed a bit more of an explanation.

"Michelle Shore," she added. "I came out here looking for someone I used to know, years ago. Her name was Amanda, Amanda Irving. Do you know her?"

The girl looked at Michelle as if she spoke complete gibberish. Michelle studied the girl, and noticed for the first time that the girl's hands were covered in dried blood. A shard of broken glass was in her hands. How had Michelle not seen this earlier?

"You've cut yourself!" Michelle said, stepping closer. The girl's head jerked up, and she tensed.

What had happened then? Michelle struggled for an answer in her aching mind. Michelle had tried to help, and there had been an unexpected struggle, the girl thrashing — flinging Michelle backward with a sudden, powerful strength, the impact of the floor had come next, and that liquid sleep washing over her...

The flashlight trembled in Michelle's hand. Its beam slipped from her face to the dirty bathroom sink full of mirror shards. She half-stumbled out of the bathroom. She didn't know what was happening, but she knew one thing: she had to leave this place.

Through the kitchen was the exit route. She hurried down the length of the hallway, shining the light in front of her, but the sound startled her to a halt, and a great form crossed the flashlight's beam. The room went utterly dark.

Michelle gasped and backpedaled, almost stumbling. Startle became dread, and dread, with the acceleration of her heart's pounding, might soon turn to panic. *Something was in the kitchen. Something horrible.*

Michelle ran back up the hallway. She grabbed a doorframe and spun into one of the side doors, smacking the frame and whirling into darkness. Before she lost her footing altogether, she caught herself against a wall.

Her head still hurt, and now her arm ached after scoring against the doorframe, but these concerns fled Michelle's mind for the greater concern of that thing in the kitchen.

"What in the name of —" she whispered, and further words failed her. A voice in the dark answered her.

"You can see it now, too," came the girl's voice. Michelle pulled back and brandished the flashlight as if to defend herself from an attack, but she saw only the thin girl from earlier sitting there, leaning against the wall as she had been before.

Michelle shook her head, without a clue as to where she might begin.

"I saw — *something* — in the kitchen," Michelle managed. "What was it?"

The girl regarded Michelle in quiet. Michelle could still feel her heart pounding. She almost became angry at the girl's deliberation and opened her mouth to fire some impulsive reprimand at her for the delay, but the girl finally answered.

"Now you know the secret of this house," the girl's tone was neutral. "But I guess it isn't exactly a secret anymore." A sadness threatened to spill from her, Michelle sensed, but here, alone in the house of that unknown monstrous thing in the kitchen, the girl had mastered her emotions.

"We *have* to get out of here," Michelle whispered. The girl just looked at her.

"We can't," the girl replied.

Michelle stood still for a moment despite the strangeness of it all, how it appeared that, since her bout of unconsciousness, she seemed to have awoken in a different world from the one of before. After all, she hadn't seen the thing upon entering the house; why now? And *what was it?*

"There must be some way out," Michelle said, desperation leaking through her voice.

"Through the kitchen," the girl said. "That's the only way. The front door is on the other side of the kitchen."

Michelle stared at the girl. Tears threatened to spring forth. She held them back as best she could, but the combination of helplessness and frustration that poured through her was overwhelming.

She stopped, forced herself to take a slow, deep breath, and searched for a foothold on her sanity. "Amanda," Michelle said. "That was my friend's name. That's why I came here. What happened to her?"

Once again, the girl took a long look at Michelle. "There is no one else here. Just us and *it.*"

The girl wasn't making sense. This house didn't make sense! It was madness.

While there was still hope of saving herself, Michelle knew she had to try to escape. Her mind raced. How? The house had no windows, she remembered.

"Is there a back door?" Michelle asked, but she already guessed what answer she might get, if anything. To affirm this, the girl, her eyes still locked on Michelle's, gave another shake of the head.

Michelle turned to face the door that led back into the hallway. She had to try. She had to. What else was left? She couldn't stay here forever. Sooner or later, she would have to step into the kitchen and face it.

She thought, before she went back to that dreaded kitchen, to ask the girl one more question. "How long have you been here?"

The girl's answer: "Days."

The quiet girl was left behind in the room. Michelle's every step along that hallway brought a fiercer clamoring within her chest.

Possibilities assaulted her imagination. Trying to deny the fear only made its presence more powerful.

She faltered in her steps, but forced herself onward. She knew that if she stopped, she might not be able to continue.

The flashlight. It would see the flashlight!

In a hurry, Michelle switched off the flashlight. Everything went black. If the uncertainty had been stifling before, it was now asphyxiating.

She couldn't see a thing. Her ability to judge distance was lost with the extinguishing of her sole light source. She feared, beyond anything, the moment that she stepped into that kitchen, the domain of...

Whatever it was.

She took another step. As quietly as she could, she took another. The kitchen shouldn't be much further, she thought, and took another step.

An immense rustling sounded. She screamed. The thing in the kitchen came forward to meet her, and Michelle turned and ran.

A hard surface struck her. She staggered backward.

She caught her balance, felt around to lay a hand on an unseen wall, and in grasping about, made out the cobweb-ridden frame of the doorway. She grabbed it and rushed through.

She fell against a wall, listening, but could hear nothing but a ringing in her ears. Hadn't that creature been coming for her? She was confused.

She waited almost another minute before turning the flashlight back on. The light shone across the room to bring into pale illumination the familiar red circle painted upon the wall.

Michelle had been foolish to turn off the light, she realized. That *thing* — light or darkness made no difference to it. Somehow, she understood this, although she didn't understand why it never pursued her beyond the kitchen.

Maybe it wasn't there to catch her, swallow her or hurl her into some measure of unthinkable torment. Maybe it was there to keep her from leaving.

"I told you," the girl said. "There is no escape for us."

"I — I don't understand."

"How could you? How could either one of us? We're only human."

"And what is *it?*"

"I don't know, but I do know that it's a part of this house. When I first came here, like you, I didn't see it, but I felt something. I had a feeling about this house. I didn't know why. If only I had left right then. I still wonder, though. What if I had? Would I have been able to?" The girl shook her head. "Maybe I'll never know. I'm sorry. This sounds bad, but — I'm glad I'm not alone here anymore. The longer I stay here, the worse this place seems, and the harder it is for me to leave." She drew a shuddering breath, and Michelle saw in the girl, for the first clear time, a tangible fear. "You can feel it, can't you? The craziness in the very air of this place? Can't you feel it?"

Michelle looked around the room, from the red circle on the wall to the bits of broken glass scattered into a corner to the remains of the light fixture which hung from the ceiling. Bewildered and frightened still, Michelle thought for a moment of sitting down, but was reminded of the dried blood on the girl's hands and the piece of glass clutched in them.

Michelle decided to remain standing, and kept her distance. She didn't seem to be getting anywhere with her questions about the thing in the kitchen. She decided on another approach, both for her own hopeful benefit and to distract herself from thoughts of that monstrosity.

She crossed her arms and backed against a wall but kept both the room's sole door and the girl sitting on the floor in her line of vision. Her eyes still roaming, Michelle thought about snatching up a piece of that broken glass — to use as a weapon? What good would it do against a monster the likes of that in the kitchen? She didn't know. Nothing, probably.

"It is not of this world," the girl said. "Believe me."

"What do you know about it?" Michelle asked. Her eyes stopped their wandering and fell upon the teenage girl.

"Like you, I didn't see it when I first came here," the girl said. She looked toward the door with a pause. "It wasn't until my eyes adjusted to the inside of this house that I started to hear it. The first night, sleep was easy, but I dreamed of those circles, and after that, I couldn't leave. It's like, every time I closed my eyes, I would see the circles on the back of my eyelids. I couldn't stop thinking of them. I still can't. But do you know what's *really* weird?"

"The whole situation is weird," Michelle replied, "and that's an understatement."

"The weirdest thing of all is that I still have no idea what it looks like."

"The monster in the kitchen?"

"Yeah. I've never seen it. I've only heard it."

"I saw its outline," Michelle said. "It was — huge. Gigantic. It blocked the light of my flashlight. When I saw it coming, I ran."

The girl nodded. "I've seen a dark form, darker than the darkness in here. This place has no windows, you must have noticed, so that's..."

The girl looked up. "Really dark," she finished.

"But you couldn't describe the creature in detail?" Michelle pushed.

"No."

"You mentioned the circles," Michelle said. She surveyed the large red circle painted on the wall. "Well, *that's* a circle."

"I'm the one who painted it. I picked up this piece of glass, thinking I could defend myself, and then I realized how silly that was. That's when I cut myself. It wasn't long after that when I started painting. I've painted circles in every room so far, except for the kitchen. I don't know whether you've noticed."

"With your own blood?"

The girl didn't answer.

Michelle swallowed. "Why?"

"I'm trapped here. Trapped forever is my guess, and I can't think of much else while I'm here. I thought I could try to exorcise those circles from my mind in some way. This place is making me crazy."

"We can't stay here," Michelle said. "I have a life. I have a home, back in Kansas City — I have friends and family, people who count on me. I can't stay here forever."

"And just what," the girl said, "do you think you're going to do about it?"

"I'm going to get out of this place."

"You've already tried that."

"I'm going to try again. You said that the longer you stay here, the harder it is to leave. If I'm going to get out of here —"

The girl gave a soft laugh. It wasn't malicious; rather, it was resigned. By it, and the words which had come from the girl's mouth so far, Michelle knew that this lost girl had already given up all hope of escape.

"If I'm going to get out of here," Michelle repeated, "it's now or never. And you're coming with me."

"What? No. I can't."

"You have to. You can't stay here alone, with nothing to eat or drink, no way to survive. There is nothing here but us and it. You said so yourself."

The fear was still in Michelle, but also, there was outrage for her predicament and for the girl's acquiescence to defeat. Into this anger Michelle delved for everything she needed to battle her fear.

"You," she said to the girl, approaching, "are *coming with me from this place.*"

"No."

"Yes." The piece of glass in the girl's hands didn't even frighten Michelle at this point. Before the girl could blink again, Michelle slapped it out of the girl's hands. It nicked the heel of her hand in the process, and she fired a curse, seeing a trickle of blood forming on the edges of the cut.

She slid the flashlight under one arm, and crouched to grab the girl. With both hands, Michelle hoisted her to her feet.

"Please," begged the girl. "Don't make me go into the kitchen. Please."

"Your fear," Michelle whispered to the girl, holding her close, "is what is keeping you here."

Michelle went for the door, and dragged the girl along. The girl's efforts to resist only prompted Michelle to yank her along all the more roughly.

She entered the hallway. The girl fought with a sudden surge of panic and knocked the flashlight from Michelle's grip. It struck the ground and erupted into pieces.

Darkness consumed the hallway. The girl screamed.

Heedless, Michelle knew she couldn't stop now. She pushed along the blackness in the direction of the hallway's end.

The girl continued struggling, but she was too weak for lack of nourishment. She swung and managed to land a blow against Michelle's back, which stung, but Michelle ignored it.

Neither Michelle nor the girl could see a thing. Maybe that was for the best, Michelle thought, because she now suspected they were nearing the end of the hallway.

The girl began to cry. When Michelle's shoulder bumped the side of the doorway, she knew they were there. Her fear surged, and her doubt along with it.

When she heard the rustling, she almost lost it. The voice, Michelle's voice of indignant fury, propelled her from the back of her mind.

Keep going!

She gulped and ventured a meek step toward the kitchen. The girl dug her heels into the floor, grabbed the doorframe, and held on.

Michelle anchored a more secure grip on the girl and lifted her, finding her to be unnaturally light. She, even more than Michelle, had to get out of this place. This lit Michelle's resolve.

With the girl trembling in her arms, Michelle pushed forward. The heat of the kitchen startled her. It was an aspect she hadn't noticed before, another element which hadn't been present upon her entering the house, just like the monster itself.

The rustling stopped dead. The girl cried out. Michelle ran as fast as she could with the girl in her arms. She could only hope she wouldn't stumble, because she couldn't see, and because the creature was here.

The heat intensified. Even in the darkness, Michelle could discern the shapes. *Circles.*

She caught a glimpse of light, the tiniest trace of it beneath a closed door. She ran for the light.

The circles became larger. She tried her best to avert her gaze, but it seemed that wherever she looked, she saw the circles.

Michelle heard another scream, aware from some distant place that it was her own. Her legs worked of their own accord in the mad dash of fear, spurred on by Michelle's own deeply buried determination which she could only grasp at in her desperation to be free. The heat burned at a near-unbearable level.

"It's coming!" the girl screamed. *"The Zurzupwus!"*

The girl went limp in Michelle's arms. Against the overwhelming terror of the nightmare in the darkness, its circular eyes and that gaping circular maw, Michelle went for the light of escape and kicked hard against the front door until it crashed open, light flooding into the room and dissolving the circles from her vision as she tumbled away into the evening's fading sunlight.

Hours later, Michelle was still unable to relax or to escape the visions of that moment. She sat in Jefferson Memorial Hospital, her hands fidgeting in her lap. When the medical personnel approached, she looked up.

"Ma'am?" the older woman, dressed in gray with dark brown hair pulled into a bun, spoke.

"Yes?" Michelle was unable to hide the conflict and concern in her eyes.

"She's going to be all right."

Michelle sighed, relieved.

"Her parents are on their way. They want to speak with you. Could you please wait here?"

"Um, sure."

The woman left. Michelle looked around, nervous. She was glad the girl was all right, after the bout of unconsciousness that came with their escape from that cursed house.

The girl, Amy Baxter was her name (it was almost amusing in an unusual fashion to learn her name *after* they had been through their ordeal together), was a runaway. Her parents were no doubt horrified to learn that their daughter was in the hospital, but at the same time, overcome with relief that she was alive.

They knew nothing about the house of the — Michelle didn't want to think about its name. She didn't want to think about the circles. When she closed her eyes, though, that's all she could see. Circles.

Michelle knew that it still possessed that house.

She didn't want to talk to the girl's parents. She didn't want to try explaining what had happened. It would sound like madness. That's what it sounded like to her, and really, that's what it was: madness and fear greater than any human could bear alone.

At least Michelle had found Amy, and she was free, though not completely, because neither of them would be able to forget. As it was, Michelle doubted she would be able to sleep at night without those circles reminding her that *it* was still out there.

The hospital personnel had asked Michelle to wait for the girl's parents to arrive. Michelle hadn't thought of leaving before, but now that she did, it sounded much easier than trying to tell the story of that house and relive a terror best avoided in any way possible.

Amy would be fine. Michelle rose and left, and was soon back on the road.

She almost avoided the Hematite area altogether, but at the last second, she made a sudden decision. She stopped to purchase a gas can, and filled it before returning to the house of circles by night.

She had to do it, because if she didn't, she would never feel safe again.

The house was just as she had left it, abandoned, in disrepair, and smelling of filth and rot. She thought of the kitchen inside, its old chairs and table covered with dirt and insects, the way it had been when she first entered, and then the dark place of horrors that it had revealed itself to be.

She would never step into the house again. She would make certain that no one else ever did, either.

She walked the perimeter of the house with the red can, sloshing gasoline across the old wood on all angles of it until the can was empty. She struck a match, allowed the entire matchbook to catch aflame, and tossed it against the side of the house. Fire erupted, and Michelle hastened to her minivan and sped away.

The heat reminded her of the heat that had permeated the kitchen during those last moments. She glanced into her rear-view mirror, and saw the house burning in the distance behind her. Michelle hoped that the events of the day were behind her, as well.

Only one question remained. What of Amanda Irving?

Michelle had no answer. She could only hope that she had been wrong about the address, where it was clear that there lived no regular resident. She didn't want to think about any other possibilities.

Sometimes, we make friends, and sometimes those friends take different paths through life than we do. Sometimes, we never see them again. Maybe that's just the way it was. That's what she told herself, anyway.

While a frightened little girl woke to her parents' arrival in a white bed in Jefferson Memorial Hospital, and a house filled with smoke and fire and burned to the ground, Michelle drove north and then west, bound for her apartment, quiet, safe, and familiar, which waited for her back in Kansas City.

GRANDPA'S STORY
Curtis Thomas

I never much liked visits to my grandparents' house. For one, if we were there, my cousins were there, and my brothers and I didn't have much in common with them. We enjoyed video games and books, they enjoyed guns and dead animals. Something of a bridge to gap there, conversation-wise. Plus it smelled kind of funny.

There was one highlight to going to my grandparents' house, though. Something I never claimed to love then but cherish now, looking back into the haze of the past. Those were my grandpa's stories.

He'd be in his recliner, feet propped up, hands folded across his belly. His TV would usually be on, though turned down; newscasters or hunting experts would provide the background music to his tales. We'd be talking about who-knows-what, and then, without any warning or introduction or disclaimer, he would start telling a story.

"I was about you all's age, I figure. Summertime. That meant working the farm, starting at four in the morning." Our eyes would widen in horror. "Had to take care of the cattle – make sure they were watered and all. Then me and my brother would bale hay for most of the morning, before it got too hot out.

"But, come the afternoon, we'd usually have some time to ourselves. Most days we'd play tag or football or wrestle in the yard. Just fooling around, you know. We didn't have video games and 600 channels on the TV and computers to keep us inside all day." He said this with a glance towards my brothers and I. We kept our eyes in our laps, guilt and judgment brought to bear on our heads.

He'd continue. "Some days, though, a girl about my age would come down from the next farm over. I could never say why – always seemed like she hated my guts, the way she teased me and scolded me and wrinkled her nose at me. And I teased her right back, sometimes even going so far as throwing sticks and pebbles at her." He'd laugh as he said this, a laugh brought up from deep in his chest, a laugh that would shake his belly. "Not hard, 'course. Just to bug her. I guess she had nothing better to do at home, though, 'cause she'd just keep coming by.

"Now, there was another house on the other side of our property. Old one. Real big, too. It'd been abandoned for years – boarded up, paint peeling like a bunch of old scabs, a few holes in the roof

"I didn't know much about who lived there, but what I did know was that moaning would float up from it at night when the wind was strong, and the other kids would talk about how it used to be an insane asylum. The old kind, the ones where they'd shove 'em all in a dank basement and leave them to starve and claw at each other. Others were closer to the truth, and said a family used to live there, and that the mother went crazy one night and stabbed her husband and five children to death with a meat thermometer. Whatever the story, most agreed it was haunted. I didn't believe the stories, of course. I was too smart for that.

"Well, this old house came up one day when this girl was over. We started arguing about whether or not we thought there were ghosts. She believed in them, she said. They were in the Bible.

"I remember laughing, throwing a clump of dirt at her. I said, 'The Bible? There ain't no ghosts in the Bible.' Granted, I hadn't read much of the thing, and I didn't pay much attention in Sunday school, but I think I'd remember any ghost stories in our lessons.

"That didn't go over well. I don't know which exactly, but she started citing verses, and I just kept laughing and throwing dirt at her. She dodged them, but she was getting mad. I guess I was too. Eventually, she said, 'Well, if you're so sure there ain't ghosts up there, I s'pose you won't have any trouble staying the night up in that old house, now would you?'

"At first I told her I wasn't gonna sleep in a drafty, creaky old house just to prove her wrong. But then she started calling me chicken and sissy, and that got me pretty mad. I knew there weren't ghosts, and I sure as hell wasn't a chicken."

We would all squirm in delight when he cursed. He didn't do it often, and Grandma would have raised some hell of her own had she heard it, but it was one of our favorite parts of his storytelling.

"'I'll stay in that old house, then,' I said. ' One whole night, by myself.'

"And I did.

"I told my parents I was staying at a friend's house a few miles down the road. Around dusk, as the sun was dropping below the ground, that girl came stomping up the drive to walk me over there. She said it was to make sure I kept my word, but I think she was just a little bit scared for me. I would have died by a rusty spike to the gut before I admitting it, but I was pretty scared, too. We cut across a nearby field. Soon enough, there it was, looming up out of the ground like a sore.

"It sat there, frowning at us, silent. Its giant windows were shattered, the remaining jagged teeth blood red in the setting sun. The front doors had been removed – where they should have been was only a gaping black hole. You couldn't see a thing inside. We were about thirty feet away when she stopped walking. By then it was getting dark.

"'Well,' she said, 'you'd better head on in there. And if I find out you didn't stay the whole night, you'll be sorry. I'll tell everyone at school what a wuss you are.'

"I told her she didn't have to worry about that. I wasn't a wuss. Or a chicken. Then, trying to look braver than I felt, I stuck my chin up in the air and marched straight into the darkness. I didn't even look back. 'That'll show her,' I remember thinking.

"I walked about a third of the way into the foyer before stopping, trying to get my eyes to adjust to the darkness. It took a while, but the sky was clear and despite it being a sliver of a crescent, the moon gave off enough light.

"If the outside had looked rough, the inside was even worse. Smashed furniture and rubble lay thrown around the house. Broken bottles, probably the work of some older kids, sneaking up there to have a few drinks and fool around, had been tossed into one corner. There were drapes against the windows that were torn to shreds, more hole than fabric. They swayed in the cool night breeze.

"Right in the middle of the room was the biggest staircase I'd ever seen. It led up to a landing about half the size of the foyer, where doors and halls led deeper into the house. I listened carefully for any moaning, but the only sound was the soft rustling of the drapes. I wasn't much comforted, though. There was still plenty of nighttime left.

"I figured I'd better find someplace I could lay down for the night. I wasn't gonna stay in that big ol' drafty foyer. I walked 'round past the stairs, thinking I'd start with the first floor. Off to the left was a hallway. It was pitch black, but on the other side I could see the silvery-soft glow of moonlight.

"It led to a fancy dining room. A huge chandelier hung above a long, long table. Cobwebs clung to the thing, so many they almost touched the table.

"Another door and I was in the kitchen. Two big wood-burning ovens, counters that went on forever. There was another door, on the other side of a rusted icebox. It looked even older and more decrepit than the rest of the house.

"Out of all that cookware that old kitchen must've had back in its time, there was just one thing left. Something that gave me the willies and sent me straight back through that dusty dining room and back down that pitch-black hall.

"A knife, crusted over with something dark enough to be blood, stuck into a countertop. Big one, too. Just sitting there. Felt like the empty kitchen had been built especially for that knife – protecting it, like the cove of trees I imagine surrounded Arthur's sword when it was still stuck in that stone.

"I couldn't tear my eyes from it. And then it was silent. Mind, it had already been quiet as death, but this was something else. Like I'd suddenly gone deaf and could feel the lack of sound. And then, just as quick, voices broke through the deafness. Whispers calling out for blood and pain, and then there was this wailing, like a hundred thousand hearts had just been broken, and a scream that made my teeth shatter to the point of cracking. My stomach leaped up past my eyeballs and I split, just as that bloodied knife began to quiver in its resting place.

"So I was back in the foyer, out of breath and scared out of my britches. Damn hallucinations,' I said to myself."

We squirmed in our seats again, caught between the thrill of the "damn" and the stomach-churning fear of the knife and the scream.

"It was darker now, or it seemed that way to me. I headed up the giant staircase. I'd had enough of the first floor for a while.

"The upstairs hallway led further into the house to either side. Both were dark, but I had brought a box of matches with me. I headed down the right hand side on a whim. When it got so dark I couldn't see my feet, I struck a match. The flickering light barely reached the walls and stretched about a step ahead of me.

"There was a door up ahead and to my right. My match went out, singeing the tops of my fingers before I threw it to the ground. And, as if on cue, soon as the darkness swallowed me up that wailing echoed across the house. It sent goose bumps racing down my arms. It grew faint, and then was gone.

"I fumbled as I tried to light another match. The little flame brought nothing but uncertainty to the surrounding darkness. I stood there for a spell, too scared to move, knowing somebody was going to walk out of the blackness any second. But nobody did, and I was able to convince myself it was the wind, or a stray cat outside. I tried the door – locked up.

"The others were, too. I finally reached the end of the hallway. A simple wooden door stood against the far wall, a clown's face painted on the front.

"It was a bedroom. A small one, but with enough space for a little bed, a bookshelf, a nightstand, and a little rocking chair in the corner. They all looked worn with age. Covered in dust, too.

"It looked as good a spot as any though, so I threw my blanket on the floor and closed the door. I lit a match to get another look at the room. It must have been for a young kid – it was covered in old circus decorations. A parade ran 'round the top of the walls, lions standing on their hind legs, front paws on shoulders in front of them, bears, elephants, men in top hats, clowns, all marching in line.

"There was an overturned picture frame on the little night stand. I picked it up and lit another match. Four faces peered back at me in the orange glow. A man, what must have been his wife, a little girl not older than two, and a boy about my age. All smiles, standing in front of a big painted sign that read 'The Farrelli Family Circus – Magic and Wonder for All.' I set the picture back down.

"I was tired and cold. I lay down on the blanket in an attempt to sleep. I lay there for a lifetime but I must've nodded off at some point because something woke me up. I shivered.

"I wasn't sure what had woken me. I thought I remembered dreaming, and that maybe the crying in my head had done it. I remembered the moaning from earlier and shivered again.

"But it couldn't have been a dream because just then, as I sat in the darkness, too scared to breathe, I heard it again. A soft crying. A sniffling sort of crying. The kind you get made fun of for doing at the schoolhouse after you've been whipped.

"A girl was standing in the corner, by the rocking chair. Little girl, younger than I was, holding a teddy bear against her chest. I'd be lying if I told you I didn't jump. She didn't seem to notice though. A soft glow like moonlight surrounded her. I stepped toward her.

"She didn't look up 'til I was close. Her eyes were brimming with tears.

"'What's the matter?' I asked. She didn't say anything, just kept sniffling. But she did move her teddy bear.

"Dark, dark red. She'd been hiding a bloody gash in her chest. It looked deep. My eyes must've looked like a couple dinner plates.

"'We need to get you to a doctor,' I said, reaching for her arm and trying not to lose my cool. She backed away, shaking her head, crying a little louder. 'C'mon, we have to. Don't it hurt?' She shook her head again.

"'Knife hurt,' she said, 'But Bubby okay.'

"'A knife? A knife did this to you?' Then, 'You don't look okay to me.'

"She just kept saying it, over and over. ' Knife hurt. Bubby okay. Knife hurt. Bubby okay.' I didn't have a clue what she was talking about.

"But I remembered the bloody knife in the kitchen and the wailing coming from the basement. Almost seemed like it wasn't me remembering but someone remembering for me.

"'The knife in the kitchen?' She bobbed her head up and down. 'Okay then. So who's Bubby? Not you?'

"But she only shook her head and kept up the same line she'd been repeating, frustration creeping into her voice. ' Knife. Bubby okay. Bubby!', speaking as if it should have been plain as day who Bubby was. I could tell she was getting mad at me. She glanced around, trying to come up with some way to make me understand. It was then she saw the picture, grabbed it, and pointed to the boy. 'Bubby,' she said. Because I can be a bit dim-witted at times, it wasn't until then I noticed the girl standing in front of me was the same little girl in the picture.

"'So that's Bubby,' I said. The wailing echoed in my head again. 'And is this Bubby in the cellar? Is he downstairs?'

"She nodded.

"I swallowed.

"'Okay. And . . . you want the knife in this Bubby? Like it was to you?'

"Then she really lost it. Started crying at the top of her lungs, shaking her head enough to make me dizzy just watching."

My grandpa scrunched his bushy eyebrows together and crossed his eyes at that point, making us laugh. It wasn't that funny, but we needed something to laugh about and were thankful for the excuse.

He smiled and continued.

"'Then what?' I asked. 'What do you want?'

She was really getting pissed. 'Bubby okay! Bubby okay!'

"A light was starting to come on in my head, slowly, like the sunrise on an ice-cold morning. 'You want me to tell this Bubby that you're okay?'

She nodded again, up and down and up and down.

"I didn't understand why she wanted me to, but if she didn't want to go to the doctor then I figured I'd pass her message along. Maybe I could get this Bubby, whoever he was, to get her some help.

"Okay, little girl. I'll go tell him. You stay put, all right?'

"As I turned away, I glanced out the window. There wasn't a star in sight, much less the moon.

"I shivered, grabbed my matches, leaving the little girl behind, pretending not to notice that she was still glowing, softly.

"The house was quiet and dark as ever. I ran down the hallway, my eyes closed most of the way. I made my way back down the stairs and headed for the kitchen. Everything seemed…still. Not that anything was moving before, but now the stillness seemed intentional. Not even the ratty curtains moved. I ran down the foyer hallway, straight into the kitchen. And there it was – that old, bloodstained knife, stuck into the countertop.

"As I stepped towards it, that moaning cut across the stillness of the place, echoing off the walls. I took a deep breath but couldn't stop the shiver that raced up my spine. I figured I might need something to protect myself, in case things went bad, so I reached for the bloodstained handle.

"Soon as I touched it something entered my brain. I don't really know how to describe it. It was like a gnarled root wormed its way into my head, right to the center of my skull. And then it was like that root opened up, bloomed inside my head, but instead of petals there were pictures, and sounds, and smells.

"I saw a boy – same boy as in that picture, in fact. He was holding a knife. He threw it, fast as an arrow. Then things got fuzzy, and I felt a scream – felt, mind, not heard, it was something that dug its way into my bones, clawed behind my eyes – and there was the girl on the floor with the red of blood pooling around the boy's feet. He ran into the inky darkness.

"It was over, and the root pulled its way back out of my head with a snap. I was drenched in sweat and panting, the knife still in my hand.

"I didn't know how I saw what I saw. But I'd seen it, and it made me mad. I was supposed to tell that guy that everything was okay? After he'd knifed that little girl and ran away like a coward? I had a better idea. One involving that same knife.

"I pulled it from the counter. It felt wrong in my hand, like I was holding a severed arm, but I needed it. Another moan, this one softer, came up from the door behind me. The one that lead into the cellar.

"I stood at the door for what felt like an hour, holding that knife. Breathing fast and sweating. I almost talked myself out of it, but that girl kept popping up in my head, and the picture of her dying, and that scream that made my joints itch.

"So I opened the door. A wooden staircase dropped down into the darkness below. I pulled the matchbook out of my pocket, struck one, and stepped inside. The little flame barely gave me enough light to see down the step ahead of me, but it would have to do. I could feel the darkness holding its breath.

"I reached the bottom of the stairs. It smelled like dirt and something that had been dead a long time. Moldy and rotting. I lit another match. Out of the corner of my eye, I saw something move. I raised up the knife, but I'd be a liar if I said my arm wasn't shaking.

"I could hear breathing now. Labored, raspy breathing. Faint, too. Then darkness again, and I fumbled to strike another match, my own panicked breathing drowning out the other. I finally got it struck. I screamed.

"He was inches from my face. Or it. A shadowy thing, eyes pale yellow like two tiny moons. No mouth, no nose, no nothing. Just those eyes surrounded by shadow. I tried to say something, to ask what it was. I couldn't get the words out. I just lifted the knife, hoping it would speak for me.

"When the shadow saw that rusted, bloody thing in my hand, its moon-eyes grew twice as big, and it shrieked. It moaned and screamed and screamed some more, tearing at its face, beating itself. I tried to back away, to run back up the stairs, but then it was gone and then it was there again, only right on top of me, pinning me to the ground, its hand wrapped around my throat. My match had long since burned out, but I could still see its pale eyes in front of me. Then, like lightning, the shadow was gone and the pale, glowing face of the boy was in front of me, angry or sad I couldn't tell, but only for an instant before the shadow swallowed it back up.

"The anger I had felt after seeing him kill that little girl came pouring back out of my chest. I struggled, but I couldn't breathe, much less move. It squeezed, tightening its grip, bringing tears to my eyes. I tried to pry his hand off but couldn't. I squirmed and kicked and beat against the shadow but it didn't loosen its grip. I started to black out.

"But the knife was still in my hand. I squirmed, fought against the weight of the darkness, fighting to stay awake at the same time. Just when I felt myself going, when I thought I was gonna die there on the dirt floor of that cellar, my arm came free of my side. I plunged that old knife right into the thing's belly. He let go of my neck, howling and screaming like the wind through stubborn trees. I twisted, pushed the knife up to the hilt, felt something warm flow across my hand.

"I was running on adrenaline. It was kill or be killed, and the hunter in me wanted to make sure it was dead. So I stuck him again, in the only place I could see him. Right between those yellow eyes.

"The root wormed its way back into my head and the pictures bloomed again. It was the boy. This time I could tell that he was on a stage. He bowed at a crowd of people, who hushed and settled into their seats, waiting. A drumroll started up somewhere backstage as the boy reached for a knife. Not the one now stuck in his head, but similar. He took a breath, and, faster than I could follow, flicked it like a dart and sent it spinning across the stage and into a large target on an easel – bull's-eye. The crowd clapped, and he bowed.

"He took two steps back, grabbing another knife. A breath, a pause, and then a flicker of motion. A second knife quivered in the target, right next to the first. More applause, louder this time. A whistle echoed from somewhere in the back of the crowd.

"Another two steps back. He was on the opposite side of the stage now, as far from the target as he could get. He picked up a third knife – the same knife I had just stuck between his eyes moments ago. He took a breath. The crowd tensed in anticipation. I did too.

"He threw it, but as he did so a shout came from offstage. Sounded like "Bubby." The noise made his eyes move from the target for a second. Just a second. But it was enough.

"The knife went long, whizzing past the target. The scream, the one from earlier, burrowed down to my bones once more. She came stumbling out from behind the curtain – the little girl, clutching the knife, blood running down her front.

"The boy cried out and ran to her. She fell into his arms, and, as tears fell down his cheeks, onto her colorless face, she died. Things started to get fuzzy again, but I thought I saw angry faces surround the boy as he got up, angry faces that ran after him into the darkness.

"I stepped away, panting, the knife lodged in its head. Slowly, the eyes faded away and darkness swallowed me up again. I couldn't believe what I'd done. I told the darkness that I was sorry, that I didn't know it was an accident, that I'd made a mistake. And, not knowing if there was anything left to listen to me, I did what I should have done from the start. I passed the little girl's message along. I told the dark what she said – that she was okay, that she wanted him to know it. Nothing but a quiet dripping somewhere in the distance was my answer.

"I just wanted to leave. Go home and crawl in bed and forget I ever took that stupid dare. But it wasn't over. Not quite yet.

"A strange whistling sound filled the dark cellar. It started softly, but it grew louder, and louder, until it made my legs vibrate and my head throb. I lit another match – I was almost out, but I wanted to be ready for whatever else was coming my way. The pale-eyed shadow was gone, with only that bloody old knife laying there in the dirt. Only it wasn't bloody anymore – it looked brand spanking new. Gleaming in the light of my little firestick.

"And then he came walking into the light. It was the boy, looking just as he did in that picture upstairs. He picked up the knife and tucked it into his britches. I backed away, looking around for something I could use as a weapon, finding nothing but dirt.

"My match went out.

"I scrambled to light another. When I did, the boy was right next to me, tears streaming down his face.

"I said the first thing that came to mind. 'She says she's okay,' I told him. 'She wanted you to know.'

"There were still tears in his eyes, but I guess they were the good kind, because he was smiling and nodding. 'Thank you,' he whispered.

Before I could say anything else, he ran past me and up the stairs. Not wanting to be alone in that dingy place any longer than I had to, I turned to follow.

"He was nowhere to be seen when I made it back up to the kitchen. I figured there was one place, odds are, where I'd find him. I headed for the little bedroom. No moaning echoed down the halls this time.

"But I was wrong. The room was empty but for the early morning sunlight. I went to gather my stuff and found a little locket resting on my blanket. It had a bear engraved on the front, balancing on a ball. I couldn't say how, but I knew that girl wanted me to take it.

"I had spent the night in that old house like I said I would, and I was ready to go home. I headed back down the hallway one more time, it being far less scary now that the morning sun was filling it. The foyer was almost cheerful looking, though the tattered curtains and smashed bottles did their best to balance things out. I practically ran down that staircase, taking them two at a time, and bolted out the door.

"I shouldn't've been surprised, but there she was – that neighbor girl, standing there with her arms crossed, up at the crack of dawn to make sure I hadn't chickened out. I strutted up to her, chest puffed out in what I thought was a pretty tough look. She didn't seem impressed.

"'Well,' she said. 'Were there ghosts or weren't there?'

"I stared at her for a good long while before I answered. 'Nope,' is all I said. I smiled, knowing that would tick her off.

"I don't know what compelled me to do what I did next, but then I held my arm out, locket glistening in the early morning light. 'Found this old locket, though. I don't need it.'

"I think that surprised her. She mumbled a thank you as she cautiously took it from my hand. But it only took her another second or two to put her guard back up. 'But if there ain't ghosts in there then what's causing all that moaning?'

"'Stray cats,' I said. 'I scared 'em off though.'

"She huffed, did an about-face, and marched off toward home. I did too, after one more look at that big, shabby house. The broken windows looked more like a toothy grin that morning than any kind of grimace. When I turned to leave, I could have sworn I saw what looked like two kids, arms around each other, out in the field. Watching the sunrise. But I blinked, and no one was there, so I walked home and was sound asleep before I even stepped into my room.

Grandpa laughed at this point, and leaned back in his La-Z-Boy. Just then, my grandma walked in. "Is he filling your heads with his nonsense?" she asked as she passed around a plate of homemade Rice Krispy treats. "Don't believe a word he says. It's all a bunch of baloney."

As she leaned over to offer me one, I noticed something gold handing off her neck. It looked like a locket, and though I couldn't be sure, and there might have been a bear engraved on it, balancing on a ball.

My grandpa's eyes twinkled. "I was lying to you then, Grandma," he said. "But honest to God, I'm telling the truth now!" And he laughed, and laughed, and laughed.

GHOST IN CELESTIAL BLUE
Donna Duly Volkenannt

On a warm day in late September, Marie shakes off a chill when the tour bus exits the highway. Her eyes widen as landmarks of her old North St. Louis neighborhood spring into view. Like a runaway dog coming home to die, Marie is returning to the place where she first saw the ghost.

Fifty years ago, her hair was long and dark, her body lean and limber. Now, she's silver-haired, overweight, and has a weak heart, but her desire to see the spirit once more burns strong.

To soothe her jittery stomach, she sucks on a peppermint. Thumbing her crystal rosary, she prays, "Hail Mary, full of grace, the Lord is with thee. Blessed art thou among women . . . ."

Katie, the tour guide, taps a microphone, interrupting Marie's prayer, "May I have your attention, please?"

Two dozen senior citizens men snap to attention.

The guide begins, "At the top of the hill on the driver's side you can see the Bissell Mansion, where we'll be eating lunch."

Goosebumps race across Marie's shoulder blades at the thought of reliving the experience that has haunted her for half a century.

While passengers gawk, Marie finishes her Hail Mary. "Pray for us sinners now and at the hour of our death. Amen."

The guide grabs a clipboard. "But first, we'll check out some other famous St. Louis landmarks. Straight ahead sits one of only seven historic standpipe water towers left in the United States. Three are located in St. Louis, and we'll visit two today."

Katie directs the driver down East Grand. Lumbering over the wide street, the bus passes debris-strewn lots with boarded-up brick buildings overtaken by tangled bushes, tall grass, and graffiti. Marie closes her eyes and remembers the street as it used to be: a Tom Boy Store, a bakery, and girls playing double Dutch on sidewalks in front of tidy yards with lush rose gardens.

Katie reads, "What you're seeing now is the Grand Avenue Water Tower, which, because of its age and white coloring, is also known as the Old White Water Tower. Constructed in 1871 under the direction of Thomas Whitman, the brother of poet Walt Whitman, Old White has been described as the only perfect Corinthian column of its size in the world."

After taking a sip of water, she continues. "In the 1920s and 30s, beacons were placed on top of the tower to direct pilots to Lambert Field. According to legend, Charles Lindbergh once used the lights to find his way home after flying in a Mississippi River fog."

The bus idles along a curb, and Katie drones on about the tower's staircase, cost of construction, and renovation. With sunshine on Marie's face, she visualizes the not-so-famous landmarks that shaped her childhood.

On the corner of East Grand and 20th Street, Pete's Pool Hall once stood. Pete's was the place where neighborhood bad boys sporting Brylcreemed duck butts drank cold beer and flirted with fast girls who smoked minty Newports and wore tight sweaters and bright lipstick.

Back in high school, a teenager who hung around the pool hall disappeared; her body was found near the Bissell Mansion. The neighborhood was terrified. Children were kept inside, and Marie had nightmares for years.

To keep her mind occupied, she focuses on other memories. The empty lot across the street was once home to Velvet Freeze. The busy ice cream parlor everyone called Velvet was a favorite after-school gathering place for Marie and her girlfriends, who giggled about boys while they slurped fountain cherry cokes.

Velvet was also the place where, after Sunday morning Mass on November 24, 1963, a woman ran inside shouting, "Some guy named Jack Ruby just shot and killed Lee Harvey Oswald in Dallas."

When the bus stops, Katie announces, "Now's the time to take pictures."

Marie and a few others step into the late morning sun. While cameras and Smart phones click away, she wanders down the block. Standing in front of the former Most Holy Name of Jesus Church, she chokes back tears and says, "Such a waste."

Like Marie, the once beautiful church is a shell of its former self. In the 1980s, the century-old Irish parish church was desanctified and sold by the archdiocese. The rooftop statue of Christ on the cross -- with the Blessed Mother and Mary Magdalene weeping at his feet -- has been lopped off. Struggling to catch her breath, Marie re-boards.

At the intersection of Blair and Bissell Avenues, the guide announces, "Here's the Bissell Water Tower, also known as the New Red Water Tower, the tallest n St. Louis. Built in 1886 and designed in the form of a Moorish Minaret . . ."

While Katie relays details about doorways, the spiral staircase, and lookout platform, Marie recalls childhood days when she raced up Blair from her house on John Avenue, past corner taverns and confectionaries to play at Gloria's.

Marie and Gloria met at in Holy Name School, where Marie was the new kid in sixth grade. One of the nicest girls in class, Gloria invited Marie to pajama parties at the mansion. It was during one of Gloria's PJ parties that Marie saw the ghost.

When the bus parks in the Bissell Mansion parking lot, chills run down her spine. In the crowded dining room, a server ushers Marie, another woman, and a man to a small corner table. When Marie starts to place her purse on the empty chair, the man plops his USMC Vietnam Veteran cap there, claiming the territory as his own. After the couple introduces themselves as husband and wife, Marie tells the former Marine, "My late husband spent a tour in Vietnam. And some of my classmates died there."

"I did two tours," he says then asks about her husband's branch and duty station.

"He was in the Air Force, stationed at Cam Ranh Bay."

"Easy duty," the former Marine says before slathering butter on a hot roll.

After drinks are served, Marie's hand trembles. To calm her nerves she slides a pill into her mouth and takes a gulp of iced tea. She picks at her salad while chatting with the vet's wife about the dining room's chandelier, fireplace mantle, dark woodwork, and pocket doors. By the time the main course arrives, her appetite is gone.

While servers clear the tables, Katie picks up a microphone. Over clinking glasses and silverware scraping against dishes, she announces, "Now that we're done eating, it's time for the most exciting part of our tour."

A tall man wearing a white polo shirt rubs his salt and pepper beard. Katie points to him and says, "I'd like to introduce our host, Mr. Peter Heim. Pete is part of the group that owns the mansion. He's going to share some history about the place, including tales about things that go bump in the night."

"Welcome to Bissell Mansion," the host begins.

Marie's stomach rumbles, so she chews an antacid while Pete recounts the story of Captain Lewis Bissell and his distinguished military family, including their connection to Lewis and Clark, President Thomas Jefferson, and westward expansion.

Wishing she hadn't drained that second glass of tea, her mind is on the bathroom, but Pete continues, "Bissell lived in this house for more than four decades and died here in 1868. Over the years, the building has changed hands a number of times, and despite a few close calls, it has been saved from the wrecking ball."

Marie wrings her hands when one of the tourists asks, "What can you tell us about the ghosts?"

Pete says, "According to legend, Captain Bissell wanders around, keeping an eye on his property. But he's not the only ghost that's been spotted. A mysterious woman dressed in a long white gown has been spied inside the mansion. Some speculate she's one of Bissell's wives."

Another asks, "Are the spirits good or bad?"

"Both have been described as friendly, but strange events occur whenever they're around."

"What kind of events?" Katie asks.

"The most common are items being moved around. Wine glasses fall off shelves or disappear then reappear days later unbroken."

The marine vet nudges his wife and says, loud enough for everyone to hear. "Sounds like somebody's got a drinking problem."

When his wife glares at him, he says, "There's no such thing as ghosts."

"Ah, we have a skeptic," the host says. "I used to be one myself."

The vet pushes out his chair and searches underneath the table. "What happened to my hat? I know I put it on that chair."

His wife whispers, "You probably left it on the bus. Stop being rude."

"I'm going out for a smoke." He stomps off.

Marie glances at the empty chair, where she remembers he laid his hat. In its place sits the spirit Marie met decades ago. The spirit's still golden-blond hair is held back with a silk ribbon, and she wears the same celestial blue dress. The girl smiles and points to the man's cap, which is on the floor behind a potted plant.

Overcome by the sight of the ghost who saved her life, Marie's throat constricts. She takes deep breaths, hoping to calm her fears.

While Pete hands out brochures about the mansion's dinner theater schedule, he asks, "Any more questions before your bathroom break and tour?"

A man asks, "Was anyone ever murdered here?"

Pete shrugs and shuffles his feet. "Our murder-mystery theater productions aside, there is one unsolved homicide connected to the mansion.

Back in the mid-1960s, the body of a teenage girl was found on the grounds. Days before the girl's death, a boarder who had been living in the mansion was evicted for being a Peeping Tom. A witness identified him as talking to the girl the night she was murdered. The boarder was arrested, and everyone was certain he was the killer, but police didn't have enough evidence to charge him."

Someone asks, "So, he got off Scott free?"

"Not exactly. A few days after his release his body was discovered floating in the Mississippi. Police suspected the girl's father exacted his own form of justice, but they couldn't prove that, either."

Marie blurts, "What do you know about the girl in the blue dress who haunts the mansion?"

"Not much." Pete puts on his glasses and peers at her. "Have you been here before?"

Marie's face flushes. For moral support, she turns to catch a glimpse of the girl, who's vanished. "I grew up not far from here."

"Can we talk afterward? I love hearing stories from people who lived in the neighborhood."

"Of course." Marie stands and picks up her purse.

"Listen up, people," the tour guide claps her hands. "If you want to see more of the mansion, you've got twenty minutes before the bus leaves."

While tourists line up to use the restroom on the main floor, Marie climbs the wooden staircase to the tiny bathroom on the second story. At the top of the stairs, she pauses to catch her breath before turning the antique doorknob and opening the door. After relieving herself, she walks to the pedestal sink, washes her hands and splashes water in her face. From the corner of an eye, she glimpses a swirl of blue.

"Hello," Marie says, "I never got a chance to thank you."

The ghost's eyes sparkle.

"Do you remember the night we met?"

The spirit leads her to the narrow window overlooking the side of the house with a distant view of the Mississippi River.

Marie says, "It was a hot night in August during one of Gloria's sleepovers. I woke up to use the bathroom. When I walked in, you were looking out the window. You told me not to be afraid then gestured for me to join you. We stood in the dark watching the most brilliant shooting stars I've ever seen. At first, I thought it was all a dream."

Leaning against the windowsill, Marie says, "Then you showed me the peep hole hidden in the floral wallpaper. Do you remember what you said when I looked through and saw the boarder's room on the other side?"

The girl whispers, "Beware. He's a bad man."

"When I looked through the hole a second time he was staring back at me, stark naked. I screamed, ran downstairs, locked Gloria's bedroom door, and pretended to be asleep. The next morning when I told her mom about the hole in the wall, she evicted him. Until today, that's the last time I was in this house."

Someone twists the bathroom doorknob. "Are you done yet? There's a line."

Marie answers, "Sorry. Stomach problems."

After footsteps retreat, Marie sits on the edge of the tub.

"The next week, he followed me from Velvet Freeze. He rolled down his car window and yelled, 'You're the one that snitched on me. I'm going to kill you.' Then he hopped out, grabbed my arm, and tried forcing me into his car, but a bright light came out of nowhere, distracting him. I thought it was a police spotlight, then, as clear as a church bell, you welled, 'Run!' I twisted away and cut through a neighbor's yard. I hid under their porch until his car speed off in the opposite direction."

Overcome by sadness, Marie's tears flow. "I was too scared to tell my parents about what happened because I was ashamed that I'd seen a naked man. Until just now, I've never told anyone. If I had, that other girl might not have died."

"It wasn't your fault." The spirit brushes a tear from Marie's cheek. "And it wasn't your time."

Marie blows her nose and says, "I don't even know your name."

The girl points to a painting on the wall of a starlit night.

"Is your name Star?"

She shakes her curly hair.

"Something to do with a star?"

She nods.

"Is it Stella?"

She points to the caption beneath the painting.

Marie reads out loud, "Celestial Night."

"Celeste? Is that your name?"

A grin spreads across the girl's pale face. Marie reaches out to hug her, but she disappears.

The tour guide pounds on the door. "Hurry up. The bus leaves in a few minutes."

Marie flings open the door and rushes past Katie. By the time Marie reaches the bottom floor, she is winded and her head is spinning. When she stumbles, Pete catches her and leads her to a chair.

"Are you all right?" he asks.

"Just a dizzy spell. Give me a minute. I'm the one who asked about the ghost in the blue dress. You probably think I'm a crazy old woman."

"Not at all." He leans closer. "I've seen her too. She's beautiful."

Marie starts to say something, but a pain shoots up her arm. Her chest feels heavy. As she falls off the chair, she knocks over a vase of fresh flowers.

Pete yells, "Call 9-1-1. I think she's having a heart attack."

Before blacking out, Marie sees a thousand fireflies. When she opens her eyes, Celeste has an arm around her.

"It's time," she says.

"Time?" Marie asks.

"To go home." A cluster of shining stars swirl behind Celeste.

When Marie blinks, they are replaced by bodies floating in the distance. At first, she thinks they're passengers from the tour bus until she recognizes her husband, her parents and grandparents, childhood friends who died in Vietnam, and the murdered teenager whose photo was in the newspapers.

Gesturing for Marie to follow them, their glowing faces turn into brilliant orbs rising heavenward.

In the background, Marie hears the buzz of a thousand bees and feels someone rub cold liquid on her chest. "Clear!"

With a jolt, she sits up then falls back down. When she opens her eyes, she's back at the mansion, lying on a stretcher. Two EMTs lean over her.

In a soothing voice, Pete says, "Hang in there."

Marie motions for him to come closer and whispers, "The ghost in the blue dress. Her name is Celeste."

Pete smiles knowingly.

As Marie's body is rolled out of the mansion, the scent of roses envelopes her. Celeste holds her hand, and Marie's heart feels light. Closing her eyes and taking a deep breath, she whispers a prayer before joining the shooting stars.

SARAH'S HOUSE
Anna Roberts Wells

The streets of University City wear their early Twentieth Century elegance with ease. Nowhere is this truer than in University Heights, that portion of the city where red brick structures sit a few steps back from the sidewalks on carefully manicured lawns. Its gracefully curving streets are overhung with old trees that form a cool green tunnel for the fortunate residence to pass through on their way home. It was this feeling of calm security that first attracted Evan and Olivia Compton to the area. It was also close to Clayton where Evan had transferred to work in one of the brokerage firms while Olivia completed her PhD in English at Washington University.

The Comptons had been married for seven years and were the doting parents of four-year-old Sarah. While Evan was a man of non-descript coloring, his wife was a natural blond with a classic profile and beautiful silvery blue eyes. Both had been somewhat amazed that Sarah had emerged from the womb with fiery red hair and hazel eyes. They had to look back three generations on both sides to find where this had come from. By age four, she was a ball of fire with a quick temper and an even quicker joy in life. She giggled and pranced her way into the hearts of all but the sourest of individuals. When the Comptons found the two story brick house on Stanford with its fenced back yard and perfect little girl's room, they knew they had found their home.

By the standards of the area, the house was more modest than some of its neighbors but not so much as to bring attention to itself. It blended into the community and offered the Compton family a place for rest, study and entertainment. In short, it was home from the moment they moved in.

It took several weeks between class scheduling, finding daycare, and unpacking for Evan and Olivia to meet the neighbors. They were all in the backyard on the third Saturday when the lady who lived in the house to the south of them came out and introduced herself. After Evan had told her his and Olivia's name, their daughter came bouncing up wearing a pale green sundress and a grin. The lady, Ellen Barks, immediately leaned down and said to the child, "and you must be Sarah."

"How did you know that?" Olivia asked with a puzzled look. She was quite sure that Sarah had not been out without either she or Evan or by herself.

"Oh, I just guessed," came the enigmatic reply.

Olivia thought that the real estate salesman must have mentioned their names and forgot all about it. Shortly after that, Evan had an experience that he reported to his co-workers as "just plain weird." Evan was a disciplined sort, good with numbers, conservative and concrete in his thinking. One of his few indulgences was a love for cinnamon toast lightly buttered with his morning coffee. He only ever allowed himself one slice, but he savored each bite. The Monday after meeting the neighbor, he prepared his toast while Sarah sat eating her breakfast and chattering away. Olivia was upstairs getting ready for school. She had a position as a student assistant teaching a freshman English class on Monday, Wednesday and Friday. She would come shortly and get Sarah to get her ready for daycare while Evan finished his toast and coffee. It was a well-orchestrated routine that generally allowed everyone to leave on time and in fairly good moods to begin the day. After preparing his toast and leaving it on a saucer, he turned to the coffee pot where he poured himself a cup. He stopped long enough to give Olivia a quick peck as she moved on to pick up Sarah and return upstairs. He went on to the refrigerator and got out the cream and added it to his coffee. When he turned around, his saucer was where he had left it but the toast was gone. Not even a crumb was on the plate. He turned to the counter where he saw that the bread bag was still open, the butter still in its dish, and the knife showing the remains of the butter he had swiped across his bread.

"That little imp," he said as he walked to the foot of the stairs and called, "Did you let her have my toast, Olivia?"

"Your toast is right there on your plate," she called back.

"No, it's not."

"But I saw it as I walked by," Olivia sounded genuinely puzzled. "Maybe we knocked it off as we went by, but you'd think I would have noticed. Check the floor by your place."

Evan went back to the table to do just that but was stopped in his tracks. There on the saucer sat the toast just as he'd prepared it, and it was still slightly warm. It would plague him the rest of the day.

Several days passed during which the toast incident faded as daily life took hold of the family. It seemed that Sarah had begun to have what many children have, an imaginary friend. She told her parents that they played together in her room. When they asked her what her friend's name was, she replied, "Sarah, just like me."

"What does this Sarah Number 2 look like?" Olivia asked her daughter.

"Well, she doesn't look like me, but her hair is like mine, and, Mommy, she isn't Sarah Number 2, I am. She's Sarah Number 1."

Evan and Olivia exchanged indulgent looks at how very clever and charming their Sarah was. They enjoyed listening to her tell about the other Sarah's antics and suspected that their Sarah was transferring guilt for some of her own naughtiness onto her invisible friend. They smiled at her infantile slyness. Several weeks later, Olivia tucked Sarah into bed after reading her favorite bedtime story and turned out the light leaving the door ajar and the hall light on. She returned down stairs where Evan was watching a Cardinal game and she got busy grading papers for her class. About an hour later, Evan looked up and called out, "Back to bed, young lady." With a tinkling of laughter and the sound of footsteps running back up the stairs, the child went back to her room. At least, that is what he thought. The same thing happened just as the game was ending and he and Olivia were turning out the light to retire for the night. First, they heard the laughter then the running on the stairs.

"I'll take care of this," Olivia said as she headed for the stairs. "You lock up."

Moments later when Evan got to their bedroom, Olivia was sitting on the bed with an odd look on her face. "What's up?" Evan asked as he began to unbutton his shirt.

"She's sound asleep. She couldn't have gone back to sleep that fast, Evan. Something else must have happened. Do you think she is sleep-walking?"

"Well, maybe because we certainly heard something."

Olivia decided to call the pediatrician the next day to find out if this was normal behavior and how to deal with it. The doctor assured them that many children have imaginary playmates and they often are a way for children to feel they have an ally in new situations. Olivia also asked about the sleepwalking but he showed no concern for that either saying that she would probably outgrow it in time. Armed with assurance, Olivia decided to just keep an eye on her and see that she didn't hurt herself although they had never actually caught her wandering about at night.

The night noises from Sarah continued, but neither Evan nor Olivia paid much attention to it. That was not as disconcerting as the other things that seemed to happen in their house. While the toast incident didn't repeat itself, other objects tended to disappear only to be found again right where they were supposed to be. They car keys disappearing really annoyed both of them. They got out the spares and began to carry them on their person because the frantic searches for the others had caused one or the other to be late on several occasions. Olivia had a coral colored sweater that she was particularly fond of. She would fold it carefully away after wearing it only to find it the next morning hanging off the back of a chair or once even in the bookcase. The thing that finally sent cold chills down her back was the class papers. When she corrected her students' assignments, Olivia made a point of stacking the graded papers in alphabetical order so that when she returned them to her students no one would be able to discern a fellow classmate's grade based on the order of her stack. The night before her class, she would place the stack in her grade book and put all of her supplies for the next school day together in a book bag on the kitchen counter by the back door. One day in the late fall, she walked into her classroom and after roll call began to hand back the corrected assignment. She got through the letter "G" then realized that the next letter was "R". What had happened to the middle of the alphabet? She looked for the papers among all of her things. They were not there.

"Class," she said, "I seem to have left a few of the papers at home. I'm not sure how it happened; but if you wish to know your grade before the next class session, please, see me after class."

No matter how she tried to figure this out, she couldn't seem to find an explanation. Evan had left with Sarah before she had that morning and she recalled that her materials looked just as she had left them on the counter the night before. No doubt, if Sarah had bothered them, they would have been in a mess when she went to get them. She finished her teaching and her classes for the day, met with her faculty advisor, then swung by the grocery store before going home. She knew she would have a good hour or more to get dinner on the table before Evan would arrive from work bringing Sarah from her daycare. She parked the car in the garage located off the alley and crossed the backyard digging out her house key while juggling the bag of groceries and her book bag. She was still preoccupied by the morning events as she unlocked the door and pushed it open. She dropped the bags she was carrying and stared in horror at the floor. There just a few steps in front of her, fanned out as perfectly as a professional card sharps hand, lay the graded papers. She sank to her knees and just stared until her head snapped up to the sound of a child's tinkling laughter and footsteps on the stairs. She couldn't stay there another minute. She grabbed her purse and ran for the car. On her way, across the yard, she saw Ellen Barks clipping dead flowers from her chrysanthemums. Ellen called out, "Mrs. Compton, you look like you've seen a ghost."

Olivia stopped in her tracks and turned toward Ellen. "I didn't see one but I may have heard one. Oh, heavens, I sound like I'm losing my mind" she gabbled.

"Not at all, my dear," came the calm reply. "I think you've just encountered the permanent resident of that house. She's perfectly harmless I assure you although the family before you turned tail and ran because she frightened them so. I've lived here through several families living there. Except those silly cowards before you, the other owners would tell you that she a friendly, though mischievous little ghost. I bet you've noticed how things disappear and the running on the stairs. Don't you fret," she smiled. "You'll have wonderful tales to tell by the time you move on."

"But Ellen, why weren't we told before we bought this house? Although I doubt that either Evan or I would have believed it."

"No, probably not. May I call you Olivia?" she got a nod in reply. "Olivia, we are far too modern and sophisticated to put much stock in such tales. Oh, yes, and did I mention that apparently every family who has lived in your house since it was built in the 1920's has had a redheaded daughter named Sarah?"

"That's how you knew our daughter's name." It was a statement not a question.

"Absolutely," Ellen smiled back. "The minute I saw her I knew that things were just as they were supposed to be. You go on back in there and don't be afraid. She means you no harm, and the long time neighbors have been wondering when she'd show up."

Olivia returned to the house to find that the papers were neatly stacked on the counter and the grocery bag had been picked up and refilled with its spilled contents. She spoke into the silent house, "Sarah, we need to come to an understanding. We won't bother you and we would like for you to not annoy us too much." Her voice echoed in the silent house.

After dinner and Sarah's bedtime rituals, Olivia sat down with Evan and told him of her day. He did not quite believe her but accepted that nothing that had happened so far had done anyone any harm. He guessed that they could live with silly pranks, and they did.

Over the next three years, there was frequent evidence of their resident ghost. There would be fingerprints in the icing on cakes. Toys placed far too high up for their daughter to have put them there. The laughter and stair running became so common to them that they no longer woke up to it. They laughed when they came down on Christmas morning to find all of the ornaments brought down to their Sarah's eye level. On Sarah's sixth birthday, no matter how they tried to keep the candles lit, a little puff of wind would blow them out immediately. Sarah just laughed and declared that that was Sarah Number 1 playing tricks. That summer, friends from their hometown, Little Rock, called to say that they would be stopping for a few days in St. Louis and would love to see them. Evan asked them if they would like to attend the MUNY, explaining what it was and that the week they would be in town, *Fiddler on the Roof* was playing. It sounded like a great idea, and Evan ordered their tickets giving his credit card information to the ticket office over the phone. When the tickets arrived a few days later, he checked them against the receipt. He then tucked the tickets into the frame of the master bedroom mirror. On the night of the performance, their friends arrived just as Olivia walked in from taking Sarah to a neighbor's home to spend the night with their daughter. After a celebratory drink, Evan bounded up the stairs to get the tickets. They were nowhere to be seen. He called down to ask Olivia if she had put them in her purse.

"Are they missing?" She sounded exasperated.

"That silly imp has them," Evan stormed back down the stairs and grabbed the phone. He dug the receipt out of the desk and called the box office. He simply explained that he had the receipt and had lost the tickets. He was assured that if he brought the receipt, his credit card and driver's license with him, they could place them in their purchased seats. As they drove to the MUNY, they related their home's history to their disbelieving friends. After the performance and a stop for a late dinner, they returned to the Compton house. With their friends in tow, they went to their bedroom and Evan switched on the lights. The tickets were just as he had placed them, days before, sticking out of the mirror frame. After a moment of shocked silence, his friend of many years breathed an awe inspired, "Wow."

The following year, Olivia finished her doctorate and got a job teaching at the University of Arkansas Little Rock. She had to report for the summer session. She and Sarah moved in with her parents while she taught and house hunted. Meanwhile, Evan remained in St. Louis to get the house sold. When he was able, he would transfer back to the Little Rock branch of his brokerage firm. It didn't take long for the new real estate agent to find a buyer for their house in U. City. She called him with the exciting news only a few weeks after the house went on the market.

"A lovely little family has made a solid offer on the house. They knew that several other people were interested so they are offering asking price and they are pre-approved. I think you should accept this offer" She spoke with confidence that there would be no problems and he could soon rejoin his family.

"I'll call Olivia right away and we can get started on the necessary paper work," he agreed.

"Great." She replied. "They really are a darling little family. They have the cutest little redheaded girl."

"Really," mused Evan. "By any chance is the child's name Sarah?" he asked.

"Why, yes," she sounded astonished. "How did you know that?"

"Oh, I don't know. Just a lucky guess," said Evan hanging up the phone with a smile on his face.

THE DEVIL'S PROMENADE
Dacia Wilkinson

"I've seen it," the old woman said and flicked her cigarette. Ashes flew and scattered across her lap. Some fell to the floor, a few landing on my Converse tennis shoe. I shook them free.

"What did you see?"

Her eyes left my face and wandered up as if she were staring at the blinking exit sign in the far right corner of the room. A student of facial expressions and body language, I knew it was not the lit sign that she held in her vision, but visual construct of the past. Her still dark eyebrows pulled together and I saw fear register in them. With narrowed eyes, she held her stare, and the moment ticked on.

"Grace," I said with a gentle tone and reached to touch her knee, hoping to draw her back to looking into my eyes, where I would work to keep her attention with my expressions of interest. "What did you see?"

Turning back to me, her face changed in the movement and she smiled again, finding my eyes. "It was a long time ago," she said and her bony hand came down over mine. She squeezed and then patted, never leaving eye contact. "A long time ago." The smile she bore fell into a pursed grip of lips and I knew my window of opportunity shrank in the passing seconds.

"I'm going there." I announced and sat up straighter in my seat, keeping careful contact with her eyes. Her cheek flexed and with slowness, her right eyebrow arched. She removed her hand. No words came from either of us, only an exchange of facial muscles twitching, indicating the standoff taking place in our minds. She broke the silence.

"I've seen it."

"You have?"

"Yes," she said and her chest lifted with a deep intake of breath, which she exhaled, then removed her eyes from mine. "It was a long time ago."

She repeated herself. A grandfather clock chimed from the lobby and it rang clear, reminding me of my grandparent's home and spending the night as a young girl. It chimed the hour every hour and I never tired of the sound. Behind me now where I saw in a music sitting room, it floated and in and out of the rooms along the hallways, all branching from the main lobby of the home. The chimes rang out and I felt them – my heart fell in tune and its beat matched the tone and I pictured Grandpa sitting next to the clock at the dining table, motioning me to join him in a game of Boggle. I felt the small smile curve on my lips and touched it, feeling for him in a way, trying to bring back that day, stifling the emotional flood threatening beneath my finger-clasped mouth.

"Johnny, Frank, me, and Mabel. We saw it."

Grace's voice spoke the names slow, with purpose and my mind snapped back from my memory bank where Grandma's cookies were just about done in the oven and I smelled their sugary concoction.

"The four of you?" I asked, back in tune with her eyes, which sat deep in her once beautiful face. Still beautiful, but aged, and her eyes were much smaller than the photos I'd seen in her room. Standing next to her husband in their wedding photo, her eyes were the largest feature of her face – bright and alluring, now small and fearful.

"Johnny borrowed his dad's car that night, told him that he and Frank had to study at the library, that he needed the car to pick Frank up. Said it'd be a late night, because of Final exams. Johnny's dad never questioned him, just let him go. Mabel asked could she go and Johnny tried to say no, but his dad said he should take his sister – the library would be good for her." She paused and tilted her head down a bit and looked up at me with darkening eyes. "Mabel was fifteen, thought she was twenty. Johnny always told me and Frank about the trouble she caused him. We were seventeen, the three of us. Me, Frank, and Johnny. So, Johnny showed up at the library with Mabel in the back seat. Frank and I had been there waiting a while – see, Frank lived a couple doors down from me on Wall Street, real close to the library, so we walked there together. Funny that Johnny's dad never knew where Frank lived." Her eyes became soft and I wondered among the three musketeers if any romance ever sparked. Such a ridiculous romantic, and I did an inward eye roll at myself.

"Sounds like he was happy to get the kids out of the house," I said.

"Yes, he was. Had a drinking problem," she said this as a conspirator might, with a low whisper, leaning in close to me, not wanting to reveal that secret to anyone in the room. I smiled, knowing Johnny's father had been long gone for a good, decent amount of time. Grace, across from me, was pushing ninety.

"Did they have a mother?"

"No," she said and shook her head. "Poor man. He gave me the willies." A shiver ran through her and I saw it begin in her shoulders and run down to her feet. I had to bite my lip to keep from laughing. A spark lit her eye and I said, "Why?"

"Always lookin'," she said. "Looking at me and other girls. I saw him. Paid him no attention and stayed away, always telling Johnny to meet us at the library. His dad must have thought Johnny was going to be the Valedictorian." A deep laugh escaped Grace and the twinkle in her eyes deepened, and then changed, a faraway look took them over, and she put her cigarette into the ash tray next to her, bobbing it a couple of times before releasing it. "At the library, we stood around in the parking lot trying to decide what to do. I wanted to see a picture show. Frank wanted to get sodas and dance. He nudged me when he said it. Frank was always sweet on me."

"And were you sweet on him?"

Grace drew back and looked at me – I saw in her eyes first trust then distrust and I wondered why. She chose not to answer and kept telling her story.

"Johnny said we could do both, but Mabel called us dull, saying we should do something exciting, like go find the Spiva pool. I tried to sound sophisticated and said we'd done that. We hadn't, but I'd heard stories and I wasn't going near the place. My cousin and her friend George almost fell off the ledge of a cliff there in the dark, trying to find it. I'm afraid of heights, always have been, so the Spiva pool was a no. Mabel was undeterred. She said we had to go see *it*. She emphasized 'it' and I didn't like the way she said it. It was wrong somehow."

"It? The Spooklight?"

With a deep breath, she answered, "The Devil's Promenade," and her eyes clouded a second. I waited, and while I waited, I pushed record on my cell phone, not wanting to miss a thing. Garnering eyewitness accounts of the Spooklight was the next step in my research. I'd already spoken with some teenagers, a few middle-aged people, a gas station attendant, all who claimed to have seen the light that goes by several names. The Hornet Light, the Devil's Promenade, and the Spooklight.

"Frank said that actually sounded like a good idea and Mabel cheered, then tugged on Johnny's arm, asking him, can we please. Johnny searched my face and I shrugged, not really knowing what to think. My cousin and George had been there too, but they'd not seen anything. Some people say they saw something, others weren't sure. We had four hours before any of us were missed. Johnny said let's do it and we piled into his car, me in the front next to Johnny and Frank and Mabel in the back."

"Were you sweet on Johnny?"

"My dear, you sure are a romantic, aren't you? Why do I need to have fancied one of those boys? They were my friends."

"I'm sorry, Grace – it's just who I am, I suppose."

"That's alright," she said. "It was twelve miles south of Joplin and it took us a spell to get there, but we tried to sing the lines from songs in "Broadway Melody," Fred Astaire's newest movie – we'd seen it the week before. We did that part of the drive and we were horrible." She paused and reached for her pack of cigarettes on the sofa beside her, picked it up and shook it against the palm of hand, knocking one free from the pack. With unsteady fingers, she lifted the cigarette to her lips and placed it between, holding it there. The pack went back to its place and she looked back to the nurses' station. Without having to say a word, the orderly attended to her cigarette, lighting it for her. He smiled and she nodded thanks, then focused back toward me with a long drag on the cigarette. Her eyes seemed lost, so I spoke up. "You were singing in the car ..."

"That only last so long. Then Frank told us what he'd heard about the Hornet Light. It wasn't always called the Spooklight. Frank said some people believed that the Hornet Light was the souls of two Quapaw Indians kept from loving each other and their souls forever on that road searched to be together. Johnny laughed at that idea. He said no way was it going to be a romantic story that he'd believe, he said that it wasn't even clever. Frank said, all right, other people said that a miner in the area back in the early 1800s had a run in with some Indians and that a few days later his children went missing. That he never found them, and that the light is him searching for his children – a girl and a boy, both teenagers, the boy older than the girl. Johnny said that sounded better. I said nothing. Mabel squealed with delight, clapping her hands and hanging over the back of the seat, her face too near my own, and Johnny turned the car down a dark road. The road sign said E-50. I remember my heart started racing and I gripped the door tight. The only light anywhere around us was the car's headlights. I said to Johnny that I didn't think it was a good idea. Frank laughed at me. I'll never forget that he laughed at me." And her eyes went up to the ceiling, off to the right and she winced.

"Grace?"

Back staring at me, she shook her head as if making a decision, and continued her story, "We crept into the darkness down the road and I asked what we were supposed to do. Frank said, nothing, that the light would find us. Mabel told Johnny to drive farther down the road and park, that she wanted to get out, sit on top of the roof of the car. He laughed and I knew I wouldn't be able to convince him to go – he was enjoying his sister's excitement. Okay, he'd said. And we moved slowly into the darkness. Around us, I made out branches of trees and they closed in on us the farther down the road we moved – they came nearer the road and my heart seized in my chest and I know the trees moved, they bent down to the road and then back up, all together they did, and there was a light shining then. Mabel said, "Stop the car!" and when Johnny put the car into park, she opened the door and climbed on the roof of the car. Frank followed her. Johnny asked me if I was coming. I could only stare at the light and stay in the car.

"It just hung there in the air suspended, dancing almost, just a ball of green light. At first, it was small and whether my eyes adjusted or it grew, then it was larger. It moved to the right and stopped, then moved back to the left and then it disappeared, covering us in complete darkness. I could see nothing for a few seconds, just blackness. Mabel pounded her disapproval on the roof of the car, yelling for the light to return. I just stared, trying to see something, anything. Frank said, "Grace, come out here," and I saw it again, this time closer, larger, and it was blue. Johnny and Frank let out a whoop in unison. Mable said she wanted to run to it and before Johnny could stop her, she slid off the roof and ran down the road ahead of us. I could only make out her figure for a second and then she disappeared into the overwhelming dark. The light went out and nothing. An owl hooted off in the forest and everything stood still. Johnny called out, "Mabel!" and Frank said, "Get back here, Mabel!" They stood outside the car and argued about who would walk after her. "Mabel!" I remember Frank called out again and Johnny cursed. He opened the car door and slid into his seat. Frank got in next to me. Johnny cursed again. We sat there without Mabel, scared.

"He started the car and the headlights bore a hole through the darkness down the road. No Mabel. We crept forward, nobody speaking. The trees bent in over us. Their fingers scratched the roof of the car and I clung to Frank's arm – he didn't notice, his eyes searched the forest. "Mabel," he said into the darkness - it broke and brilliant light filled the car. White light, flashing blue, then green, it radiated around my face, and it was hot. It moved inside me and through me. It knew me and I felt myself lift into the air. All goodness and warmth were in the light and I welcomed it, wanted it, and I lifted myself to it, rising there in the car and I was flat against the ceiling of the car, Frank and Johnny holding my arms, pulling me down and I didn't want them to. The light changed red and burned my skin, angry it was and they pulled on me more and both boys were speaking – I don't know what they said. I have no idea what they said. The light pulled me toward the window, changing from red to green to colors indescribable, and I wanted to go … it was beautiful and I wanted to play in the light, dance in it, to revel in it, but Frank yelled, "No!"

"The light screeched and I fell into the window, cracking the glass, and Frank's arms went round me and he yelled, "Johnny, move!"

"The car went backward – I remember that and the light left me, dropped me, it rejected me…. It followed us down the road, hovering over the hood, taunting Johnny, playing at the window in front of his face and then it went up and disappeared. Johnny stopped the car and I felt myself crying, lying crumpled in Frank's arms there in the pitch black. My skin burned all over and my clothes stuck to my skin, my hair dripped droplets of moisture onto my face. Frank held me, his heart raced. I know that. I felt it and I heard it as the car shook and the light came down behind us, looming over the road, taunting, daring. And then it moved to Frank's side, flickering there, holding still, and it whispered foreign words, but not words – it was hauntingly beautiful music as it danced by Frank, flickering from green to blue to purple to white. Johnny tightened his grip on the steering wheel, pushed on the accelerator just as Frank loosened his grip on me and opened his car door. We were moving, but Frank was there and then gone, just the light remained and it glowed brighter still – and it split into two, hovering close together and there was music to their dance – it pulled at me and I place a hand toward the open door. Johnny tossed himself over me and pulled the car door closed, with a glare into my face. I saw the whites of his eyes, wide and frightened. The moment hung, we sat frozen in the car, no longer moving, just Johnny and me. He put the car into reverse and the tires spun, sending pebbles into the air on all sides. I heard them, could not see them - it was full dark again.

Flying backward down the road, Johnny kept his eyes behind us and I watched forward. Nothing. The light was gone. Only dark. Only darker spots in the dark where trees stood darkly rooted in time. The car jolted and creaked, knocked out of joint by a pothole we'd not touched earlier. Johnny cursed and I turned to look back, taking my eyes from the road ahead. The glow surrounded the car in an instant and we lifted, suspended. A figure stood there – a man, missing teeth, in disheveled clothes, he held a lantern, and he held the car, as if it was nothing more than a cardboard box. Johnny gunned the engine and it did nothing – the man roared in laughter and then her face filled the back window, but it wasn't Mabel's face anymore. Hair wild and undone, flying about her face. Her eyes white, no pupils, glared wide and bright into the car at us, changing from green to blue to fiery red. "Father's found us ," she said and her voice bit into my flesh – low, gravelly, not Mabel … Johnny revved the engine and kept his face locked on hers. "Wants you, too," she growled. "No!" Johnny said and we were on the ground again, moving backward. I felt her pass me – she raked my skin and then she was through the car and we kept going, leaving the light … leaving Mabel. Leaving Frank."

Grace's eyes closed, she crossed her arms, cigarette still in hand, and a tear trailed her cheek.

I had no words. I had heard stories about a young couple who went missing in 1940 but had not thought, had not considered their story to be Grace's . This was supposed to be a lighthearted piece about the Spooklight for my school's newspaper – a collection of Joplin's legends and tall tales from inhabitants of all ages.

"I'm sorry, Grace. I had no …"

"I've never spoken of it." She gave a forced smile and then unbuttoned the sleeve of her shirt, lifting it to reveal scratch marks over burn scars on her forearm. "From that night."

"Grace, I …"

"No more," she said and she looked away, only this time out of the window and she held a handover her scars, caressing them with her crooked, bony fingers.

"What of Johnny?" I asked, still recording and not wanting to miss anything.

From the flash of anger in her eyes, I dared not move conversation to him, but I wanted to know. *What of Johnny. Were they questioned? What about his father? Franks' family?*

"Did they ever find anything?" I risked one more question, hoping it might coax her to give away information about Johnny. Her eyes still held the anger and a muscle in her cheek flexed, her jaw squared tight. She looked me up and then down and my skin crawled, a burning sensation covered my face, and I sat up straight under the weight of her eyes. For a moment, I thought she would not answer. Then she closed her eyes and stayed that way, while I gulped from holding my breath and inhaled what I could from the smoky air surrounding us. Her eyes opened and flashed green, then blue and no pupils were there. And then red. "No," came a voice from her lips that was not hers any longer followed by a young female laugh – and Grace shook. Stumbling from my chair, I knocked it over when I stood, not bothering to pick it up. Orderlies came to Grace's side and I walked backward through them, bumping into other chairs and falling to the floor. No one noticed me.

"She's gone," someone said. He held her wrist in his hand.

The light hovered above their heads – at first, green, then blue and it danced. It danced for me and the music was sweet, gentle, and I held out my hand.

AUTHOR BIOGRAPHIES

Dr. Pablo Baum's historical fiction and story-narration focus on Missouri's dramatic history. He has sold his books and performed at the Governor's Garden, the Pershing Foundation, and Missouri's historical societies and commemorations.

Larry G. Brown has family heritage in the Missouri Ozarks, is a retired Geography Professor, and been a storyteller for approximately 30 years.

Kenneth W. Cain is the author of the *Saga of I* (*These Trespasses, Grave Revelations Reckoning*), *The Dead Civil War*, the acclaimed short story collection *These Old Tales;* and his latest short story collection, *Fresh Cut Tales*. He lives with his wife and children in Eastern Pennsylvania.

Malcolm R. Campbell is the author of paranormal short stories and the contemporary fantasy novels *The Sun Singer, Sarabande, The Seeker,* and *The Sailor.* He lives in Georgia.

Janet L. Cannon, technology instructor and avid runner, earned her BA and MA in English, and proudly has never had to say, "Do you want fries with that?" at work.

Shenoa Carroll-Bradd lives in Southern California with her brother and her dancing dog. She writes mainly horror and fantasy, with occasional sojourns into science fiction and erotica. Keep up with her progress at www.sbcbfiction.net or join her fan page at www.facebook.com/sbcbfiction.

Kathryn Cureton writes from the dark basement lair of her hillbilly mansion, three-quarters of a mile up a gravel road in southeast Missouri. She has seen two ghosts.

J.K. Dark is a writer/author residing in St. Louis, Missouri. He contributes to the E-zine magazines Taboojive.com and The Good Men Project. He is the author of three books, *Anecdotes, Short Stories & Mind Clutter; Dark Thoughts & Dark Forces*, and his latest, *Dark Harbors*.

Gerald Dlubala has spent over twenty years writing in multiple genres. His work has been published in magazines, newspapers, and books, including *Chicken Soup for the Soul, Think Positive.*

Patrick Dorsey began creating his own books in first grade by stapling together crayoned pages. President of the St. Louis Fencers Club and an UMSL English graduate, he's recently begun publishing his stories without either stapler or crayons.

Ed Farber has devoted his creative efforts to his two passionate loves – writing and painting. Ed's non-fiction book, *Looking Back with a Smile*, and a collection of short stories, *Echoes of Clara Avenue*, are available on Amazon Kindle. His artwork and a sampling of his short stories are on his website, www.farberart.com.

Nathan Feuerberg received an MFA in creative writing from the University of New Orleans. His fiction has appeared in a variety of literary journals and anthologies. Currently, he resides in San Miguel de Allende, Mexico.

Robert Holt lives within walking distance of Sylvan Springs Park. A graduate of Webster University, he has horror stories appearing in various anthologies and markets.

C.V. Hunt is the author of *Thanks for Ruining My Life, How To Kill Yourself, Zombieville, Phantom, Legacy*, and *Endlessly*. She lives somewhere in Ohio.

When Wendy Klein isn't writing stories about time travel or ghosts, she can be found drinking coffee, playing video games with her husband, or building Lego spaceships with her two sons.

John Kujawski has interests that range from guitars to the Incredible Hulk. He was born and raised in St. Louis, Missouri, and still lives there to this day.

Rebecca Lacy lives in a house in Farmington, Missouri that has a ghost, but he isn't very interesting. She's a business owner, has written a leadership fable, and is currently working on a novel, *Reinventing Holly*.

MJ Logan is passionate about reading and writing. He began writing small illustrated books made from loose-leaf paper in third grade. Today he writes fiction and non-fiction and has been published in newspapers, magazines, and across the Web.

Conny Manero is the author of two novels and two children's books. When not writing, Conny likes to play ten-pin bowling or devote time to fundraising for the Toronto Cat Rescue. Visit her online at connymanero.weebly.com.

Sean McLachlan has written numerous articles and books on Missouri history. This story explores the background of a character from his novel, *A Fine Likeness*. Visit him online at civilwarhorror.blogspot.com.

Schevus Osborne is just a guy who enjoys writing, and he would love to do so as his career as well as his passion. He lives in the Metro East.

Caryn Pine lives in New York and is a student at the Massachusetts College of Liberal Arts, studying literature. When she's not writing, she reads, watches movies, and plays video games.

Marie Robinson has a strong interest in the paranormal and is also a folklore expert. As well as being a horror fiction writer, she also writes for several websites.

J.T. Seate's stories may be told with hard-core realism or humor in order to pull his corpses from the grave. His work can be found at www.troyseateauthor.webs.com.

Jacqueline Seewald has had her short stories, poems, essays, reviews and articles featured in hundreds of publications such as: THE WRITER, THE L.A. TIMES, PEDESTAL, SURREAL, LIBRARY JOURNAL, AFTER

DARK, and PUBLISHERS WEEKLY. She has also won multiple awards for fiction, poetry, and plays.

Rosemary Shomaker is a government data and policy analyst by trade, an urban planner by education, and a fiction writer by choice. She lives in Richmond, Virginia.

Tommy B. Smith is a writer of dark fiction, and the author of *Poisonous*. His presence currently infests Fort Smith, Arkansas, where he resides with his wife and cats.

Curtis Thomas graduated from Missouri State University two years ago with a degree in English, and now teaches broadcast journalism and film at a high school in Springfield, MO.

Donna Duly Volkenannt grew up in the College Hill neighborhood of North St. Louis, where she learned the Imperial and told ghost stories during sleepovers at the Bissell Mansion. Visit her online at donnasbookpub.blogspot.com.

Anna Roberts Wells is a native of Arkansas, with a degree in English from Hendrix College. A retired social worker, she serves on the MSPS board and is a member of WSJC and On the Edge poetry group.

Dacia Wilkinson is the wife of a biker, mother of six, general education instructor for Vatterott College in Berkeley, Missouri, and writer when she finds a quiet moment here and there. She spent four and a half years in Joplin, MO and has seen, with her own eyes, the Joplin Spooklight on the Devil's Promenade.

ABOUT THE EDITORS

Robin Tidwell Robin is the author of women's dystopian novels *Reduced,* *Reused,* and *Recycled,* and lives in the St. Louis, Missouri area. She tries very hard to make it through one week at a time without a crisis.

Shannon Yarbrough resides in St. Louis, Missouri. He is the author of four novels, including the recent mash-up *Dickinstein: Emily Dickinson – Mad Scientist.* He believes in ghosts and aspires to be one someday.